THE HELLSPAWNED KNIGHT

THE HELLSPAWNED KNIGHT
HELLSPAWNED CHRONICLES™
BOOK ONE

MICHAEL TODD

DISRUPTIVE IMAGINATION

This book is a work of fiction. All of the characters, organizations, and events portrayed in this novel are either products of the author's imagination or are used fictitiously. Sometimes both. Names, characters, places, and incidents which are copyrighted, are property of their respective owners and are used under a licensing agreement.

Copyright © 2025 Michael T. Anderle
Cover copyright © LMBPN Publishing
A Michael Anderle Production

LMBPN Publishing supports the right to free expression and the value of copyright. The purpose of copyright is to encourage writers and artists to produce the creative works that enrich our culture.

The distribution of this book without permission is a theft of the author's intellectual property. If you would like permission to use material from the book (other than for review purposes), please contact support@lmbpn.com. Thank you for your support of the author's rights.

LMBPN Publishing
2375 E. Tropicana Avenue, Suite 8-305
Las Vegas, Nevada 89119 USA

Version 1.00, March 2025
eBook ISBN: 979-8-89354-624-8
Paperback ISBN: 979-8-89354-625-5

This book (and what happens within / characters / situations / worlds) are copyright © 2015-2025 by Michael T. Anderle.

THE HELLSPAWNED KNIGHT TEAM

Thanks to the JIT Readers for this version

Zacc Pelter
Wendy L Bonell
Dave Hicks
Jan Hunnicutt

If I've missed anyone, please let me know!

Editor
Lynne Stiegler

*I appreciate your love, your
support and acceptance
when you don't have a
clue what I'm talking about!*

CHAPTER ONE

Jackson McCade drove his sword forward, the blade singing a low, chilling note as it sank through the worn leather of the final bandit's armor. A strangled gasp escaped the outlaw's lips, and he sagged to the earth, joining his fallen comrades around the still-smoldering remains of their makeshift camp.

Smoke rose in twisting columns, the orange glow of dying embers reflecting the carnage left behind. Blood trickled down Jackson's left arm, but he held firm, refusing to let the pain crack his composure.

He pulled in a long breath, tasting ash and soot. The bruises beneath his battle-worn cloak throbbed. Dusk had settled over Duskwarren Rise, painting the sky bruised purple and gray. The wind carried the tang of scorched wood and a bitter hint of metal.

Luke, lanky and agile, ambled forward with a dagger half-drawn, still scanning for any threat they might have missed.

"So." Luke nudged the fresh bandit corpse with the toe of his boot. "I suppose that's all of them. Unless one of these sods has a twin lurking behind a bush. That's the kind of luck we have."

Jackson's breath puffed out in a short, humorless laugh. "Not a chance. I've counted a dozen or so. Looks like we got them all."

Luke's playful smirk widened. "I'm sure your demon-fire was a real crowd-pleaser."

Jackson winced, not missing the kernel of unease Luke's light words carried. Though they traveled together, Luke never forgot the cursed force coursing behind Jackson's ribs. No one did. Shadows on Jackson's neck shifted, runic scars pulsing with a faint glow as if the fight had stoked an infernal blaze inside him. They were a feature he never invited, and one he couldn't mask.

Jackson sensed movement to his left, but it wasn't a missed bandit. Riven approached like a silent specter, her steps hardly a whisper on the trampled grass. The wind ruffled her dark cloak, revealing lean muscles and a quiver perched on her back. Elven archers carried themselves differently than humans. They seemed to fuse with the surroundings, each breath and motion attuned to the land.

"They fought harder than I expected," she mused. "But incompetent all the same."

Luke cocked an eyebrow. "You do realize they nearly cut Jackson in half, right?"

"I noticed. Surprised your jokes didn't make them surrender."

"That would've required their sense of humor to be more refined," Luke stated, feeling a small cut on his jaw. "Bandits around here seem to prefer the 'stab first, banter never' approach."

Riven shrugged with a slight frown. "Humans have a knack for tearing each other apart. Sometimes, I wonder if it's in your blood."

Jackson forced his shoulders to relax, though something about Riven's words set his teeth on edge. "Not all humans are like these outlaws," he insisted softly. He stepped over the man he had recently dispatched, lips pressed tight. Killing was never pleasant.

He knelt, rummaging through the bandit's belt pouch. His hope was to find something for the trouble. Silver coins, a keepsake. Bandits often traveled with small valuables. Instead, he discovered an ornate bit of parchment sealed with crimson wax and bearing a crest he recognized too well.

He carefully turned the object in his fingertips, King Rodric's sigil pressed into the thick seal. Bright gold script indicated it wasn't the typical tavern flyer or petty missive. His pulse kicked up a notch. "A royal courier's dispatch?" he muttered.

"What?" Luke blinked, stepping closer. "They were carrying that?"

Riven glanced over, her elven eyes narrowing in curiosity. Her typically impassive silence found a crack. "Strange place for official correspondence."

Jackson eased himself upright, ignoring the dull ache in his ribs. "We need to see if these bandits intercepted this or if the Crown was trying to corner them. Either way, it's a problem." Perhaps the biggest problem he had seen in a while. He ran his thumb along the edges of the parchment. The seal was partially cracked but still discernible, undeniable evidence these outlaws had meddled with royal business.

Luke whistled, tapping the letter. "That's King Rodric's crest. Opening it might mark us as traitors if we're not careful. Also, ironically, not opening it might do the same if we've stolen something important. We're in that perfect spot where either choice feels like a trap."

Jackson shook his head. "Better a trap we know than one we walk into blind. We're going to open it. You two may want to step back." He grabbed a half-broken crate, slammed a boot against it to flatten it into a makeshift seat, and sank down. The tepid glow of embers lit his features in a copper hue.

Riven's gaze darted between the letter and Luke's pensive stare. "Do it quickly, before the dying light hides any clues."

After taking a careful breath, Jackson worked a finger under the brittle seal, trying not to destroy the crest while breaking it free. Beneath the wax lay a few cramped lines of text. The edges looked smudged, suggesting the letter might have been handled roughly in the scuffle. He started scanning, his lips pressed thin. The writing was direct, lacking any trace of pleasantries. He recognized the royal scribe's precise script.

We urgently request the presence of Sir Jackson McCade in the capital. A matter of grave import connected to rumors of baronial unrest. Signed by the word of King Rodric.

He exhaled, folding the parchment gently. Knowing the letter was specifically for him sparked an uneasy knot in his chest.

Luke's eyebrow shot up. "Wait. That's not just any summons. It's addressed to you?"

Jackson nodded. "It is."

"How in the gods' names did a pack of bandits get hold of it?" Luke scowled at the bodies around them, some moaning softly, many no longer moaning at all.

"Bold," Riven observed. "Humans pocketing the king's letter. What did they expect to do with it?"

"Sell it, maybe," Luke suggested, gesturing with a gaunt, calloused hand. "Or intercept it on someone else's orders. Doesn't matter now. They're not going to trade anything today. Let me see that."

Jackson hesitated but extended the letter for Luke to glance at. The traveler's eyes flicked over the text. His grin evaporated as he reached the bottom. "So, we hustle to the capital, or what? When the King's Eye calls like this…well, let's say ignoring a royal dispatch is the quickest path to an unmarked grave."

Riven stepped closer, her expression betraying neither excitement nor fear. "The letter demanded Jackson specifically. Are we invited, too, or should we vanish?"

Jackson's neck scar burned faintly. "Seems the Crown commanded me alone." He glanced between them. "But I could use help. The war broke enough trust that folks might assume I'm one breath away from unleashing demon-fire on them."

Riven's gaze dropped to the ground, then she spoke in a clipped tone. "We share a common cause. Outlaws along the borders, rumors of feuding barons. If the bandits are bold enough to intercept royal messengers, the threat extends beyond your realm. I'll go, if only to ensure these scum don't creep toward elven lands again."

Luke's lips curved with a wry enjoyment. "Guess I'm in, too. I do so love charming the socks off suspicious townsfolk."

Jackson rose with a pained groan. The muscles across his back screamed in protest. "Then let's see if these bandits had anything else worth salvaging. We'll need supplies. I can't show up to the capital like a street brawler."

The three of them fanned out, poking around the smoldering camp. Old bedrolls and half-eaten rations littered the site. Most of the bandits had been living rough, judging by the ragged tents and rusted cooking pots. One corner of the ravaged camp revealed a meager stash of stolen goods, a couple of silver ingots, a few coins, and mismatched weaponry that none of them regarded with much interest.

Riven frowned at the meager pickings, running her fingers along a chipped short sword. The smell of burned cloth stung her nostrils. As an elf, her senses were more enhanced than her human companions.

Luke nudged aside a half-rotted trunk, rummaging through a pile of tangled belts and broken scabbards. "All worthless," he grumbled. "Ugh. Risked our necks for *scraps*."

"The big find is the letter," Jackson reminded him, turning a small, tarnished ring over, then weighing it in his palm. It wasn't even real silver. Perhaps iron, painted over. Worthless, some cheap trinket a highway bandit might use as a ruse. He pocketed it anyway out of habit. "We'll need travel coin, though."

"I can help," Riven offered. She knelt near the largest tent, rummaging quickly, then emerged with a modest leather pouch that jingled faintly. "At least it's something."

Luke craned his neck to see. "Well, the day's not a total bust."

They regrouped near the embers, which had cooled to a dull glow. The air carried a damp chill that cut through their cloaks. Jackson swallowed against the dryness in his throat. He cleaned his sword on a rag taken from a fallen bandit's patchwork armor, then sheathed it.

As Riven stood watch, Luke knelt by Jackson's side to check his injuries. The warm flicker of dying firelight revealed a blossoming bruise along Jackson's ribs. "Definitely going to need downtime soon," Luke quipped, carefully pressing the bruise. "Can't have you keeling over on the road."

Jackson's eyes narrowed. "It's not that bad."

"Stubborn is not a synonym for healthy."

"Means I'm still breathing." He stretched, ignoring the pinch in his side. "We have to leave soon if we want to get there before whoever set these bandits on the courier gets wise that we're coming. The capital is far."

A rustle of wind swept across the remains of the campsite, scattering ash. Riven's keen elf ears lifted slightly. Her expression grew taut. "We should move tonight. Dawn will see us slowed by travelers on the roads."

Luke brushed the dirt off his knees and stood. "Fun times ahead. Nothing says we can't catch a little rest after we're beyond Duskwarren Rise. I'm sure you can handle riding a few miles in pain, oh fearless demon knight."

Jackson shot Luke a stern look, but no actual anger was behind it. Years of living with the brand on his flesh only deepened his resolve not to lash out at harmless jests. "Call me 'demon knight' too often, and someone else might start believing it," he remarked.

Riven's gaze flicked over. "They already do," she murmured,

not unkindly. "But if you can lead us out of here alive every time, I don't care what rumors they spread."

The small compliment left the air silent. Jackson set his jaw. He had not asked for the infernal mark, but every skirmish proved a curse could be twisted into a tool of survival. He turned back to the bandit corpses. Most lay in scattered heaps around the blackened campfire. A sour tang of char drifted from the scattered debris. "Let's at least bury them," he suggested. "We're not animals."

Luke sighed. "You're right. But you'll do the heavy lifting with that freakish strength of yours."

Riven's eyes flashed, but she wordlessly moved to help organize the bodies. They worked methodically, clearing a shallow scrape in the dirt for each. Jackson's knuckles stung where he pressed them into the hard earth, muscles already protesting from the fight.

The sky deepened in color, the last purple smudging into near darkness. They said no prayers nor lingered in sentiment, but at least the scoundrels wouldn't be devoured by crows. Even a petty bandit deserved an end with a little dignity.

By the time they finished, the moon had risen, pale and cold above the silhouettes of twisted pine trees. Luke used the tip of his dagger to prod the fire's remnants, scattering sparks into the night. Riven folded her arms, glancing east, her posture tense.

Jackson shifted, muscles knotting at the memory of the courier's satchel scrap. He stooped near the bandit who had carried the royal letter, no doubt the leader of this sorry group. The man's ragged cloak reeked of old ale.

A quick check revealed a hidden pocket inside the cloak, holding a single torn scrap of cloth with King Rodric's crest. Tattered edges suggested the courier might have struggled to keep it from them. A surge of anger mingled with regret in Jackson's chest.

He rose and rubbed the back of his neck. *This never should've happened.* The war might have ended, but outlaws still roamed free. That letter was evidence. The king obviously needed something from him. And the monarch's requests weren't trifles.

Luke studied Jackson's face. "You'll answer that summons, yeah?"

Jackson clenched his jaw, remembering the king's watchful gaze the last time they met, when he'd first joined the King's Eye. "I can't ignore it." The faint glow of his markings flared in renewed frustration. "Damn it, I was hoping to stay under the radar."

Luke gave a tired half-smile. "Since when do you do anything quietly?"

Riven shot them a sidelong glance. "Humans have a flair for drama. It's how you survive your short lifespans, perhaps."

Jackson released a dry snort. "Could say the same for elves, though from your perspective, I imagine it's all foolish noise. But if you want to come with me, I won't refuse. You saved my life back there."

Riven inclined her head, acknowledging the gratitude without voicing it. She reached for her bow, checking the string and adjusting her quiver. "I go for my own reasons. The rest is convenient timing."

A breeze carried the scent of wild lavender from a nearby ridge, a curious sweetness amid the aftermath of bloodshed. Jackson stared at the letter, brow furrowed. An uneasy tension hummed through his bones. King Rodric must have known trouble was brewing. Perhaps these outlaws were only a symptom. *What else is coming?* he wondered.

Still, the letter asked for him. From the looks of Riven's calculating eyes and Luke's easy grin, the three of them might become an odd traveling party. Jackson found no comfort in that, but it was better than facing this uncertain call alone.

He glanced at Riven. "I do want to know something. Why

show up and help us at all? The bandits were a threat to the region, but you've obviously got bigger issues with humans."

She paused. "Keeping my domain free of wretched pests is reason enough. These bandits earned an arrow the moment I heard they planned to push deeper into elven territory to hide. I wasn't about to let that happen."

Luke wagged a finger. "So you're playing the ominous elven avenger type, eh? I like it."

Riven's expression didn't change, but faint amusement crossed her eyes. "And you're playing the fool, I see."

"Professionally so," Luke retorted, snapping a flamboyant bow. "I should have been a court jester. Don't know how I ended up here."

Jackson turned away from their banter and folded the letter neatly, placing it in a safe inside pocket of his cloak. "We'll worry about roads, rations, and justifying our next move when dawn breaks. For now, I need a moment." He gingerly touched the bruise on his side.

"Don't bleed out," Riven stated curtly, though her glance carried a glimmer of concern.

"Would ruin the mood," Luke added.

Jackson sank against the trunk of a gnarled tree, mind churning despite his exhaustion. At his feet, an ember popped, sending a tiny shower of sparks skyward. *Wherever the next step takes me, I can't abandon it.* His vow to the Crown wasn't easily broken, and ignoring this summons would only coil that oath tighter.

He felt the swirling presence of the same infernal power that let him slash and burn through brigands. It churned in his veins, a dark echo urging him to charge forward, heedless of the cost. He fought it as he always did, refusing to let it submerge him in rage.

Riven moved closer, shifting her weight. "You said nothing about these 'ghosts' that haunt you," she murmured.

Jackson's voice was quiet as he answered. "Those ghosts remain mine to carry." He glanced at Luke, who busied himself tying off a wound on his forearm, then offered her a shrug. "I know where I stand. The king's call can't be ignored. I'll face it, no matter what nightmares it stirs."

Riven's gaze briefly lingered on him before she turned, accepting he wouldn't elaborate. They all knew plans were in motion, though none spoke it aloud. War had ended months ago, but trouble brewed anywhere a few desperate souls stirred up chaos.

Luke shoved a stray lock of hair from his brow, then dropped onto a rock beside the dull fire. "We staying here for the night? Or do you fancy traveling in the dark with bruised bones and frayed nerves?" He pulled a dented tin flask from his belt and swigged. "I'm all for a ghost walk, but try not to blame me if I cry about my sore feet come morning."

Jackson exhaled, letting his eyes drift shut. The tension in his neck loosened by a thread. "We'll find a place to rest for a few hours, then we move out."

He pressed a hand over the parchment pocket, the chill of night brushing his skin. He could still taste the metallic tang of adrenaline on his tongue. The bandits had been no ordinary roadside rabble if they dared seize a royal courier's message. Someone wanted it off its rightful course. That was reason enough to answer quickly.

Riven adjusted her cloak, scanning the perimeter. She seemed perpetually prepared for another ambush. Luke poured a trickle of water onto the last cinders, sending a ghostly spiral of steam into the evening air.

Jackson rose slowly, ignoring the stab of pain across his ribs. "I'll need both of you," he decided. "Whatever demands the king has, it's big. Looks like we're traveling together for now, if that suits you."

Luke saluted with two fingers against his brow. "Hey, I'm a

fan of living another day. Besides, the roads between here and the capital are rumored to be crawling with scavengers looking to take advantage of weak souls who don't know how to fight back."

Riven's nod was slight. "I'll keep my arrows ready. Humans have a habit of surprising me with their stupidity."

Jackson offered a thin grin. The odd camaraderie between them felt tenuous, but it was preferable to going alone in the dark. He took a final glance at the bandit camp they'd left in ruins, the swirling ashes, the lumps of freshly disturbed earth, the stench of smoke clinging to everything. Each detail revealed how fragile Kharadorn's so-called peace remained.

At last, he turned toward the track leading away from Duskwarren Rise. Luke quietly took point, scanning for movement, while Riven walked a few paces behind, watchful as a hawk.

Jackson flexed his fingers, feeling the sting of fresh cuts across his knuckles. He patted the pocket containing the king's letter. Did this herald a new confrontation that might spark chaos in the realm? He sensed it might. *Damned if I run from it*, he thought. *And damned if I stand still.*

With a grim set to his jaw, he steeled himself. He would answer the call. No matter what ghosts waited.

CHAPTER TWO

Jackson shifted uncomfortably on the creaking plank bench, one hand gripping the wagon's wooden railing as the steam-hauled contraption hissed down the muddy road. The early morning fog swallowed most of the surrounding hills in drifting gray swirls. In the driver's seat, a gaunt operator worked the engine's levers like an overburdened conductor, each puff of smoke accompanied by sharp clangs beneath the wagon's riveted metal plating.

Luke sat opposite Jackson, legs stretched in a posture far too casual for anyone perched on a still-rumbling machine. He tapped on his thigh with every squeak of the wheels. Riven remained silent, cross-legged near the back, arms folded over her dark cloak. She stared at the passing countryside, her gaze suggesting she was thinking of a colder, more distant place.

A hill loomed ahead, its slope carved by the violence of old siege weapons. Shattered rock and weathered spikes littered the roadside. Jackson exhaled, wishing the route weren't so cragged. "Won't be making good time," he muttered.

Luke smirked. "Better than walking, mate. Although that might actually be faster if this hunk of metal keeps coughing like a sick cat."

The driver cast a wary glance over his shoulder. "She'll get you there," he fired back, voice muffled by the bandanna over his mouth. "Long as these roads don't break her first." He turned back and gave a lever a yank, sending a trembling vibration beneath their boots.

The wagon groaned and rattled on, trudging through a patch of sludge that splattered across its iron-riveted flanks. Jackson's gaze flicked to Riven. Her hood concealed most of her face, but slight tension tightened her mouth. She had used few words since they left Duskwarren Rise. The memory of those bandits still lingered.

A sigh slipped from Jackson's lips. They were on borrowed time. King Rodric's summons weighed against his ribcage like a hidden brand. The recollection of that official crest stoked a hum of dread in his chest. He'd once followed a baron's summons to the letter and clashed with a sword-for-hire. That fight ended with the mercenary's last gasp over Jackson's shocking use of demon-fire. The day left scars, both visible and not.

Luke's voice broke his reverie. "So, still reeling from the last fiasco? You look like a storm cloud."

Riven's eyes swiveled in his direction. "If you call a demon firestorm a mere 'fiasco'…" She trailed off with a scoff.

Jackson managed a half-hearted chuckle. "I was thinking about the war." He pressed a palm against his thigh. "A baron hired a killer to take me out. I was pinned down behind some old fort's rubble. The man nearly took off my head in the first strike."

Luke's grin widened. "Let me guess. You turned him into cinders?"

"Not immediately." Jackson ignored the dryness in his mouth. "We traded blows for ages in the mud. No cheering crowds, no fancy speeches, only two men trying to kill each other. I was a fraction faster and drove my blade through his chest." He swallowed. "But not before tapping into the infernal powers inside me. The poor bastard saw that swirl of demon-fire and nearly dropped his sword."

Luke's eyebrows shot up. "He was paid to kill you but didn't expect a hellspawn trick, I take it?"

Riven exhaled. "Humans never consider the consequences of meddling in dark powers."

Jackson said nothing. She wasn't entirely wrong. The endless scrapes of war wagons and the shifting allegiances had left the roads in tatters. Now, judge and jury might be whichever passing soldier wore the king's crest, or whichever outlaw held the bigger crossbow.

A sudden pothole jolted the wagon. Luke cursed, nearly biting his tongue. "I forgot how charming these roads are," he grumbled, bracing a hand against the side.

"Enough talk," the driver barked, adjusting a gear that released a hiss of steam. "Next town is up ahead. I'm dropping you folks there for a bit. Need water for the boiler."

Jackson nodded tersely. The wagon swayed, giving them a view of the upcoming settlement. Low walls circled a scatter of houses with broken windows. A small roadside inn stood near the gate, its wooden sign swinging precariously.

As the wagon halted with a lurch, the smell of burned coal drifted in. The driver motioned them off. "I'll take an hour to stoke this baby. Spend your coin or don't. I don't care. Just be back when I'm done."

A wave of relief washed over Jackson. The bench had done little for his aching back. He stretched his shoulders and hopped down. Riven landed beside him, knees bending gracefully, while Luke nearly toppled but recovered, scuffing his boots in the dirt.

As they approached the inn, curious eyes peered through cracked window shutters. Jackson's tattered cloak and runic scars always drew stares. He'd grown used to them, but something in the tension of this settlement felt sharper.

The inn's wooden door creaked, and they entered a dim,

cramped common room. A single lantern dangled from a hook overhead, swaying with each step on the warped floorboards. A handful of travelers occupied the tables. Behind the counter, the innkeeper, a lanky man with wide, anxious eyes, froze at the sight of them.

Luke offered a disarming grin. "Mornin'. Got any breakfast?"

The innkeeper cleared his throat. "We've porridge and some stale bread. That be all. Coin up front."

As Luke rummaged through a small pouch containing silver coins from the bandit stash, Jackson approached the unlit fireplace. He plucked a pipe from his belt, tapping its metal tip on the hearthstone. Riven watched him from the corner of her eye, her posture guarded.

"Two coppers for the bread," the innkeeper announced. "And don't cause trouble."

Feet shuffled across the floor. Another patron in the corner, an older man wrapped in a tattered cloak, stared at Jackson with open mistrust. A single word left the man's lips...*demon*. Barely voiced, but Jackson heard it all the same.

He said nothing, busying himself with filling the pipe's bowl. A sliver of infernal warmth danced along his neck markings. He channeled the faintest flicker of that energy to light the tobacco, an act he rarely performed openly. The faint, sulfurous glow pulsed at his fingertip before igniting. In the gloom, it looked like an ember from some forbidden pit.

The innkeeper gasped. His face blanched. One or two travelers stood from their chairs, eyes round, any talk dying on their lips.

Luke clucked his tongue. "You ever not scare the piss outta folks?" He elbowed Jackson and turned to the innkeeper. "Relax. My friend's harmless unless you pick a fight." A tight smile accompanied his words.

Jackson exhaled a puff of smoke, teeth clenched around the pipe. The innkeeper forced a nod, though tremors still rippled across his face. "D-do what you will," the man stammered. He looked ready to duck behind the counter.

Riven folded her arms. Her gaze darted around, measuring every reaction. "Humans and their fear. Always the same."

Jackson shot her a sidelong look, then set the pipe aside, letting a swirl of fragrant smoke fade. "All right," he muttered under his breath. "We'll keep this quick."

They claimed a rough-hewn table near the corner, planting themselves on wobbly stools. The innkeeper, presumably eager to remain in one piece, brought over two chipped cups and a wooden bowl of porridge that might have been warm an hour earlier. Luke tossed him a coin, more than required, and waved off the change.

The man hustled away, leaving them to the murmurs in the room. A few seats over, a rail-thin musician strummed a lute, plucking a slow tune that might have been pleasant if the strings weren't so out of tune. Jackson caught the faint melody of an old war ballad. Its lyrics, half-forgotten by most, reminded him of the kingdom's pride.

Luke scooped up a spoonful of porridge and wrinkled his nose. "Better than nothing, I guess." He grinned at Jackson. "So, about that time you nearly set the battlefield ablaze. Do you always do that for effect, or was it a special day?"

Jackson resisted the urge to roll his eyes. He sipped stale water from his cup. "That day, I didn't control it. It was more like a reflex."

"Reflex, huh?" Luke flourished his spoon. "One second the baron's hired killer was bragging about collecting your head and the next, *whoosh*. A whole circle of blackened earth around you both."

Riven tapped her fingers on the table. "Trust is a precious commodity in humans. I doubt using demon-fire in public helps engender it."

Luke chuckled. "Well, better demon-fire on our side than theirs. Right, Jackson?"

Jackson said nothing. Silence settled, broken by the occasional chord from the lute. Outside, a gust of wind rattled the shutters.

When the innkeeper returned, Luke motioned for him to stay calm and fished a palm-sized medallion from a hidden pocket. He held it face-down, letting only the innkeeper see its engraved crest, the minimal sign of the King's Eye.

The man's pupils dilated. He nearly tripped over his own feet backing away.

Luke raised a brow. "We appreciate the hospitality." His tone was measured, quietly emphasizing the Crown took notice of these parts. The innkeeper bobbed his head in a rush, wiping sweat from his temple.

"Of course, s-sir," he replied, voice trembling. "Let me know if you need anything else."

Jackson averted his gaze. Every time that insignia came out, the tension grew palpable. He wondered if it was better to remain a rumored demon than to confirm his link to the King's Eye. Still, intimidation had its uses. They needed rest without prying trouble.

They finished the meager meal in silence. The other patrons stared at their table from time to time, uneasy. Some recognized the crest. Others simply cowered at Jackson's presence. By the time Luke rose to settle the final cost, the innkeeper seemed torn between gratitude and fear, half-bowing in confusion.

Riven tossed a copper coin onto the table for the musician, who promptly ended his out-of-tune strumming. The elf glanced at the lute. "You ought to learn more stirring tunes," she muttered. "Your kingdom has enough dirges lately."

The musician gave her a grateful nod, apparently relieved to receive any coin at all, and began a quiet, albeit slightly more hopeful melody.

In the gray morning light outside, the trio regrouped by the wagon. The driver's mechanical chores had brought the engine back to a billowing hiss. The man swept a rag across his greasy brow and eyed them impatiently. "If you're done with your fancy infiltration, let's ride. Got a schedule to keep."

Jackson climbed up first, bracing against the wagon's side. Luke clambered in behind, rummaging through the small stash of bandit loot they were gradually trading for supplies. Odds and ends like cheap rings, half-filled pouches of questionable coin, and cracked and worthless amulets. Riven took her seat quietly, checking the fletching of her arrows as though expecting danger.

A moment later, they were off again, the engine chugging a weary protest. Clouds of smoke billowed overhead, blending with the drifting fog. The road unfurled before them, lined with broken fences and scorched farmland. Some houses looked inhabited, others abandoned. Occasionally, a traveler hurried out of sight at a glimpse of the wagon's passengers.

Jackson's mind wandered to the letter jammed in the pouch at his hip. The day he'd sworn his oath, he had promised to serve the realm. Even so, suspicion trailed him everywhere, thanks to the shred of infernal power licking at his bones. *A Hellspawned Knight isn't exactly the face of comfort,* he thought.

Luke nudged him. "You good?"

Jackson nodded stiffly. "Just thinking."

Riven watched them from under her hood. "Think faster. The king's summons isn't a casual tea invitation."

Luke released a laugh. "Hey, maybe it is. We show up, have a light snack, perhaps Riven entertains with her best scowl." Her glare in response made him amend hastily, "Or not."

The wagon rattled across a shaky bridge spanning a dried riverbed. The distant farmland gave way to rolling plains dotted with patchy crops. In one field, a farmer paused mid-swing of his scythe, staring warily until the wagon lurched out of sight.

It felt like an eternity, but eventually. midday sun broke through the thinning fog. Luke rummaged for a cloth and dabbed sweat from his brow. "So, question. If the capital's still on edge about war refugees, how are they going to react to your demon marks, Jackson?"

Jackson's jaw tightened. "They've seen worse," he replied.

Riven glanced at the smoldering symbol on Jackson's neck that sometimes glowed in direct sunlight. "If you let that aura slip again, we'll see how quickly their courtesy disappears."

Luke snorted. "Speak for yourself, oh Mistress of Politeness."

She stared flatly but made no retort. The wagon rumbled on, spitting sparks as the steam engine struggled uphill.

They passed a half-scorched roadhouse, graffiti scrawled across its charred boards. Jackson caught sight of the words "Demon Scourge" scrawled in white chalk. He inwardly grimaced. *Always the same fear,* he thought. At least no one here was actively hurling stones.

"Wish we had more to trade," Luke piped up, forcing a lighter tone. "Some better rations, better ale. Maybe a new traveling companion who doesn't mind demon-fire?" He jabbed Jackson's arm.

Jackson mustered a smirk. "You can always walk."

The day wore on with little conversation. By mid-afternoon, their wagon driver shoved a dented can into the boiler, cursing like a man who'd lost a bet. He hammered on the outer shell of the steam chamber until it spat more scalding vapor. Riven seized the chance to slip down from the wagon bed and pace the roadside, scanning the horizon.

The fields remained eerily quiet, a reflection of the kingdom's state. After the driver declared the contraption "barely functional," they continued, albeit with more squeaking than before. Each mile grew slower.

They stopped again near a weather-beaten stable to swap a few worthless trinkets for dried fruit and stale biscuits. The stablemaster glared suspiciously until Luke flashed the medallion again, prompting a grudging exchange. They ate as they rode,

Jackson and Riven chewing in silence while Luke smacked his lips. Jackson tried not to let it annoy him.

Finally, the outlines of travelers grew more frequent along the horizon. Caravans hauling crates, a handful of mounted scouts. The roads showed slightly improved upkeep. Perhaps the capital wasn't far. However, the tension among the three had quietly grown, curling in the pit of Jackson's stomach.

"You sure you don't want to read the rest of that letter before we arrive?" Luke asked, rummaging in a side pouch for a waterskin. "We got the gist, but maybe the full details?"

Jackson shook his head. "We know enough. The king wants me. The rest is best left intact." He pulled his cloak tighter, mind on how quickly rumors traveled. In times like these, any sign of an official dispatch might incite theft or blackmail.

Riven shrugged, drawing out one of her arrows to inspect its runic grooves. "Either way, I've no interest in your human politics. But you helped handle the bandits who threatened my territory. Now, I'm obliged until I see it's no longer worth my time."

"Charming," Luke remarked with a grin that only nudged Riven's sour mood slightly.

The evening light paled, a pinkish glow obscured by drifting clouds as the wagon crested another hill, revealing a wide stretch of road etched with wagon tracks leading deeper into Kharadorn. They heard the clang of distant blacksmiths and glimpsed a few outlying farmsteads still bearing scorch marks from old battles.

They rolled past a crooked road sign reading *Seven leagues to Kharadorn's Wall*. The driver barked, "I'll take you a bit farther, then I'm turning around for my next job. This route's done."

No one objected. Each tick of the wagon's wheels carried them closer to the city, closer to King Rodric's summons. Flocks of birds took flight over a half-flooded marsh, cawing as if witnessing something ominous.

Jackson shifted his weight, glancing at Luke and Riven. They wouldn't pass quietly for the rest of the trip. His demon-fire would ensure that. He felt the letter's shape beneath his cloak, a reminder of duty and the storms sure to follow.

Riven closed her eyes as if lost in thought. Luke pretended to doze, but his hand remained near his hidden dagger. The steam wagon hissed, forging through ruts and mud, each mile an echo of the war-torn past.

They spoke little but shared the same unspoken truth. Their travel from the inn was merely the beginning. More dangers awaited. The stolen loot they carried wouldn't buy them peace, only temporary sustenance.

The realm's mistrust of anything demonic hovered everywhere Jackson went. Beneath that weight, he steeled himself for whatever audience awaited in the capital. This journey felt like walking a knife's edge, a precarious path that might lead to redemption or a deeper darkness.

The driver spit another curse as the engine sputtered. Jackson's cloak fluttered in the breeze. Riven set her bow across her lap, studying the tree line for threats. Luke cleared his throat as if he might lighten the mood with a joke, but the tension swallowed his words.

Jackson thought it better that Luke didn't jest. He didn't have it in him to smile.

CHAPTER THREE

The driver guided the wagon into a dim alley behind a quiet row of weathered stables. The capital's outer walls loomed nearby, pitted with old battle scars but patched with fresh stone. Here, the hustle of midday traffic was little more than a muffled hum, replaced by the scraping of hooves on cobblestones and the sour smell of horse feed.

Luke hopped out first, adjusting his cloak to hide his belt knife as he squinted against the glare of sunlight reflecting off the high towers beyond the walls. Riven followed, her movements supple and noiseless even without the cover of trees. She said nothing, only tipped her face toward the battlements above.

The capital of Kharadorn was no simple fortress village. It was a sprawling domain of commerce and intrigue, and those walls spoke of hard-won resilience. Jackson exhaled, glancing at the wagon driver before dismounting. After a short nod, the driver flicked the reins and coaxed his engine-driven beast away. The job was done, so he had no further interest in them.

As the rumble faded, the trio stepped across the yard, mud clinging to their boots. The King's Eye seldom wanted a triumphant parade when returning from a mission. Secrecy was the coin they spent most. Jackson was used to discreet stops where no banners unfurled, no braying trumpets blasted. Part of him was relieved. Attention usually brought trouble.

Luke shifted a satchel over one shoulder, clearing his throat as he stared at the weather-beaten stable doors. "So, are we sneaking in through the servant's entrance, or is this the deluxe route for demon knights, surly elves, and roguish charmers?"

"A little respect for the King's Eye," Jackson replied in a low voice. The corner of his mouth curled, half amusement, half caution. "But yes, we're going in quietly."

Riven stepped around a clump of straw, adjusting her quiver. "I do not see the difference," she murmured. "If the king values secrecy, we're all unannounced visitors in his fortress."

Jackson shrugged. He gestured forward, leading them behind the stable block toward a narrow door set flush in the fortress foundation. One of the guards, who wore a nondescript patch on his cloak, let them pass without a word, merely giving Jackson a small salute.

The corridor beyond was cramped, lit with guttering brackets of flame that cast flickering shadows. They moved single file, Luke grumbling under his breath about the smell.

"This city is built like a labyrinth," Luke pointed out. "Every time I come here, I expect to get lost and never see the sun again."

Riven inspected the surfaces without a trace of humor. "Typical human design. Winding corridors, hidden sub-routes, all for clandestine dealings."

Jackson snorted. "Cities have their reasons. After the war, the Crown wanted plenty of ways to maneuver around prying eyes."

At last, the corridor opened into a small antechamber with a high-beamed ceiling. Pillars sculpted from pristine marble lined the space, engraved with subtle runic flourishes that glinted in the lamplight. A soldier in simple plate armor waited there, posture perfectly upright. The man's gaze flicked from Jackson's infernal markings to Riven's pointed ears, then settled on Luke's rakish grin for a second too long. He somehow straightened further.

Jackson gave a respectful nod. "We have an appointment."

The soldier, clearly a King's Eye attaché, opened a heavy door to reveal a broader corridor ahead. Its polished stone floor reflected a handful of tall windows that let in bright afternoon sun. Farther down, the corridor ended in dark wood double doors carved with the royal crest. Men-at-arms crossed halberds at the threshold but parted when they recognized Jackson's brand along his collarbone.

Inside was the receiving chamber. Its marble columns rose to a domed ceiling where colored glass cast swirling patterns of blue, green, and gold. At the far end, upon a dais draped in banners, stood King Rodric himself. He was broad-shouldered, thickly built, with a short-trimmed beard that shone silver in the dappled light. At his side stood Sir Cain, the ever-stoic knight commander, whose expression rivaled carved granite. A handful of silent attendants hovered near the walls.

Jackson inhaled and walked forward. Luke and Riven trailed, flanking him. The old tension coiled in his gut. Encountering royalty or anyone in high authority always reminded him how deeply his curse set him apart. The faint glow of the infernal runes on his neck itched as though responding to the presence of official scrutiny.

Before either of his companions could speak, Jackson sank into a bow. "Your Majesty," he greeted steadily.

Rodric indicated for them to rise, gaze sweeping the three of them. "Jackson McCade," he announced in a firm baritone. "I appreciate your discreet handling of the brigand situation near Duskwarren Rise."

He glanced at Luke, who offered a half-formal bow, then Riven, who inclined her head with cool reserve. The king's brow arched slightly at the elf's presence, but he did not comment.

Instead, Sir Cain stepped forward, briefly looking at Riven.

"We've heard of your marksmanship," he murmured. "It seems your arrows shaped that last encounter to a favorable end."

Riven dipped her chin. "They did."

Luke managed not to blurt anything, though his grin almost seeped out. Jackson was grateful. This was no place for comedic quips.

Rodric clasped his hands. "I summon you for graver tidings," he admitted. "Word reached me of a troubling disappearance." After a pause, he continued, "Master Runeforger Elarius has been abducted. Our scouts believe it the work of forces loyal to Lord Corgrave."

A hush settled over the chamber. *Corgrave,* Jackson thought. *He's hardly a name one forgets.* The war might have dethroned him, but not his craving for power.

Luke exhaled. "Fun. So, he's still out there playing with forbidden forging."

Rodric nodded, expression grim. Then, he turned to a small stand near the throne. Upon it sat a sealed missive. "And there is more." The king broke the wax with a quick motion and scanned the letter. "It seems a duke's son was meant to be under Elarius' protective watch, some side arrangement to ensure the boy's safety from brewing baronial feuds. Instead, the son has been discovered lifeless, possibly by poison or drunken foul play."

The king's jaw tightened. "Another line of suspicion leads us to believe Corgrave used these tragedies to stoke fear. He means to keep the rightful forging secrets out of our hands and funnel resources to a doomsday weapon. We suspect shipments of volcanic steel are flowing to the borderlands."

Sir Cain's voice was low. "If Corgrave refines that steel with Elarius' knowledge, Kharadorn might face an arsenal that tears these fragile alliances apart."

The weight of unspoken obligations clamped around Jackson like an iron band. He glanced at Riven and Luke. "Your Majesty," he started. "These two helped me handle the bandit threat. I vouch for their skill and their discretion."

Luke gave a more official bow, though his lips twitched. "Glad to be recommended, your Grace. We're not exactly amateurs."

Riven stayed silent, but her gaze flicked to Sir Cain. The older knight gave the slightest nod of acknowledgment, as though confirming her presence was acceptable. The tension eased in Jackson's chest. *At least they won't be thrown out now.*

Rodric released a breath. "Very well. If Jackson vouches for you, and Sir Cain sees no harm, you may remain for the rest of this discussion. But be warned, what we speak of here is for no ears beyond the King's Eye." A subtle emphasis in his tone signaled the gravity of the situation.

Luke shifted in place, crossing his arms.

The king looked back at Jackson. "You recall Corgrave's downfall was never fully realized. He slithered away amid the final battles, fanning out rebels to sabotage us. Master Elarius, with his forging mastery, is now in Corgrave's clutches. If Corgrave can fuse volcanic steel, Riftcrown crystals, and unholy runic practices, the result may be catastrophic. This time, we cannot risk underestimating him."

Sir Cain placed a rolled parchment on a small table near the throne. "We traced suspicious shipments of raw volcanic ore heading north, double that amount flowing east. The pattern only makes sense if someone is forging off-grid. We suspect Corgrave intends to produce a new type of weapon, some prototype that could rally exiled houses under his banner."

Jackson's gut tightened. The memory of half-formed rumors about necromantic forging sparked an uneasy swirl in his mind. He forced himself to speak calmly. "What do you require of me, Your Majesty?"

The king's eyes narrowed. "I charge you to find Master Elarius and stop Corgrave's forging efforts before they unleash a new war on this realm. The border barons teeter on the edge of revolt. If they see a chance at victory, they may seize it." He turned to Luke and Riven. "I allow your presence by Jackson's side, if you choose, but I expect only the highest loyalty. Kharadorn's peace is fragile."

Riven lifted her chin. "I have no fondness for war-bound humans, but if Corgrave threatens even the outskirts of elven territory, I'll see him thwarted."

Luke coughed. "In simpler terms, we're in."

Rodric's stern gaze swept back to Jackson. "I know your strength, Hellspawned Knight. Your oath binds you to the Crown. Will you uphold it?"

A familiar spark of infernal energy coiled in Jackson's gut, responding to the question of duty. *There's no turning away from this.* He bowed stiffly. "My blade is yours, Your Majesty."

Rodric's features softened, though the tension in the air remained. "Time is pressing. Corgrave's pawns move quickly, and the abduction of Elarius is a ploy that may be used to blackmail us or produce something vile. We cannot let that happen."

Sir Cain lifted the parchment again. "You three will have the courtesy of traveling with minimal scrutiny in the capital for the moment. I will arrange passes to move through the outer gates. One caution, there are watchers. Men who might want Corgrave to succeed. Tread carefully."

That ended the briefing. Rodric's final words were subdued but biting. "May the realm's fortune be better than it has been of late." Servants approached timidly, as though prepared to usher the group out.

Jackson bowed again, then turned away, leading Luke and Riven off the dais. The hush of the high-ceilinged chamber swallowed their footsteps. They strode back through the corridor, guards stepping aside without comment. The tension lingered even after they had left the throne room behind.

Luke released a long breath after they were outside the inner hall. "We always land in the thick of it, huh?" He cracked a grin.

"Doomsday forging, blackmail, missing runemaster. Makes your usual demon-fire shenanigans look downright trivial, Jackson."

Jackson cast him a sideways glance. "If you're regretting it, you can step back at any time."

"Not a chance," Luke replied lightly. "I want some part in saving the world. It'll beef up my reputation in taverns everywhere."

Riven snorted. "You jest, but tavern songs help your kind remember who did what in battle."

They reached the corridor that twisted toward the exit route. Jackson paused at the small antechamber, where the guard from before stood with stoic vigilance. "I need to handle something before we move out again," he explained. "I'll get you both a place to rest."

Luke rubbed his neck. "Sounds good. I'm starving, too."

Riven shrugged. "As long as it's quiet and out of the Crown's gossip."

Jackson stepped past the guard and continued down a different hallway that sloped up a short flight of stairs. They hurried through more palace corridors, less grand, more functional. Soon, they emerged into open sunlight in the outer courtyard, where a steady flow of foot traffic moved among stone archways.

No one paid them much mind. Although Jackson's raw presence sometimes drew stares, the King's Eye badge pinned at his hip was enough to dissuade casual onlookers. Riven kept her hood lowered. Luke, chatty as ever, commented on the architecture, the hawkers calling out from a distant side street, and his desire for a warm bed.

Eventually, they reached a modest row of old half-timbered buildings off the main thoroughfare. A painted sign squeaked overhead, showing the faint outline of an orchard tree. Perhaps this had once been an orchard-themed inn, though the paint was so chipped, it might as well have been a blot of green over brown.

Jackson rapped on the door. The innkeeper, a short man with a limp, answered.

At first sight of Jackson's brand, the innkeeper started. But the King's Eye medallion softened his reaction. He ushered them in, stammering. "Y-you require rooms?"

"I need two," Jackson told him. "No fuss, no rumor, no trouble. Understand?"

The innkeeper nodded vigorously. "Quiet as a mouse, sir."

Jackson passed him a few coins. "This should cover it for one night, at least. I'll see how things stand after that." He turned to Luke and Riven. "Make yourselves comfortable. Eat and rest. I have a brief errand, King's Eye business. I'll return soon."

Luke doffed an imaginary cap. "Don't let the city guards scoop you up. We have to find that runeforger, remember?"

Riven shifted her weight, meeting Jackson's eyes with a hint of curiosity. Or suspicion. Sometimes, it was hard to read her. "We will be here," she promised.

Jackson nodded. Outside the small inn's entry, he paused. The breeze carried the city's tangle of aromas. Roasted chestnuts from a cart, a blacksmith's hot forge around the corner, and the dusty dryness of stone. Above, spires rose from behind walls that once bled from catapult bombardment. *Resilient, indeed.*

He turned back to see Luke drifting toward the inn's common room, likely enticed by the thought of bread and ale. Riven remained by the threshold, gaze steady upon Jackson. She did not speak, but a question lingered in her eyes. *She wonders where I'm off to,* he guessed. *She's not the type to pry openly, but she'll be watching.*

He inclined his head to her, then stepped onto the street, letting the door shut behind him.

CHAPTER FOUR

Jackson stood in a silent corridor deep beneath the castle's grand courtyard, hands clenched at his sides. Pale torchlight flickered against damp stone walls, casting uneven shadows that stretched like grasping claws. He tried not to dwell on how uncomfortably those claw-like shapes echoed the demonic markings on his own flesh. Ahead of him, a pair of narrow doors stood ajar, revealing the dim interior of a private chapel.

Sir Cain awaited inside. The knight commander cut an imposing figure in ceremonial armor marked with the insignia of the King's Eye. His stern gaze swept Jackson, lingering on the faint red glow along Jackson's neck. A robed cleric stood at the room's far end, silent and watchful, head bowed.

"Step forward," Sir Cain invited quietly. "Your vow is overdue."

Jackson's boots scuffed against the polished marble floor. The space felt impossibly small, though it was large enough for rows of pews and a single black altar in the middle. Molten symbols glimmered on the walls, etched runes set aglow by alchemical torches. Their swirling lines rang with unspoken power. This was where the Crown renewed oaths too dangerous or too fragile to rely upon normal pledge ceremonies. In Jackson's case, both applied.

He inhaled, ignoring the spike of heat that flared in the infernal sigils on his neck. With each breath, the demonic power in his veins pulsed, restless, hungry for freedom. *That thirst is never going away*, he thought, straightening his shoulders. *But I can keep it caged.*

He advanced to the center of the chapel. The robed cleric placed a thick tome onto a marble podium. Sir Cain positioned himself beside it. A second stand near them held a ceremonial brand shaped like a polished silver rod. From the rod's tip, faint ribbons of arcane light flitted into the air.

Sir Cain intoned, "By the Crown's authority, and under the watchful eyes of Heaven and Hell, we bind you anew." He nodded to the cleric. "Proceed."

The cleric opened the tome, scanning the lines with careful intensity. Then, in a resonating voice, he read from an ancient formula. Words in an archaic language flowed, swirling around them. Jackson knew enough about the ceremony to recognize command phrases that targeted his demonic essence, shackling it to the king's cause. The runes on the walls echoed those words, shimmering with a deep luminescence.

Pressure built in Jackson's chest. Each syllable felt like a clamp bracing tighter around his spirit. It was an old, familiar pain. He remembered the moment he had first sworn fealty to King Rodric and felt invisible chains wrap around his demon side. He swallowed, tasting iron. His heart thudded in his ears.

"Speak your name and station," the cleric prompted.

"Jackson McCade," he rasped. "Knight of Kharadorn, sworn to the King's Eye."

The runic patterns on the floor flared to life. Sir Cain placed one gauntleted hand on the silver rod, pressing it against a carved indentation in the marble. The rod began to glow with the same sullen light as Jackson's neck markings. Across the chapel, the robed cleric continued chanting.

Jackson's skin tingled. Heat spread from his collarbone to his jaw, the infernal sigils blazing. *Steady*, he told himself, fists clenched so tight that his knuckles went white.

"You will repeat the vow," Sir Cain instructed. "Each time, direct your words into the rod. It will channel the spell."

Jackson inclined his head in understanding. This was the testing moment, forcing him to speak the oath that pinned his demon influence in service to the Crown. He exhaled, voice trembling with tension as he began. "I swear to serve King Rodric with unwavering loyalty, to protect Kharadorn from all that threatens her people. And to hold my demon-fire in check, unleashing it only at the realm's dire need."

The moment he said "demon-fire," the molten runes on the walls rippled. A force pressed at his chest, demanding more. Sir Cain's steady presence anchored him. The commander carefully touched the rod's tip to Jackson's neck. A searing pulse jolted him, and the demon marks on his skin flared bright crimson before subsiding.

"Again," commanded Sir Cain.

Jackson repeated the vow, trying not to flinch when a crackle of arcane energy licked his collarbone. He spoke slowly, each word layered with resolve, though his teeth ached from the strain of containing his infernal nature. Blood pounded through his veins in a frantic rhythm.

The robed cleric watched with hooded eyes, verifying the incantation's integrity. Twisting arcs of magical light spiraled upward from the floor, forming a lattice around Jackson's legs and arms. With every repetition, the lattice tightened like ghostly chains.

By the time Sir Cain indicated the final line of the vow, Jackson's chest felt heavy and scorched. His limbs trembled. Tangerine sparks flickered at the edges of his vision, as if the demon within tried to burn its way out. The vow's magic pressed back, forging a barrier that reined it in.

"Speak the final words," the cleric instructed.

Jackson's breath rattled. "I submit my sword to the rightful king, until this realm's peace is assured or my life is forfeit."

A dull ring sounded in his ears. The runes along the walls ignited in one last flare of brilliance, and the arcane lines coiling around his body converged at his heart. Heat blazed through him, sharp, scorching, then gone, leaving only a crushing sensation of something bound.

Sir Cain raised the rod away from Jackson. Pale smoke curled from the silver tip. For a moment, no one moved or spoke. The hush in the chapel felt like the calm after a thunderclap.

The commander's voice rumbled, "It is done. Return here in two seasons for reinforcement. Your demonic taint grows restless. If you delay, the oath's grip may slip."

A metallic taste coated Jackson's tongue. He managed a weary nod. "I understand."

Sir Cain exhaled, perhaps in relief, though it was difficult to read his stoic face behind the polished helmet. The robed cleric cleared his throat, stepping away to close the ritual tome. He offered Sir Cain a solemn bow, then turned to Jackson with polite respect. "Your vow is renewed. May this binding guard both you and the kingdom."

The swirling runes on the walls died down, returning to unlit etchings. Outside, the low clang of a distant watch bell signaled the passing of time. Sir Cain lowered the rod onto its stand, then gestured toward the arched exit. "Leave with caution, Knight. The oath's magic may unsettle your spirit for a few hours."

Jackson inclined his head. "Thank you."

He followed Sir Cain back to the doors. The knight commander took his leave, likely to report the ritual's success to whomever oversaw such records. Left alone, Jackson looked around the emptied chapel. His veins itched as if raw power had been pressed under layers of warded steel. *At least it's contained again,* he thought.

He steadied his breathing and slipped into the outer corridor, feeling relief at the soft glow of torch brackets. The taste of smoke and metal lingered on his tongue.

A flurry of robes caught his eye from the far end. The royal scribe. Jackson recognized the figure at once, ink-stained cuffs, pages rustling in one hand. She approached, her shy smile clashing with the intensity in her gaze. Tall taper candles, set along the corridor for evening illumination, made her eyes look like twin pools of molten copper.

"You came from the vow chamber," she noted, stepping into his path. "I heard you and Sir Cain were down there." She hesitated, as if weighing how best to speak. "He told me not to disturb, but…I waited regardless."

Jackson tried to keep his tone casual. "I appreciate the concern."

She bowed her head, the movement highlighting her slender collarbone under a half-buttoned tunic. Loose strands of hair framed her face. "How do you feel?" Her voice wavered between curiosity and empathy.

"Tired," he admitted, flexing his fingers as a wave of dull heat rippled across his markings. "But it's done. The vow holds, for now."

Her gaze flicked toward his neck, where the runes glowed faintly. She set aside the documents in her arms. "I sensed the magic earlier," she whispered. "It must have been painful."

He grunted, uncertain how to answer. Sir Cain's ceremony had been thorough, not to mention excruciating. He was about to speak when she stepped closer, voice dropping to a conspiratorial hush.

"You're risking everything carrying that demon burden." She searched his face. "We record glimpses of your missions in the archives. Never with your name, but I can read between the lines.

You save countless lives, yet no one ever thanks you." She paused, breath quickening. "I mean, I want to thank you."

Warmth stirred in Jackson's chest. "You owe me nothing," he told her.

She shook her head. "The kingdom owes you, whether they acknowledge it or not." Her free hand rose hesitantly, brushing near the edge of his collar. "May I?"

Jackson nodded. He stood still as her fingertips traced the ridges of his collarbone. The runic scars pulsed beneath her touch. She looked enthralled by the swirl of linework across his skin. Each stroke made him aware of how sensitive the demon markings were beneath the wards.

His pulse skittered. A swirl of excitement and wariness mingled in his veins. *This vow weighs on me, but so does an ache for comfort*, he thought.

"The scribes say you channel infernal flames," she murmured. "And yet you remain kind." Her words trembled with more than scholarly fascination.

He swallowed. "I struggle," he admitted. "But it's better me than letting that power run wild."

She pressed her palm gently against his chest. Neither moved. A hush blanketed the corridor, broken only by the soft crackle of distant torches. Then, she stretched on her toes, lips parting in a whisper. "You fight so hard. Let me...let me give you a reason to breathe."

Before he could second-guess the impulse, she leaned into him, her mouth brushing his in a questing, heated kiss. It grounded him in sensation beyond the vow's raw magic, reminding him of simpler desires. Something in him uncoiled. He responded with cautious fervor, cradling her face as she exhaled a trembling sigh.

Their surroundings seemed to vanish. The cold stone corridor melted into the warmth of shared hunger. His hands found the curve of her waist, and she pressed closer, lips parting to deepen the kiss. Faint scents clung to her clothes, ink and parchment and the sweet hint of soap. He lost track of time as they gave in to the moment.

When at last they paused, breath rasping, she looked up with wide eyes. A flush stained her cheeks. "I've wanted that," she confessed, laughter and uncertainty mingling in her voice. "Perhaps that's reckless."

"Reckless, maybe," he managed, voice husky. "But you've done more for my spirit than you know." He cupped her chin. "I know my path is precarious."

She shook her head, stepping back to study him with the intensity of someone memorizing a beloved painting. "I want to stand in your corner, Jackson." Her fingertips brushed a jagged scar on his shoulder. "I only wish I were braver."

He released a slow breath, still reeling from the rush of closeness. "You're plenty brave," he whispered, sliding his thumb across her jaw.

She lingered, hands tracing the lines of old claw marks across his shoulders. The fleeting sting of sense told him to step away, yet the longing in her eyes made him remain. His chest ached with gratitude, surprise, and a spark of something unfamiliar. *Hope*.

Another stolen kiss followed, this one gentler, filled with silent promises. He embraced it, letting the closeness soothe the raw edges of the oath. Her breath mingled with his, and they stood as if the entire castle had vanished, leaving only the hush of two heartbeats.

Eventually, reason pushed its way back. She shifted, cheeks flushed, awareness of their location settling in. Quiet footsteps from a distant passage reminded them they were still in royal halls.

She straightened, clearing her throat. "I should return to my duties soon," she murmured, swallowing hard. "But I'll be thinking of you. And your vow. One day, maybe it won't carry such a burden." She offered a small smile, stepping away slowly.

Jackson's demon marks warmed as though in protest to her absence. He forced a faint grin. "Take care." He dipped his head in acknowledgment. "And...thank you."

Her eyes glowed with emotion as she collected her scattered pages, turned, and slipped away into the corridor's gloom. Her form vanished behind a bend in the stone hall, leaving only candlelight in her wake.

Jackson stood rooted in place. His pulse hammered from the ceremony's furious magic and the taste of that kiss. *What am I doing?* he wondered, recollecting how precarious his existence was. The memory of her lips lingered, easing the sting of fresh incantations.

When at last he found the strength to move, he inhaled and followed the candlelit path. A new resolve formed within him.

He would continue serving Kharadorn, harnessing the flames that dwelled inside him. He would fight for a future free of Corgrave's threat and all else that endangered the realm, even if it meant he had to remain the monster at the gates. If there was comfort to be found in humble corners and stolen moments, he would cling to it, no matter how brief.

With that private resolve burning stronger than the shackles around his demon-fire, Jackson ascended toward the outer corridors. As he strode on, he could almost taste possibility in the air. That despite the shadows lurking in his blood, he might still find a measure of solace, and hold the nightmares at bay.

CHAPTER FIVE

Morning light spread across the high walls of the royal castle, its brightness muted by the hush that filled one of the fortress' lesser-known courtyards. Jackson stood near a cluster of old columns, the marble still dark from the night's lingering dew. He tugged his cloak tighter around his chest. Even in this place, secrecy reigned. Sir Cain had chosen the courtyard precisely because few guards ever set foot here, and the massive hedges made a natural barrier against prying eyes.

Luke and Riven had shown up moments earlier. Luke leaned casually against a chipped statue, arms folded, while Riven kept her posture erect near a narrow archway. Their expressions ranged from impatience to mild curiosity, as if they preferred to be anywhere else rather than in a hidden corner of the king's residence. Nevertheless, they had answered Jackson's summons quickly. Their unusual presence was expected to ruffle more than a few feathers.

Sir Cain paced the perimeter in full armor. He wore no ceremonial cape nor any sign of pomp. Only the small insignia of the King's Eye on his left pauldron revealed his station. The sound of his metal boots against smooth stone tapped out a steady rhythm.

His face looked as stern as ever, with deep lines etched near his eyes, and his brow furrowed whenever he threw glances at Luke and Riven.

Three cloaked figures waited near the central fountain. Their hoods draped low, disguising their features except for faint outlines of furrowed chins. Each wore a small ring on the right hand, a sign that they worked under the King's Eye, though perhaps not as knights or enforcers. Informants came in many shapes, from traveling merchants to simple townsfolk. Jackson knew them well enough to trust their intelligence, yet they eyed Luke and Riven with caution.

Sir Cain paused in mid-step. "We begin." He gestured for everyone to circle the trickling fountain. "The King's Eye has confirmed fresh rumors linking Corgrave's allies to contraband forging. You, Jackson, will lead a small infiltration detail outside city walls."

Luke's eyebrows lifted in barely contained excitement. "Finally, a solid mission. Beats loitering around stables."

Riven nodded. She said nothing, but her silver-gray eyes reflected keen interest. Or maybe suspicion.

Jackson inclined his head. "We have leads from the last assignment about Corgrave's movement of volcanic steel. It's time to follow them."

Sir Cain's gaze moved to Luke and Riven. "Yes. The king has given a provisional order to let you assist Jackson. You are not sworn to the King's Eye, but events require additional hands. See that you don't make us regret it."

Luke flashed a grin. "I'll try to behave. Although, some claim I have no manners." He jerked a thumb in Jackson's direction. "But ask demon-boy here. I'm the soul of politeness."

A low grunt escaped Jackson's lips. "You might not want to call me that in front of Sir Cain." He eyed Luke. "He could interpret it as disrespect."

"Disrespect would be foolish, given the mission's seriousness." Sir Cain did not look amused.

One of the cloaked informants stepped forward, clearing his throat. His voice was clipped, as if choosing words with care. "We have some intel concerning safehouses used for black-market forging. They're scattered between here and the southern roads. Corgrave's people have offered silver, and sometimes more, to keep them hidden."

Luke's grin faded. "What do you mean 'sometimes more?'"

The informant shrugged. "Rumors say certain smuggler rings get paid in war crystals or even the promise of rank if Corgrave returns to power. Greed can twist men."

Riven released a quiet breath. "Humans and their unending thirst for blood money. Most in the outer villages will fall for a few coins without thinking of the consequences."

"Some in the elven world do the same," Jackson countered gently, meeting her gaze. "Before we judge them, let's remember desperation can drive anyone."

Sir Cain dipped his head. "We have reason to believe Corgrave is building alliances with those who handle magical contraband. War crystals are indeed in circulation. If they fall into rebel hands, the casualties will be high."

Riven's shoulders shifted. "I heard stories of war crystals that amplify ranged bombardments or even enhance cursed constructs. That is an abomination. I won't let them near the elven outposts."

"I'd rather not see them used in the capital, either." Luke shrugged. "This city has lived through one war. Another would be bad for tavern business."

A faint spark of tension evaporated when Sir Cain gestured again to the cloaked informants. They produced a small folded map. Jackson recognized it as one he had glimpsed in the King's Eye archives days before.

Lines and marks scrawled in dark ink indicated possible

smuggler routes. Winding paths snaked outward from the capital's walls, curving around the farmland, bridging rivers, and disappearing near a region Jackson knew was a gateway to Riftcrown Plateau.

One informant tapped the parchment. "Several hideouts are marked, But the final route is uncertain. We only know it leads into the plateau's foothills."

Sir Cain accepted the map, studying it, then extended it to Jackson. "It's your job to confirm these leads. Find evidence to guide us to Master Elarius or anyone who might know where Corgrave's forging labs are set. This must be approached with stealth. The city is littered with watchers."

Jackson curled long fingers around the parchment. "We'll leave as soon as possible. I assume we have transport?"

The second informant inclined his head. "We've prepared an unmarked wagon. Basic rations, potions, and a few runic items for your use. Should help you pass as ordinary travelers stacking crates. Keep a low profile when leaving the gates."

Sir Cain folded his arms. "Your traveling companions will ride with you. You are authorized to coordinate the best infiltration approach. Above all, keep in mind if Corgrave's men discover your identities, they might strike back here in the city." His gaze traveled from Jackson to Luke, then to Riven. "Do not compromise the capital's security."

Riven brushed her fingertips over the fletching of an arrow at her hip, as if the mention of betrayal lifted her hackles. Luke mimed an exaggerated salute. "Understood. No loud announcements. No wild duels. Low profile. That's basically my specialty," he added with a wink, collecting an unimpressed stare from Sir Cain.

Jackson tried to mask the coil of tension in his chest. *This time, we can't afford even a small slip.* He bowed to Sir Cain. "We'll do what must be done."

Sir Cain stepped forward. "Remember, Jackson, Corgrave's

tendrils run deep. No matter how discreet you intend to be, he has eyes everywhere. That is to say nothing of the mercenary packs hungry for bounties."

"Understood," Jackson answered. The faint warmth on his neck signaled the infernal markings remained quiet for now. He handed the map to Luke, who looked it over with interest. Riven glanced at it but kept her expression neutral.

Their short meeting concluded with curt nods. The informants melted away into the shadows of the courtyard's walls. Sir Cain lingered a moment, then moved toward the opposite archway, offering a final glance at Jackson. "Bring back what we need, and keep them out of trouble." The older knight's heavy steps faded behind a hedge of creeping vines.

That left Jackson with Luke and Riven. The three stood in uneasy silence, finally broken by Luke's soft laugh. He tilted the map in the early sunlight. "We're not official King's Eye members, but at least we get to see the cool secret maps." He glanced at Riven. "Hope you're ready for fun. Or, well, the opposite of fun."

She raised one brow. "Define fun. I see only infiltration, betrayal, and possible lethal confrontations. None of that is new for me."

Luke put a hand over his heart in mock offense. "Someone forgot how to smile. Fine, we'll find different ways to amuse ourselves." His gaze flicked to Jackson. "Lead on, oh fearless demon knight."

A tired exhale eased from Jackson. "I'd prefer to keep that name under wraps until we're clear of the palace walls. Let's get to the wagon."

They left the courtyard through a series of narrow corridors that smelled faintly of morning dew and wax from the torches extinguished an hour earlier. Guards occasionally passed, giving Jackson small nods of recognition. Their stares lingered on Riven's pointed ears and Luke's carefree swagger. One or two seemed curious why the trio was traveling together. None dared ask openly.

When they emerged at an unmarked courtyard gate, an old man in plain clothes waited beside a simple wagon. Wooden boards formed the back, stained from years of hauling. Two stout horses nickered as if unimpressed by their new riders. Beside them, a small stack of crates bore no symbols, only rough rope tying them shut.

Jackson stepped forward. "We'll need to load everything quickly." He sank his hands under a crate to test the weight. It was heavy, but not impossible. "Luke, check the potions and runic gear. Riven, keep an eye on the gate."

Riven reached to help with the second crate, her movements quiet and efficient. She seemed calm, though her gaze skipped across every corner of the yard. Luke pried open a small trunk and whistled. "Four healing potions, three stamina tonics, plus…" He turned up a small metal sphere. "Runic flash bombs. That'll keep us on our toes."

Riven lifted one of the local cloaks. "We should wear these to blend in. If we look like merchants or travelers, no one will suspect a thing."

Jackson nodded. "Do it. A guard might ask questions if we appear as a random band heading out. Let's keep it simple."

They spent a short time arranging the crates, double-checking that the trunk with the flash bombs remained accessible toward the front. Luke folded the map into a pouch at his belt. After hooking the horses to the wagon's hitch, Jackson took the driver's seat. Riven and Luke positioned themselves behind him, half-hidden by the cargo, ready to pass as assistants.

They started toward the main gate. The city's streets bustled even at this hour with vendors opening stalls and townsfolk moving produce carts. The heavier clamor of blacksmiths in far alleys filled the air. Sparse sunlight crept across tall spires overhead, as if the city was slowly waking to new business.

Jackson steered the wagon down a narrower side street. A few people glanced at them, uninterested. He focused on keeping his posture relaxed, a mere driver ferrying goods. He peered at the shapes of thick stone towers near the city's perimeter. No trouble so far.

Ahead, a pair of guards manned the eastern gate. They wore the king's standard but appeared distracted. Luke released a small sigh. "Let's hope they don't pick a random wagon to search."

A brief hush fell. The wagon rolled onward. Hooves clacked upon cobblestones, and the faint squeak of wheels echoed in the confined street. Riven secured her hood, only her eyes visible. The gate loomed, tall and thick, with a raised portcullis wide enough for one wagon at a time. Jackson tightened his grip on the reins.

One guard raised a hand. "State your business."

"Delivering produce crates," Jackson replied calmly, tipping his chin to the lumps of cargo behind him. He was thankful the crates were sealed. If the guards tried to open them, the potions and bombs might raise suspicion. He forced himself not to look away.

The guard's gaze flicked behind Jackson, where Riven and Luke sat. "Those two your helpers? Or watchers?"

Luke cleared his throat, feigning offense. "I'm the best packer in the kingdom, friend. You want to buy onions or salted fish, I can get them for half-price." His face broke into a broad grin that looked so genuine, Jackson almost believed him. "But we got no extra supply right now, sorry to say."

The guard raised an eyebrow at Luke's chattiness but said nothing more. He stepped closer to the wagon, glanced at the crates, then stepped back in apparent disinterest. "Move along, produce man. Next time, keep your workers from joking with the city watch."

Luke gave a mock salute. Jackson clicked his tongue, spurring the horses forward, and the wagon rolled on. Riven watched behind them until the guardhouse fell away from view. No alarm came. No shout to stop them. The path lay open, leading toward farmland and beyond.

They followed a winding road over a broad stone bridge, where the water below glistened in the early sun. The day stretched ahead under a sky that promised fair weather. Each passing moment put more distance between them and the capital's fortress towers.

Luke kicked back on the bench, giving a lazy wave at Jackson's shoulder. "We did it. We are so stealthy." A sly grin flashed. "A pity, though. That guard actually looked hungry for some onions."

Riven sniffed. "Your performance was convincing enough, but next time, less jesting might be better. Especially when our real cargo is lethal."

"Don't kill the mood." Luke chuckled. "Anyway, demon-boy didn't flinch, so that's a win."

Jackson sighed. "We made it out. That's what matters." The knot under his collar eased. *Proper infiltration. So far, so good.* He guided the horses along the curving road. Small farmhouses came into view in the distance, and the city walls shrank with each turn of the wheels. Soon, the bustling capital was a mere memory.

Riven drew back her hood, letting the breeze stir stray strands of hair around her pointed ears. She seemed pensive. "With luck, we'll find the next clue about Elarius. He may not have time for us to fumble around."

Luke nodded. "Agreed. We gotta pick up the pace. If Corgrave's men have him forging something nasty, time is not our friend."

Jackson set his jaw. "We'll see this mission through."

They continued down the dusty track until the city's gates were no more than a faint silhouette on the horizon. None of them looked back. The light guided them farther from regal promise and deeper into a tangled realm of secrets, where a single misstep could derail their fragile alliance. Yet for the moment, they rode as one, a wagon of half-hidden contraband, an unlikely band bound together by a single goal. To find Master Elarius before Corgrave's shadow snuffed out the chance for peace.

They pressed on, unmarked and unnoticed, rolling into the vast countryside and beyond.

CHAPTER SIX

Morning draped the small city they'd stopped in to resupply in a pale haze, softening the weathered stone of the old walls and the crooked lines of crowded merchant stalls. Jackson led the way through the bustling thoroughfare, shoulders set and cloak drawn close to hide any rogue flicker of his infernal markings. At his side, Luke bobbed in and out of the crowd, grinning at every new sight. Riven trailed behind, sharp-eyed and silent.

Vendors hawked their wares in eager voices that overlapped in a constant din. Racks of salted meats, patterned blankets fraying at the edges, and tarnished relics from the war. A tinkerer near a leaning fountain caught Luke's attention with a polished metal contraption spread across a makeshift table. It whirred and pulsed, small runes etched around the rim.

Luke's eyes brightened. "One runic compass, you say?" He fingered a spare coin. "It finds forging sites, right?"

The tinkerer, a wiry woman in a soot-stained apron, nodded. "Pulses when volcanic steel is near. Senses the metal's arcane signature. Costs more than a few coins, though."

Luke offered a half-smile. "Sure it does." He gestured for

Riven to keep watch, then leaned in to haggle. She opened her mouth, likely to warn him against some con, but he waved a hand in mock seriousness. "Relax. I'll pay for the real deal." He lifted the device carefully. Its runes glowed with a faint greenish hue. "Feels genuine," he muttered.

While Luke closed the purchase with a string of exaggerated pleas about being "a poor traveling hero," Riven surveyed the passersby. Several sets of eyes lingered on Jackson's broad frame, perhaps because of his cloak's suspicious bulk or the quiet tension around him. The King's Eye might have been a secretive force, but its reputation had spread through every tavern and alley. One or two bystanders actually backed away when Jackson stepped near. He pretended not to notice.

"Jackson," Luke called, returning with the runic compass. "We're all set." He flashed a toothy grin. "She didn't fleece me too badly."

Jackson nodded, guiding them onward. At a side street, they paused beside a pair of horses tied to a simple wooden wagon. The animals stamped restlessly. Overhead, the city's looming siege towers cast crooked shadows across the courtyard, a reminder of old battles. Jackson inspected the wagon's supplies, confirming spare rations and a trunk. "Sir Cain's ledger?" he asked.

Luke set the compass aside and flipped open a ragged ledger. He ran a finger down lines of ink. "More shipments of volcanic ore, all traced back to the Riftcrown region. The scribbles match everything Cain said." He shut the book with a grimace. "Guess there's no denying it. We need to follow the smuggling routes."

Riven placed a hand on the wagon's side. "If we approach Riftwyn Manor openly, we can request House Riftwyn's aid," she suggested. "They might know more about the missing runeforger."

Luke tapped the ledger's battered cover. "Or we slip in quietly. We find Corgrave's allies first."

The three of them fell silent, weighing the risk of revealing themselves too soon.

Jackson's gaze flicked to the old siege towers overhead, then lifted the reins. "We'll decide on the road." He gave Riven a nod, and she hopped into the back. Luke scrambled up after her.

After they guided the wagon through the gates, Jackson stole one last glance at the city's walls. *No more stalling,* he thought. With a quiet click of the reins, he guided the horses forward. A crisp wind cut across his hood, and the gates shrank behind them.

They followed a dusty road winding away from the city, sunlight creeping higher over farmland stubbled with old fences. Beyond that lay rolling hills patched with autumn-brown grass. Riven kept her bow on her lap, scanning each ridge. Luke occasionally consulted the runic compass, though it stayed dull for now.

By late afternoon, the terrain grew rockier, the path curving around outcrops of stone. The sky took on a sharper clarity, and broad expanses stretched out beneath them. Riven twisted upright in the seat when a massive, dark-winged bird soared across their path, its shrill cry echoing off the cliffs.

She nocked an arrow swiftly. Jackson tensed, but before he could protest, Riven aimed and loosed. The arrow met its mark. The bird dropped, wings folding, and vanished behind a thicket of shrubs

Luke released a surprised laugh. "Impressive. But why?"

Riven flicked him a flat look. "I'm tired of beef. I want varied meat before we reach the plateau."

Luke opened his mouth, then closed it again, eyebrows raised. "Well, dinner's on you, then." He grinned. "At least roast bird beats stale bread."

The trio dismounted near a tangle of boulders that formed a natural hollow. An overhang of stone gave them partial shelter from the wind, and ragged shrubs provided enough cover to hide a small fire from distant eyes.

Riven retrieved her prize, a hefty, black-feathered, hawk-like creature with thick talons. While she plucked feathers by the wagon, Luke rummaged for the cooking pot. Jackson set about gathering dry kindling from beneath nearby shrubs. The rocky ravine was treacherous. One wrong step could send a tumble of loose rocks clattering down. He kept the horses tied close, watching for signs of spooking.

The fire crackled soon after dusk settled, its glow dancing against the stone. They ate in subdued silence at first, picking the last bits of roasted bird. A gentle breeze stirred the embers, and the thick darkness beyond the ravine seemed to hold every rustle in the grass. Jackson caught himself listening for footsteps or the scrape of boots. *Constant vigilance,* he reminded himself.

Luke finally shook off the quiet. "So, big guy." He waggled a half-finished morsel of meat at Jackson. "I've always wanted to know more about the glory days. Before you had those glowing neck tattoos." Real curiosity lurked beneath his cheeky grin. "Were you always a knight? Or was there some turning point?"

Riven's withering stare told Luke he was straying into personal territory, but Luke pressed on. "Heard rumors of you in that big war, fighting alongside…what was his name, Boromar?"

Jackson exhaled. He disliked dredging up old conflicts. Still, they had little else to do beneath the stars. "Boromar was the Great Barbarian," he explained, gazing at the flicker of the flames. "He stood on the opposing side. Wasn't always loyal, just brutal. The man led raids that left entire outposts in cinders. We faced him at the siege of Hollowcrest. That was before these," he added, tapping the edge of his collar where the demon markings lay hidden.

Riven set her plate aside. "Twenty-three knights died subduing him, if I recall the stories."

Jackson bowed his head. "Yes. He was monstrous in size and

skill. People called him unstoppable." He paused. "I was a plain soldier then. No magic, only my sword. We pinned him in a ravine, cut off his escape. Even then, we lost good fighters. But he fell that day."

"And that's when you earned your spurs, right?" Luke asked, leaning forward. "A big, heroic stand?"

Jackson didn't answer right away. The shadows of the ravine pressed in, and the embers glowed a dull orange. "We were desperate," he replied at last. "He had no mercy. We had to find ours somewhere. It was the kind of battle that leaves a permanent mark."

Luke nodded. "Ah. That kind of fight."

Riven gazed off into the darkness, bow resting across her knees.

Finally, Luke stretched with a dramatic yawn. "Long day," he announced, rummaging in the wagon for a blanket. "If you two don't mind, I'll grab the first chance at shut-eye."

Riven arched a brow. "No argument from me," she responded curtly. "I'll watch after midnight. Jackson, you take the first watch?"

He nodded. "Yes. Get some rest."

Luke placed the ledger and runic compass near Riven's pack, then settled by the fire. Within a few moments, he was dozing, one arm draped over his eyes. Riven set her bow aside and closed her eyes too, though Jackson guessed she might not be completely asleep.

Jackson rose, shaking off the lingering chill. He picked his way to the ravine's edge and stood where the moonlight touched the rocks. The slope beyond fell away, revealing a vast sweep of starlit country. The wind tugged at his cloak, and occasionally, a distant coyote howl echoed.

He glanced back at the faint glow of their campfire. *Duty or not, we press on,* he thought. They were beyond the city's walls now, riding into uncertain territory. Yet resolve flickered in him, acceptance that he would do what had to be done.

Quiet hours stretched. He did not sway from his post, attention fixed on every slope and outcropping. The next phase of the journey lay ahead. For now, he would guard the fire and the fragile thread of hope they carried for Kharadorn's future.

CHAPTER SEVEN

Jackson, Luke, and Riven rode in uneasy silence for most of the morning. Ahead, the broken hilltops gave way to a vast, windswept plateau. The horses snorted as they climbed the final ridge, the wind tugging at manes and cloaks alike. Sunlight struck angled rock outcrops, reflecting odd shimmers that rippled across the path.

Luke tipped his head, curiosity dancing in his eyes. He slowed his horse and glanced at Riven, who rode astride behind Jackson. "Think we'll find a big pot of gold here, or just shining rocks?"

Riven stared back. "Everything is about money to you, isn't it?"

He put a hand over his heart, feigning offense. "Money, excitement, random tavern adventures. I'm a man of varied but simple interests."

Jackson exhaled, letting the bickering wash over him. The wind carried a crisp, mineral tang that set his nerves on edge. Thin wisps of pale dust swirled around the horses' hooves. A scattered line of crystalline shards dotted the path, rough lumps that glowed faintly in the midday sun.

Farther ahead, a gorge sprawled in a chaotic patchwork of

color. Iridescent crystals jutted from the rock in tall spires, flashing pink or violet or shimmering blue. Even from a distance, they looked as if they had soaked up the sun's radiance and gleamed with captured brilliance.

A startled breath escaped Jackson's lips. *That must be the Riftcrown.* He rarely allowed himself wonder at the world's beauty, but this was difficult to ignore. The landscape beyond the crest of the path looked like a shimmering field of prismatic glass.

Luke squinted. "Well, that is something. Not merely shiny. More like a kaleidoscope exploded across the rocks."

Riven's posture went rigid, her pointed ears twitching. "The air feels different. Like magic is leaking. We should be cautious."

Jackson pressed his palm against the reins. "We will be." He tried to keep his voice steady. The plateau's stark beauty hinted at power but also hidden danger. They were here to investigate reported suspicious drilling for contraband crystals, not to admire the view.

They continued at a measured pace. With each passing moment, the swirling glow at the edges of the path deepened. The heat of midday caused faint ripples in the air, turning the horizon into a wavering mirage. More than once, Jackson thought he glimpsed distant figures hunched over strange equipment near the crystal-littered gullies. However, when he looked closer, the shapes vanished behind stony ridges.

Luke cleared his throat. "I'm not imagining it, right? People are out there."

Riven nodded. "Working on contraptions, from the look of it." She narrowed her eyes. "We could be dealing with smugglers. Or maybe House Riftwyn's patrols."

Jackson urged the group forward. The path fenced in around them with spurs of luminous crystal flanking both sides. They passed a half-collapsed sign that bore the faded insignia of House Riftwyn. Beyond, a gentle slope led into a wide bowl, where the wind carried sparkling dust motes.

At the heart of the basin, a small party of riders appeared. They wore matching cloaks trimmed with elegant embroidery and carried slender spears. The lead figure, a woman in dusty traveling leathers, slowed her mount and raised a hand. Tall in the saddle, she observed Jackson's group with poised calm. She was young, fine-boned, and regal in posture, almost certainly a noble. A silver pendant gleamed at her throat.

She spoke first. "Travelers in my father's lands? You do not look like simple tourists."

Jackson reined in his horse. "We come on behalf of the King's Eye." He reached inside his cloak and drew out a small, coded token, careful not to appear threatening.

The woman's eyes flashed with recognition. She gave a short nod. "Lady Elinora Riftwyn." Caution filled her greeting. "Reports came that the King's Eye might show up. Still, I want to see proof of your intentions, if you have it."

Luke piped up with a carefree grin. "Shiny rocks, Lady Elinora. We heard they were, uh, extra-shiny this time of year."

Her gaze flicked to him, unimpressed. "We do not greet intruders lightly. Lately, too many have tried to steal our resources. I need more than your word." She settled her stare on Jackson, ignoring Luke's half-smirk. "You claim the King's Eye? Then present your credentials properly."

Jackson pivoted his horse forward and extended the token with slow, deliberate movements. "We are investigating rumors of stolen crystals, yes. This token is coded, bearing the King's Eye insignia. It grants us the authority to root out contraband. We believe Master Elarius' abduction may tie to these smuggling operations."

Elinora accepted and studied the token. Her expression hardened, but she made no move to hand it back. "We've had trouble with contraband. My patrols found disturbed mine shafts. Miners speak of hearing voices in the tunnels, accompanied by unauthorized drilling." She paused. "The King's Eye has wide powers, Sir Knight. My mother will want to confirm all this. But if you are who you say, we may share a common problem."

Jackson bowed his head. "We welcome any guidance you can give."

She gestured for the group to follow. Her riders, five stern-faced fellows, formed a loose escort around the trio. In silence, they cut across a portion of the plateau where the crystals jutted so high they formed natural pillars. Streams of colored light made the ground shimmer, almost like stepping through a dreamscape.

After a short ride, they arrived at a well-worn footpath leading to a sizable stone complex perched on a rocky ledge. A low wall circled the perimeter, embedded with decorative crystal shards that served as a subtle warning. House Riftwyn guarded its territory. Inside the courtyard, waiting with arms folded, stood a regal woman who bore a striking resemblance to Elinora, though older and with sharper angles to her face. Her embroidered gown displayed the Riftwyn crest in bold colors.

She cast a withering glance at Luke and Riven before settling her gaze on Jackson's neck, where the faint swirl of infernal markings peeked above his collar. Her lips thinned. "So, these are the arrivals. You must be the Hellspawned Knight we've heard rumors about."

Elinora halted and slipped off her horse, then gestured for Jackson and his companions to do the same. "Mother, this is Jackson. He has a token from the King's Eye." She inclined her head. "Baroness Seraphina Riftwyn."

Seraphina released a measured breath, then addressed Jackson directly. "You come here in search of contraband, but I know the King's Eye doesn't only concern itself with petty smuggling. There is more to this." Her voice was carefully controlled, each syllable precise. "Your presence suggests you're after larger fish. Or you are the larger fish."

Jackson's gaze flicked to a line of guards behind the

baroness. *She does not trust me.* He had grown used to that. "We serve the Crown's interests," he replied. "We believe rogue agents might be stealing Riftcrown crystals for a scheme tied to Lord Corgrave. We also suspect Master Elarius' abduction is linked."

Seraphina's jaw clenched upon mention of Corgrave. "That man's name still reeks of treason. If he aims to sabotage my estate, I'll not tolerate it." Her gaze moved to the token Jackson held. Then she eyed Riven. "And the elf?"

Riven inclined her head. "I stand with Jackson for the moment. My interest is ensuring these crystals do not fall into destructive hands."

Seraphina offered a guarded nod, then turned to Luke. "Finally, the jester, I assume." She said it without a shred of humor.

Luke gave a polite bow. "At your service, Baroness. I can amuse, I can sneak, and I can do the occasional hero act if needed."

Seraphina raised one eyebrow. "Let us pray you do not require heroic measures in my courtyard." She addressed Jackson again. "Our plateau once suffered scorched crystal fields when infernal magic ran amok during the war. I hope we will not see a repeat."

Jackson spoke quietly. "I have no desire to burn anything. My mission is infiltration, not destruction."

Elinora broke the tension by taking a step forward. "We've had incidents, Mother. Miners disappearing, or returning babbling about armed strangers in the deeper shafts. The plateau cannot afford more losses." She looked at Jackson. "If the King's Eye is offering help, we need it to rid ourselves of these thieves. And to uncover the truth behind Elarius' possible captivity." Her gaze softened. "I will show them the entrance to the old caverns."

Seraphina drew closer, so she and Elinora nearly stood shoulder to shoulder, facing Jackson. "Do not think we are helpless," she warned. "My knights patrol day and night. If I sense any treachery, you and your associates will find yourselves unwelcome."

Jackson gave a curt nod. "We understand." Then, he lifted the token again. "The Crown's authority is not meant to intrude on your rightful sovereignty. We only aim to uproot the threat that lurks underground."

Seraphina sighed and produced a small medallion etched with the Riftwyn crest. "Take this as well. It marks my grudging agreement. Return it when you leave. It may spare you from being skewered by my knights if you encounter them below. Do not mistake it for a blanket pardon, though. If you start trouble, they will respond."

As Jackson accepted the medallion, Luke coughed. "Out of curiosity, Baroness, do you have another one for me? In case I go wandering on my own?"

Riven muttered under her breath. "There it is again, the golden fool." She smirked.

Seraphina did not bother replying to Luke's request. Instead, she moved away, calling for a scribe to record the discussion. Before she returned inside, she called, "Lady Elinora, see to our guests. Ensure they do not cause more harm than good."

Elinora nodded and watched her mother depart. Then, she lifted her chin, directing her words at Jackson. "Come. We will walk the perimeter, and I will show you the mine entrance. A regiment is stationed nearby. I do not want them alarmed by your presence."

Moments later, they dismounted and followed Elinora through a small side gate that led to a worn footpath. They passed an outcrop where a single, enormous crystal jutted from the ground, its surface carved with House Riftwyn's sigil. The edges glinted with a faint blue aura under the sunlight.

Local workers bustled around a small cart loaded with tools. Many paused to stare, especially at Jackson's gauntlet and his hooded form.

"Do not mind their stares," Elinora stated without turning. "They are suspicious or frightened. Some saw infernal magic scorch our crystal veins years ago. They still fear it might happen again." She led them toward the plateau's edge, where the land fell away into jagged ravines layered with crystal. "If you truly serve the King's Eye, you can help us ensure that never recurs."

Jackson nodded. *They have every right to be wary.* He glanced at Luke and Riven. They seemed on edge as well.

"Will we have help from your knights for the search?" Riven asked as they neared a wooden railing overlooking the ravine. The vantage point revealed a vast network of tunnels below, some clearly natural, others artificially enlarged. Wagon tracks curved into darkness.

Elinora shrugged. "They can guard certain passages, but my mother's priority is keeping the main plateau safe. Venturing into the oldest shafts falls to you if you insist on investigating. Frankly, my mother wants no part of having her knights vanish in the dark."

Luke peered down. "That's a lot of ground to cover." He rested an elbow on the rail. "And you suspect stolen crystals are being taken from which section?"

"We do not know for certain," Elinora admitted. "However, we heard heavy drilling at night. One miner swore he saw men loading crates onto an unmarked wagon. Then, they vanished into the deeper shafts." Her voice lowered. "He also claimed to see strange lights, possibly wards or illusions."

Jackson studied the ravines. *This place is huge.* The darkness in some tunnels looked impenetrable, even with midday sun overhead. "I see. We may need a day or two."

Elinora's expression remained cool. "Time is not our ally. If Corgrave's men are snatching crystals, they are likely planning to move them soon. We stand to lose an entire season's worth of crystal trade and face the risk of sabotage if the thieves undermine the veins. That would cripple the plateau's economy."

"Then we start at once," Jackson decided. "We will need the location of the miner's last sighting or any vantage point near these unmarked wagons."

She nodded. "Come to the manor's entrance. I will have a guard direct you." She pivoted, heading back along the footpath. "Gather provisions and any gear you need. The caves can be treacherous." After a few steps, she paused and glanced back. "For what it's worth, I hope your presence truly is to resolve this. We cannot afford half-measures."

Jackson inclined his head in understanding. Luke shot him a subtle grin, as though to say, *We're in the thick of it again.* Riven's expression remained impassive, but tension radiated from her posture.

They returned to the courtyard, where a handful of stable hands took their horses. A small retinue of House Riftwyn guards eyed them from a polite distance, hands never straying far from sword hilts. Elinora exchanged quick words with one of the guards, who then hurried off into a side corridor in the manor's outer wall.

Through it all, Jackson felt the watchful presence of Baroness Seraphina. Though she was not visible, some intangible chill lingered, like an unspoken reminder that every step they took on her land was under scrutiny.

In short order, a page approached, offering a basin of fresh water and a few towels. Luke and Riven drank from a separate pitcher, brushing dust off their leathers. Luke patted his satchel, then checked his runic compass. He gave Jackson a pointed look. "Shall we go find these hidden smugglers, big guy? Or would you rather lounge in a lovely courtyard for an afternoon?"

Riven snorted. "I doubt the baroness wants us lounging around. We should push below while the daylight remains. Maybe we catch them off guard. That is, if you want to get started."

Jackson dried his hands. "Yes. No reason to wait." He glanced at Elinora. "We're ready."

"Then follow me. The mine entrance is not far." Her gaze flicked between them, lingering briefly on the swirl of Jackson's demonic markings. "I will guide you to the border of the old shafts. After that, you're on your own. Do not provoke the knights or damage our property."

Luke raised his hands in mock innocence. "Damage? I would never."

Riven shook her head. "We'll see how long that promise lasts."

A smile touched Elinora's lips. "Keep your jests to a minimum belowground. Noise travels, and if these thieves are armed, they will not appreciate intruders." Her posture stiffened, and she gestured for them to follow toward a ramp that descended into the labyrinth. "We should go. Something about this day feels too still."

They walked past the outer gate. The path angled downward, hugging the plateau's slope in a wide arc until it reached the lip of a wide cavern mouth. Veins of color glowed in the rock overhead, an unearthly mosaic of swirling crystal. The floor was dark, dusty, ominous. Hints of damp air wafted out, touched by the metallic tang of machinery. Shadows played tricks against the rocky walls, as if illusory silhouettes were dancing.

Elinora paused at the threshold. "Bring lanterns, if you wish, but expect deeper wards inside. My people have heard echoes, groaning metal, stifled voices. We do not know how many are down there."

Jackson inhaled slowly. "We will be mindful."

From behind them, a faint rustle indicated an approaching figure. Seraphina's voice cut in, stiff and cool. "Remember our agreement. Return with our token, or do not return at all." She stood at the top of the ramp, arms folded. "I will not spare more men to chase you if you vanish. House Riftwyn has enough to guard."

Jackson nodded. "Understood."

Luke flashed a confident smile at the baroness. "We're a resourceful bunch. Wouldn't dream of causing trouble, right?" He winked at Riven. "Assuming our elf remembers to be nice."

Riven's eyes narrowed. "Do not make me regret sparing your life, Luke."

A huff of air escaped Elinora, almost a laugh, though she kept it stifled. She tucked a stray lock of hair behind her ear. "Best of luck, then. I will wait for news." She gave Jackson a measured look. The faint lines of tension around her eyes betrayed more concern than she cared to admit.

Jackson and his companions received simple lanterns from a nearby guard and lit them. The glow carved flickering shapes across the cavern walls. Luke tucked the runic compass at his belt, testing its dial. Riven adjusted her quiver, an arrow half-drawn in readiness. Adrenaline coiled in Jackson's muscles as they stepped toward the darkness.

Together, they advanced.

Their footfalls echoed against stone as they followed the tunnel's gentle slope downward. The air grew heavier, the smell of damp rock and pungent mineral drifting with each step. Riven, usually expressionless, wrinkled her nose. The scents were stronger for her. Loose shards crunched underfoot, sending up faint sparks of prismatic light.

They had come to the Riftcrown Plateau in search of hidden theft and contraband forging. Yet the deeper they went, the more Jackson sensed something else lurking, unseen and dangerous. *We will find out,* he told himself. *Or die trying.*

CHAPTER EIGHT

Jackson paused at the edge of the yawning cavern mouth. A raw, metallic scent clung to the chill air, and the ambient glow from distant clusters of crystalline ore cast wavering light across slick walls. He raised his lantern, revealing a steep path descending into the darkness.

Riven stepped forward, bow across her shoulder. She kept her fingers near the quiver strapped to her hip. Luke hovered behind her, peering over her shoulder and making an exaggerated face at the dripping stalactites. "Lovely. Damp tunnels in the middle of nowhere. This is definitely how I thought I'd spend the week."

Jackson scanned the long corridor ahead. "We should keep moving. If Corgrave's smugglers have been operating here, we need to see how far these tunnels go."

They moved in single file, boots crunching on loose gravel. Occasionally, the crystals embedded in the walls gave off faint pops, like heated stones in a dying fire. The deeper they went, the colder the air became, and the echo of dripping water filled the silence. Within minutes, they reached a wide junction where pickaxes, long abandoned, littered the ground.

Luke nudged one with the tip of his boot. "Looks like they ran off in a hurry. Or they didn't care to tidy up after themselves."

Riven crouched beside an overturned crate. She brushed aside dust to reveal a faded sigil. "That matches one of the marks we saw on those merchant ledgers. This place was definitely part of the smuggling route."

Luke tried peering into the open container but only came away with a handful of splinters. "No more loot here. Clearly, people have been hauling contraband for a while."

Jackson pressed on, leading them deeper down a narrow passage. The lanternlight skipped across the walls, revealing half-harvested crystal veins. Some strips had been gouged out with rough tools, leaving jagged edges. Others looked carefully cut and chiseled, as though a skilled hand had removed large, valuable chunks. He touched a broken crystal, feeling a faint tingle of arcane energy. "Whoever came here knew exactly what to harvest. These crystals aren't random scraps."

Riven knelt and ran her palm across her quiver of ward-piercing arrows. The feathers bore intricate markings, etched with tiny runes. "I told you about these," she stated without looking up. "My old enclave once faced wave after wave of constructs shielded by wards. I learned to craft specialized arrowheads under a master fletcher. We hammered in a neutralizing matrix so the arrowheads could punch through magical defenses."

Luke leaned forward. "So you can drop wards almost like they're paper walls?"

Riven gave a curt nod. "In theory. They're not foolproof, but if there's something warded up ahead, these help. I prefer not to rely on them unless I have to." She brushed a fingertip along the rune lines. "Takes patience to carve them."

Jackson's gaze lingered on her quiver. "Good that you have them. If Corgrave's men rigged anything down here, those arrows might save us."

She rose, and they continued. Ahead, a series of old wooden beams buttressed the corridor. Loose stones had tumbled across the path, forcing them to pick their steps carefully. Sagging timbers crossed overhead.

A sudden glint caught Riven's eye. She raised a hand to halt them, then carefully examined the ground. "Tripwire," she breathed. A thin runic filament stretched between two rock outcroppings, nearly invisible beneath the dust.

Luke whistled. "Who sets something like that in a random mine passage?"

"Smugglers who don't want guests." Jackson reached forward, trying to track the filament to its anchor. At the end sat a small, cracked rune stone. "Looks like it's already been triggered. Maybe a previous group set it off. Or the runic matrix went inert over time."

Riven tilted her head, listening, then placed a hand against the stone. She narrowed her eyes. "Not fully inert," she whispered. She closed her eyes and inhaled. "I sense a faint hum. Residual magic. I can cast a detection to see if anything else is active."

Jackson and Luke stepped back, letting the elf concentrate. She settled on one knee, bow across her lap, then extended her free hand. Slowly she traced a pattern in the air. A soft blue luminescence gathered at her fingertips. She whispered phrases in her native tongue. The words carried an odd resonance that echoed off the cavern walls. Wisps of energy drifted around her hand, then spread outward like ripples across water.

Jackson's skin prickled. Beside him, Luke muttered, "I'll never get used to that."

Moments later, the glow subsided. Riven stood, eyes grim. "There is a strong magical signature deeper in. Something big. Possibly charged with stolen energy."

Luke frowned. "Great. More fun. Maybe it's another caved-in passage waiting to fall on our heads."

Riven shook her head. "This is pulsing. Engines of some sort or a guardian with a power source. Not static."

Jackson touched his infernal markings, feeling a subdued heat respond. "We'd best see what it is." He nodded at Riven. "Lead on. We'll watch your back."

They continued into the main cavern, stepping over shattered crates and bits of broken wards. The path curved around a corner. Beyond, a wide chamber spread out, lit by the eerie sparkle of half-mined crystals protruding at odd angles. A hulking form in the center leaned against a crumbling support column. It looked like a heap of rubble until a flicker of arcane light crackled across its limbs.

"Uh, please tell me that's a statue," Luke commented.

With a hiss of grinding stone, the massive shape lurched upright. It stood at least eight feet tall, its body made of rough slabs of rock fused with metal plating. Ragged arcs of energy hopped from joint to joint, illuminating a faint stylized C hammered near its shoulder. Its head turned slowly, as if powered by clockwork or a crude magical mechanism. In place of eyes, two glowing cracks blazed a dull red.

Riven drew an arrow from her quiver, glancing at the runic anchors scrawled along the walls. "They've been recharging this sentinel with stolen energy. It's a guard dog. A dangerous one."

Jackson tightened his grip on his sword. "Corgrave's crest is there. That confirms who it belongs to." He tried to shift to the side without drawing attention, but the sentinel's head snapped toward him. A low hum pulsed from within its chest, flaring arcs of electricity across the broken metal.

"That is not a friendly hum," Luke suggested. "We might want to—"

The sentinel charged. Its heavy strides rattled pebbles loose from the ceiling. Jackson lunged to block it, sword scraping against the creature's stony claw. Sparks exploded on impact. He clenched his jaw as his infernal markings flared with heat.

Riven ducked behind a boulder, arrow nocked, scanning for a weak point. Luke scrambled onto a fallen timber to get some height. "Take it down quick," he called. "I'm not in the mood to be smashed."

The sentinel roared with a grinding rasp, swinging a massive arm that nearly caught Jackson's side. Jackson sidestepped, returning a fierce slash that glanced off the thing's plating. The demon-fire within him surged. The sword's tip glowed faintly as it sliced deeper this time, shedding sparks. "Riven," he barked. "Aim where the plates overlap."

She nodded, stepping out to release a ward-piercing arrow. The projectile drove into a seam at the sentinel's shoulder, and a brief splutter of disrupted runes sparked along its upper arm. The sentinel staggered but did not stop. Instead, it swiveled, swinging again.

Luke hopped from one timber to another as the creature's arm smashed the spot he'd vacated. Splintered wood flew, raining debris. "That was too close," he yelped. "No one wants a splinter in the face."

Jackson ducked under another swing, the creature's claw thunderously colliding with the rock wall. "You talk too much," he growled. He saw an opening and drove his blade at the sentinel's torso. Energy crackled along the weapon's edge, but the impact sent Jackson skidding backward. He sucked in a breath, ears ringing.

Luke gave a sudden mock cheer. "Go, sentinel! You big, rocky brute. Keep it up!" When Jackson shot him a glare, Luke shrugged. "Sorry?"

Distracted by Luke's commentary, Jackson barely noticed the sentinel's next attack. Its arm whipped around, slamming into him with bone-rattling force. He flew back twenty feet, crashing into a crate. Shards of splintered wood flew in all directions, and his lantern clattered away.

Riven exhaled sharply and launched another arrow, this time

striking the sentinel's chest. The runic inscriptions on its plating glowed bright, then flickered. The arrow's runes pulsed, boring through a conjured ward. Sparks erupted. Lightning crackled over the sentinel's frame.

Jackson pushed debris off his chest, coughing. He ignored the pain throbbing along his ribs as he watched the sentinel flail. A heavy limb crashed into a stack of crates, sending them tumbling. "Gah," he grunted, forcing himself up.

His infernal markings flared again, heat spreading across his shoulders. He moved in close with a surge of demonic power, sword raised. In two swift strikes, he struck the sentinel's outer plating. Cracks webbed outward across its midsection.

From a perch on a boulder, Luke decided to help by hurling a throwing knife at the exposed joint. The blade pinged off the edge with little effect. "I tried," he muttered. "Go, Riven. It's all you."

She drew a third arrow. Her gaze was coldly focused, an archer at peak concentration. She loosed the shaft, and it plunged into the sentinel's lower core where the swirling energies converged. A sharp jolt of lightning flared, then sputtered out. The sentinel reeled, staggering sideways before dropping to one knee. Stone limbs seized in place, arcs of stolen energy bursting around it in a final, crackling surge. With a thunderous crash, it collapsed face-first.

Jackson lowered his sword, panting. "Definitely not a leftover doodle," he managed. "Corgrave's agents must have built it to guard these smuggling routes."

Riven stepped closer to check the unmoving mass. "Volcanic steel," she stated, discovering shards of it among the shattered rock. "So they used both the crystals and stolen steel to power this monster."

Luke hopped off the boulder, dusting off his hands. "That's some serious arrogance. Branding it with a personal crest? Might as well shout, 'Hey, I'm Corgrave, come get me.'"

Jackson grimaced. "He must be sure of himself to leave his mark to taunt us." He sheathed his sword and surveyed the wreckage. "We should get a piece of that plating. Proof of his contraband forging."

Riven knelt, prying off a chunk with the tip of her knife. Arcane residue still sparked along the broken edges. She wrapped it in cloth and stowed it in her pack. "We have what we need."

They looked around the chamber. The fight had nearly brought down part of the ceiling. Cracks in the walls allowed drafts to stir up dust. A bruise was forming along the side of Jackson's jaw, and the front of Riven's bracers were blackened from a close brush with one of the sentinel's electrical surges. Luke's hair bristled with static, making him look more disheveled than usual.

Jackson inhaled. "Let's get out of these tunnels. We did enough damage."

Riven nodded. "Agreed. There may be more constructs deeper in." She brushed her palm across her forehead. Sweat and dust clung to her skin. "We found enough evidence to confirm Corgrave's using the crystals for forging weapons. We should report this."

Luke rubbed his shoulder where he'd slammed into a jagged outcrop while dodging. "I second that. My body is complaining." He flicked his gaze at the unmoving sentinel. "At least we gave that rock pile something to regret."

They retraced their path, picking among the scattered crates. After they passed the collapsed tripwire station, a hint of fresh air drifted in from the mine's entrance. The climb up felt longer than before. Each footstep jarred weary muscles. At the upper levels, the gloom lifted enough to show the faint gray swirl of daylight beyond the wide opening. The group stepped out into the crisp plateau air, letting the daylight chase away the chill.

Luke exhaled. "Remind me never to volunteer for a friendly spelunking trip again."

A faint grin tugged at Jackson's mouth. He set down his lantern, looking to Riven. "You all right? That was a tough fight."

Riven brushed off lingering dust. "I'm fine. What about you?" She gestured to the crimson welt under his jaw.

Jackson touched the tender spot, wincing. "I'll manage. The sentinel swung like an angry troll."

Luke cleared his throat with a dramatic flourish. "For the record, I did my part, yes?"

Riven regarded him flatly. "Some part. Maybe an eighth."

He put on a faux wounded expression. "Ouch, your words cut deeper than my knives."

Jackson smirked and stepped away, checking a tear in his cloak. As he did, Luke moved to Riven's side. "I could help, if you want me to check that bruise on your arm," he offered. "A gentle prod of medicinal skill…"

Riven leveled a frosty stare. "Do you think I want your fingers near me? What would you take?"

Luke blurted the first thing that came to mind. "Your virginity?"

A horrified hush fell. Luke slapped a hand over his mouth, eyes bulging. A spark of danger flashed in Riven's gaze. Jackson passed between them, meeting the elf's furious gaze. In a tone only she could hear, he murmured, "You have to admit. That was actually pretty funny."

Her eyes narrowed, ice-cold. Luke gave a meek shrug as if praying for a merciful outcome.

"I'm more experienced than I look," Riven quipped.

Jackson kept walking, a faint, exasperated grin tugging at his lips.

CHAPTER NINE

They had scarcely left the mine's mouth when a chattering sound pricked Jackson's ears. He stiffened. Faint, high-pitched squeaks carried on the breeze. Ahead, scraggly silhouettes hunched behind a cluster of rocks.

He halted, raising a hand. "Kobolds," he murmured. He counted four scaly figures, small but agile, clutching crude spears. Their reptilian snouts twitched at the slightest scent. A scuffle here was the last thing he wanted, but none of them looked like they intended peace.

Luke eased forward with a wry grin. "Danger never takes a day off, does it?" He drew a short sword, spinning it lightly. "I vote we scold them for existing and move on."

Riven's lips curved. "These creatures often raid travelers. Perhaps they see us as easy pickings."

Jackson flexed his shoulders, ignoring the dull throb from their earlier battles. The faint demon-fire along his throat began to pulse, but he kept it contained. "We'll try to scatter them fast." He signaled for Riven to take the left.

One kobold hissed, brandishing a spear. Luke stepped forward, intending to taunt them away from Riven's approach.

"You lot," he called. "Fancy turning back? We have nothing you'd want, unless you like armor and sweaty tunics."

The kobolds hissed, advancing in a wave of snarls.

Riven fired a warning arrow that clattered off a rock near their leader. The creature paused. Its companions looked around with wide eyes before one barked an urgent cry. Then, all four charged in, swinging their spears with frantic intensity.

Jackson drew his sword, parrying the first thrust. Rivets of pain flashed through his wrist, ignoring his body's protest from the earlier fight. *We can't waste too much energy here.* He swiped low, forcing the kobold to stumble back.

Luke ducked and spun under a clumsy swing. "At least they're predictable," he noted. He jabbed the hilt of his short sword into one kobold's ribs. The creature yelped and went sprawling.

Riven released a second arrow. It lodged in a kobold's shoulder, sending it reeling. She advanced in a fluid motion, delivering a swift strike with her bow's tip to knock the spear aside. "No time for theatrics," she muttered.

Jackson stepped to the side, harnessing enough of his infernal strength to sweep his sword in a controlled arc. One kobold, squeaking in panic, danced back, but too late. The blade caught it across the chest. Another lunged from behind with a desperate hiss, but Riven's arrow stabbed it short.

Soon, the small clearing fell still. Two kobolds lay unconscious, and the other two scurried off, cradling their wounds. Luke wiped sweat from his forehead and exhaled. "Three battles in two days. My legs might quit on me."

Riven retrieved her spent arrows, kneeling beside a limp kobold to make sure it still lived. It had only been knocked cold. She frowned in mild disgust, then rose. "We should keep moving. I want a proper wash soon, or you two will smell worse than these beasts."

Jackson nodded, taking a moment to catch his breath. The scattered scuffle had been draining, but not lethal. *Let's hope the rest of the journey is quieter.* He motioned for the group to continue up the winding path.

They made it to Riftwyn Manor by late afternoon, sweaty and covered in dust. The stone walls and ornate gate gleamed in the waning sun. A pair of House Riftwyn guards hastened to unlatch the gate, recognizing them, alarm clear on their faces when they noticed the grime and faint streaks of blood. One guard bowing deeply to Jackson coughed. "You've returned safely, my lord. The baroness and Lady Elinora await inside. Also, merchants are here."

Luke snorted at the word "lord," but Jackson merely nodded. The trio climbed the manor's steps. Servants rushed forward, eyes wide with concern. An older steward wearing House Riftwyn colors escorted them through a side corridor to wash before meeting any guests. "This way, please," he muttered politely. "We've been instructed to accommodate you with haste."

They trudged into a small washroom with a row of steaming basins. Riven paused, glancing at Luke. "Don't even think about touching me," she warned. She set her bow aside.

Luke flashed an insolent grin. "I'd do it purely out of courtesy, you know. Scrub your back in gratitude for saving my hide." He flexed his fingers with mock flourish. "I have the gentlest hands in—"

"Did you need a bloodletting before cleaning?" Her calm, flat tone held a hint of threat.

Luke raised his hands in surrender. "I'll be over here." He wandered to a separate basin, only to notice an attractive maid lingering by the door.

She gave him a warm smile. "Would you like your back done, sir?"

Luke's eyes lit up. "I would love it!" He followed the maid, leaving Riven to shut the door on him with a roll of her eyes. She muttered something about men being fools, then set to shucking off her clothes.

Jackson looked away, not embarrassed but wanting her to have her privacy. Riven undressed with precision, no shame coloring her cheeks or hands covering parts of her. Like most skilled warriors, she considered her body a vessel. A body was a body, and hers function how it needed to.

She dipped into the water and set to scrubbing the caked dirt from her arms. Meanwhile, Jackson found an unoccupied washbasin at the far end. He peeled off his cloak and dunked himself in soapy water, feeling relief at last.

He flinched at the bruises across his ribs. Carefully, he wiped away layers of dust, letting the warm water cut through the aches. He only paused once when he felt the demon-fire stir again. *Stay quiet.* He inhaled slowly and brushed the last bit of grime from his collar, revealing the swirling infernal marks he tried to keep hidden.

After emerging from the washroom, Jackson found Elinora waiting in an adjoining hall. She wore a classy yet understated ensemble, though the worry etched on her face was impossible to miss. "You're late," she remarked tightly. "A few merchants arrived before midday. They're anxious about rumors of contraband, and you know how they get around House Riftwyn's enforcement powers."

"Sorry," Jackson answered, adjusting the clean but still-torn collar of his tunic. "We had some unexpected delays." He noticed her gaze flick to the fresh bruise along his jaw. *She's trying not to appear concerned.* He cleared his throat. "Lead on, then."

Riven joined them a moment later, ignoring Luke, who lagged behind with a self-satisfied smirk. His bath had taken the longest. In short order, a pair of servants led them to a broad parlor. Chandeliers overhead glinted off the polished floor, and a cluster of traveling merchants stood near a small table laden with refreshments. Their conversation halted when Jackson stepped inside with the others.

Jackson could almost taste the tension. Several of the

merchants exchanged uneasy glances when they caught sight of the faint red glow at the rim of his collar. *Calm, keep it calm.* He forced a polite smile. "Greetings. I understand you came seeking an audience regarding crystal exports?"

A middle-aged man in tailored robes cleared his throat. "We came, yes. We had no idea…" He paused, gazing from Jackson's gauntlet to the swirl of demonic scars. "We had no idea the King's Eye would be personally involved." His voice trembled, either from wariness or from the rumors about the Hellspawned Knight.

Another merchant, a tall woman with braided hair, added, "Forgive us if we sound unsettled. Our caravans run through many routes, and we've heard about…accidents. Bear attacks, wagon failures. Some folks say Corgrave's men orchestrate them to stifle competition."

Elinora stepped forward, her posture crisp. "This isn't the time for vague rumors. If you're in my parlor, you're aware House Riftwyn has authority over crystal exports. The King's Eye is here to ensure no contraband robs us, or any law-abiding trading partners, of security and fairness."

Despite her confidence, the merchants kept shooting guarded stares at Jackson's collar. The group parted as though giving him a wide berth in case those infernal lines erupted into flames.

Luke, watching from the side, decided to break the tension. He clapped in a friendly manner. "Folks, let's keep perspective. You worry about demon magic? Think how Corgrave's men might treat you, or your caravans, if you fail to pay them hush money or smuggling fees. They have a habit of staging 'accidents' when you don't comply. I'd say having a Hellspawned Knight on your side is less of a problem and more of an advantage."

A wiry man near the table sniffed. "Corgrave's men are real enough, but demon-fire is also real. Why should we trust him?"

Luke threw a playful shrug. "Because this demon-fire happens to answer to the Crown." He crooked a grin, tilting his head toward Jackson. "If you're worried about safety, let me personally assure you. I've traveled with this fellow for months. He's only scorched about…oh, three people. They all deserved it, mind you, and it was more of a light toasting than a full incineration. You want your caravans on the right side of that line."

Jackson resisted the urge to elbow Luke. *At least he's defusing the tension.* The merchants exchanged hesitant murmurs. Some looked unconvinced, others curious.

Elinora nodded in agreement with Luke's speech, though she wore a subtle, wry smirk. "Indeed, Corgrave's bounty hunters are no myth. They've attacked shipments of Riftcrown crystals in the deeper tunnels. We believe they mean to disrupt trade and smuggle these crystals out for their own forging experiments." When she mentioned forging, a few merchants paled. Everyone knew how lethal runic weaponry could be.

Riven stepped closer, carefully placing a few scraps of runic-inscribed cloth on the table. "We found these in a secret corridor beneath the mines. They match shipping marks that appear in some of your manifests." Her voice stayed cool. "Obviously, we'd like an explanation."

One of the older merchants, wearing a polished signet ring, inhaled sharply. "What do you imply? That we knowingly help Corgrave?"

Elinora arched an eyebrow. "I trust honest merchants have nothing to fear. However, if someone uses your guild's caravans to move contraband crystals, that draws House Riftwyn's ire. Our licensing controls the export of such materials. We could revoke the guild's privileges." Despite her measured tone, steel lurked behind her words.

The merchant group stood silent. At last, the tall woman with the braided hair sighed. "We see no profit in smuggling. But some among us noticed suspicious crates, marked with half-legible runes, mixed into legitimate shipments. There might be unscrupulous elements taking advantage of our established routes."

Elinora's expression hardened. "Where do these mysterious crates go?"

Another merchant fidgeted. "They vanish at Thornreach Bluffs, or so the records suggest. The route's known for dangerous cliffs, so few dare follow. Some deliveries are mislabeled as standard inventory, but the volumes are too large. Then they end up on small barges or hidden wagons. We neglected to investigate more closely. Out of caution."

Jackson let a hint of demon-fire show in his eyes. "Caution, or willful ignorance?" He pinned them with a stare, but he kept his voice steady. "Even if you didn't knowingly help Corgrave, you'll help us stop him now."

The merchant with the ring swallowed. "No one wants to see a new war. If you can keep us safe from Corgrave's retribution, perhaps we can share details. But we need real protection. We can't risk our caravans being—"

"Corgrave's men are less likely to target you if the Crown stands behind you," Luke jumped in. "Think about it. The King's Eye plus House Riftwyn equals deterrence. Sure, you might see a spark or two of demon-fire, but that's a small price if it saves you from forced 'accidents.'"

A few looks of reluctant acceptance spread among the merchants. One by one, they nodded or mumbled their agreement. Riven produced a small notebook, setting it on the table. "Show us exactly which shipments had questionable cargo. Dates, recipients. We'll handle the rest."

Glances were exchanged. Finally, the tall woman pulled a ledger from her traveling cloak. "We wrote cryptic notations for fear of spies, but we can decipher them here." She flipped through pages, pointing at symbols. "See there? Three shipments in the last month, all bound for Thornreach. Marked with these half-runic glyphs. We assumed it was a private code for a new client. Possibly a noble from that region."

Elinora's eyes narrowed. "Those glyphs match the scraps in the mines. Corgrave's network is bigger than we suspected."

The merchants shifted uncomfortably. They realized they were now squarely in the middle of a conflict.

"We'll verify everything," Jackson stated. "No one here will face reprisal if they cooperate fully."

Riven folded her arms. "Remember, House Riftwyn's licensing is at stake. If you keep anything crucial hidden, you lose your rights to trade crystals. Understood?"

"Understood," the merchant with the ring muttered, looking resigned. "We'll comply. Just keep your demon curses away from us, yes?"

Jackson showed a forced smile. "I'm not in the habit of cursing people for breathing, friend." He sensed Luke stifling a chuckle. "Accept a measure of trust, and we'll see your caravans pass safely."

Elinora guided them to a side desk, where a House Riftwyn scribe waited with quill and ink. By signing an impromptu agreement, the merchants vouched to provide full logs and updates. In return, they would receive official protection under House Riftwyn's banner. If Corgrave's men dared to strike, they would face the combined wrath of the Crown's Knight and Riftwyn's defenders.

As the final strokes of ink dried, the tall merchant exhaled in relief. "You have no idea how tense this has been. Whispers of sabotage, bounty hunters lurking along trade routes. We look forward to an end to this madness."

Elinora dipped her head. "Your cooperation is appreciated." Her tone softened slightly. "House Riftwyn doesn't wish to harm legitimate trade. We simply can't allow saboteurs free rein."

Luke ran a hand through his damp hair. "Think we've

scrounged up enough gloom for one day? I'm starving, and I recall someone mentioning dinner."

A faint smile lifted Elinora's lips. She offered Jackson a glance of relief tempered by caution. "I arranged for dinner in the main hall. You all look like you could use rest as well."

The merchants, evidently eager to maintain goodwill, bowed and murmured their gratitude, saying they would share a meal if invited. Elinora waved a hand. "You're welcome. Remain in the manor tonight. Safer that way."

Jackson's relief came like a slow breath escaping his chest. Tension still curled around the edges of his thoughts, but for now, they had forced the guild's cooperation. *Better to have them on our side than left alone and frightened.* He gave a polite half-bow to the merchants. "We'll discuss details more tomorrow."

Servants guided everyone along the corridor, the house's glow tinged with the softened orange of early evening. The hush that settled spoke of uncertain calm between harrowing truths and the promise of deeper entanglements.

Luke couldn't resist a final aside as they walked. "Told you, folks appreciate a flaming demon more than roving bounty hunters if you spin it the right way." He winked at Riven, who shook her head. "Sometimes, all they need is a friendly salesman."

Jackson released a tired chuckle. *It's progress. But we're stepping into an increasingly tangled web.* He straightened his shoulders, pushing thoughts of Corgrave aside for the moment. The evening's dinner awaited, along with a chance to breathe before the next stage of this unraveling plot demanded their attention.

CHAPTER TEN

Morning sunrays crept across the steep cliffs of Riftcrown Plateau, igniting faint sparkles in the crystal-veined walls. A crisp breeze carried the scent of pine and frost. In the courtyard of Riftwyn Manor, stable hands hurried about their chores, stacking feed and brushing down the horses. Laughter and hushed conversation floated through the air, until a slow, rhythmic hum drew every gaze skyward.

From the eastern horizon, an airship appeared, looming against the pale blue sky. Its hull was carved from reinforced oak and plated with a metallic sheen. Four runic propellers circled each side like glowing paddles, churning the air with a shimmering arcane pulse.

As it descended toward the courtyard, stable hands staggered back in awe. A breeze laced with magic whipped through cloaks and tousled hair.

Riven's vigilant eyes darted over the craft, her posture rigid with mistrust.

Luke, usually brazen in his remarks, quieted. He lowered his gaze, almost in reverence. "That carriage flies better than the ones in the capital," he muttered. A rare flicker of respect crossed his features.

Elinora was already present, standing near one of the stone arches that framed the courtyard. She watched the descending vessel with perfect composure, though her heart hammered under her embroidered cloak. *Sir Cain*, she thought, and recognized the King's Eye insignia emblazoned on the side. *It must be serious if he has come himself.*

A gust of wind kicked up dust when the airship finally settled. The propellers slowed, shedding bright motes of magical residue. A ramp clanked down. Sir Cain appeared at the top, armor immaculate as always. He wore a polished breastplate displaying the King's Eye crest, and a heavy cloak draped from his broad shoulders. As he strode off the ramp, every guard snapped to attention.

Jackson stood near the edge of the courtyard. At first glance, he seemed composed, but Elinora noticed the muscles in his neck tense beneath his collar. The infernal markings shimmered in response to the strong magical aura surrounding Sir Cain.

Elinora stepped forward to greet their visitor. The morning sunlight glinted off Cain's armor, highlighting faint runes etched along the gauntlets. He regarded her with cool authority, offering a respectful nod.

"My lady," he stated in a baritone voice. "I have urgent business here on behalf of High King Rodric."

She inclined her head. "Sir Cain, your presence honors House Riftwyn. I trust your flight was smooth."

He shifted, scanning the courtyard with sharp vigilance. "As smooth as a sky route can be," he replied. His gaze landed on Jackson, who stood behind Elinora. "Jackson McCade."

Jackson exhaled, then stepped forward, inclining his head in deference. "Sir Cain."

Cain gestured toward the manor's interior. "I require a

private audience. There is news from the capital that concerns you and your current operations. Lead me inside."

Without further ceremony, he followed Elinora into Riftwyn Manor, moving past the open oak doors into an austere reception hall. The polished marble floor shone with reflected morning light, and portraits of the Riftwyn lineage stared from the walls. Tall windows overlooked the plateau's crystal-studded cliffs, though none of the spectacular view seemed to distract Sir Cain.

He dismissed Elinora's attendants with a curt motion. Only Jackson, Elinora, and Cain remained behind when the thick doors groaned shut. Even the golden candelabras lining the walls seemed to lose warmth under Cain's steady scrutiny.

"You have matters for me?" Jackson asked, folding his arms. His voice was respectful but taut.

Cain regarded him. "You realize the stakes of what you are meddling in. Corgrave's men are poised to move shipments of volcanic steel. They will soon funnel these metals and stolen crystals into clandestine forges. I suspect Master Elarius' knowledge is fueling more than one hidden workshop." His gaze swept to Elinora. "Lady Riftwyn, your family's plateau is now the crossroads of a looming crisis. I hope your house is prepared to cooperate."

Elinora drew a breath. "I will do whatever is necessary to stop the illicit activity in my domain. We have uncovered partial ledgers from traveling merchants. However, they are incomplete, and many markings are coded." She paused, uncertain how much to reveal, but Cain's steady regard left her no choice. "We suspect multiple routes disguised as legitimate shipments."

Cain's face did not change as he faced Jackson. "You are to continue your investigations, but be warned. Do not let your infernal power slip out of control. There was once another knight tainted like you. He believed he could wield those flames without consequence. It ended with a city block reduced to embers and dozens of innocent dead." He paused, letting the words weigh heavily in the silent hall. "The King's Eye was forced to eliminate him."

Jackson's shoulders tensed, and his gaze flicked downward. His infernal marks burned slightly, sensing the tension. "I understand."

Cain gave a curt nod. "Your vow binds you to the Crown. If your control fails, then we will have no choice but to deal with you accordingly." He turned to Elinora. "As for House Riftwyn, keep me informed of any suspicious movement. I will station two of my knights at the base of the plateau in case an evacuation or direct interception is necessary."

Elinora inclined her head solemnly. "We are grateful for your support, Sir Cain."

"Do not be grateful. Simply be thorough." He walked to the door, pausing to glance back at Jackson. "I depart in two hours. If you need me, contact one of my knights. Good hunting." With that, he left the pair alone.

Jackson exhaled, releasing tension from his chest. A faint sheen of sweat lined his brow.

"You have to be careful," Elinora cautioned. "Luke can joke all he wants, but Sir Cain's warnings are not mere threats."

Jackson nodded. "He's right. We have to keep the demonic side in check, no matter what. I would prefer not to end like that other knight." He schooled his features into composure. "Let's see what progress we can make on those ledgers. If Corgrave plans a bigger operation, we need to find it before it takes root."

They spent the day in her father's old study, a high-ceilinged room lined with bookshelves. Dust motes drifted in beams of light as Elinora laid out a large table covered in half-deciphered notes and shipping lists. Riven joined them briefly to deliver a small, coded ledger snagged from a merchant. Luke hovered near the back, cracking awkward jokes or complaining about the dryness of old parchment. Yet whenever Elinora or Jackson found a crucial detail, Luke swiftly grabbed a quill to cross-reference it.

The hours stretched. Page after page of jumbled runes. Arrows scrawled in the margins indicated possible routes. Some ended in question marks, others in the dreaded brand of Corgrave's crest. The sun traversed the windows, sinking lower until shadows swathed the shelves.

Elinora's stomach growled. She glanced at Luke. "Fetch something from the kitchen, would you?" Tired humor touched her voice. "We might starve before finding the right code."

Luke snapped to attention with a mock salute. "At once, my lady. I shall return with bread, fruit, and possibly a chunk of cheese if the cooks do not chase me off with ladles." Then, he ambled away.

Riven drifted after him, presumably to keep watch and to avoid further tedium deciphering trade routes. That left Jackson and Elinora standing side by side at the table. The quiet crackle of a wall sconce replaced the usual chatter. She glanced at him, noticing the faint lines of fatigue etched around his eyes.

He shifted, meeting her gaze for an instant. Warmth flickered there. He had a strong presence, and it didn't help that he was attractive as well. It wasn't merely his honed, muscular body and chiseled face. She thought of his voice and the way his presence drew her attention no matter what else was going on in the room.

Get it together, she admonished herself. *This is not the time.* She wasn't prejudiced toward knights like him, not like others were. But entangling herself with one was off the table. She cleared her throat and bent over the ledgers, focusing on the scribbled runes.

Eventually, they reached a natural stopping point. The sun had descended into brilliant orange across the plateau. Outside the tall windows, the last streaks of daylight kissed the shimmering crystal spires. Elinora stacked the parchments. "I think we have a direction. Tomorrow, we can…"

Her words faltered as a sudden, impulsive thought took hold of her. "Jackson, I would like to speak with you privately tonight. If you can spare the time." She kept her features neutral. Inside, her heart pounded. She had no clear plan, only the press of curiosity and a low, simmering attraction she had fought to ignore. All right, maybe it was *on the table*.

Jackson hesitated, aware of the unusual invitation. "Of course. Where shall I meet you?"

"My study," she replied. "After dinner." Without waiting for his reaction, she turned on her heel and left.

Night settled thickly across Riftwyn Manor. Torchlight and a scattering of magical sconces illuminated the corridors. Servants hurried about, cleaning away the day's chaos. The distant laughter of guards drifted from the courtyard. Riven had disappeared to do her usual perimeter checks. Luke, content after an ample meal, had wandered off mumbling something about "finding a good spot to rest."

When Jackson reached Elinora's study, he knocked quietly. She called him in at once. The room was small but elegant. Shelves brimming with tomes lined the walls, and a single window overlooked the starlit plateau. A modest table in the center bore two plates covered with domed silver lids. A candle's warm glow accentuated the subtle lines of worry on Elinora's brow.

"I had the kitchen prepare a late meal." She motioned for him to sit. He removed his cloak, setting it aside before taking a seat across from her. The old wooden chair creaked softly underneath him.

He lifted the lid from his plate. Steam wafted into the room, carrying the aroma of seasoned meat. The dish was rift-fowl in a rich gravy, served with roasted root vegetables. Elinora uncovered her own plate, a gentle swirl of savory scents filling the air. Jackson had eaten already but obliged her. For a few moments, they ate in comfortable silence, each uncertain how to broach the real purpose of the invitation.

At length, she spoke quietly. "I know your vow to the king weighs heavily on you. I see it in your eyes."

He paused, setting his fork aside with a soft clink. "The vow is necessary. My nature needs oversight. Without it, I might..." He stopped, exhaling. "There are risks. Cain's reminder was hardly subtle."

She nodded. "I also know the weight of a family's expectations. My mother has strict notions of what House Riftwyn requires, especially now. If she discovered any closeness between me and a knight like you, she would not react kindly."

Jackson's heart pounded. "So, why risk meeting me here alone?"

She exhaled, gaze flicking to the single candle. "Because I trust you more than I should. You have proven yourself. You stand in that corridor with your infernal power under such tight control, and I admire it. It stirs curiosity in me. And something else."

Their plates remained half-eaten as she rose, moving around the table. Her emotions swirled between caution and longing. Without fully thinking, she placed a hand on his shoulder. He looked at her, searching her face, uncertain whether to step back or tilt closer.

"Perhaps we are both making a mistake," she murmured. "But if so, I do not care." She placed her fingers along the collar of his tunic, feeling the lingering heat from the demonic marks.

He stood, breath catching in his chest.

She slid her hand up to the side of his jaw, and raw tension flared. He inhaled her perfume, the faint citrus notes mingling with candle wax. Then, bracing herself, Elinora tugged him to her. Their lips met in a sudden, fierce kiss. Heat rushed through them. Their arms shifted, searching for an embrace that felt both inevitable and precarious. She pulled him closer, and his back encountered a tall bookshelf.

He groaned, the sensation of her pressing against him overwhelming. His gauntleted hand found the small of her back. She captured his lower lip, kissing more urgently, as though all the tension they had bottled throughout the day needed release. One of the books from behind them dropped with a soft thud, but neither broke contact.

When at last they pulled apart, both drew ragged breaths. A wave of conflicting feelings clouded the air. Relief, desire, caution. Elinora's cheeks were flushed, her gaze bright and searching.

"They would disapprove," she whispered. "My mother, Sir Cain, everyone. But let them. Tonight, I wonder if we can be ourselves. If only for a little while."

Jackson's pulse thundered. *Spirits, what am I doing?* He gazed at her parted lips, at the regal tilt of her chin. "Here and now, I will not say no," he managed to reply. His arms remained around her. The slightest shift in his stance revealed how every part of him wanted to keep her near.

They kissed again, gentler this time, a promise rather than a demand. She leaned into his chest, heart pounding. For a few moments, they simply existed in that hush, ignoring the magnitude of what might follow. Her hand slipped lower, resting against his collar as if feeling for a tremor in the infernal power. He inhaled, careful not to let the flame spark beyond control.

Eventually they separated, the walls of the study coming back into focus. She stepped away, glancing self-consciously at the scattered books and the plates of half-eaten food.

"This cannot be easy," she stated, touching her lips. "But I do not regret it. Do you?"

His voice shook only slightly. "I regret nothing. If it complicates matters, so be it."

Silence lingered between them, warm but tinged with worry. Neon flickers from the crystals outside played across the study walls, reflecting the array of conflicting hopes in both their hearts.

Finally, Jackson cleared his throat. "I should go before we court more trouble than we can handle."

She nodded, expression torn between relief and disappointment. "Yes. It is late, and we need rest. Tomorrow, we continue the fight. If we are careful, we can find ways to…"

He touched her cheek, halting her words. "Tomorrow," he repeated. Then, with one last fleeting look, the corner of his mouth tugged into a faint smile as he stepped through the door.

The corridors of Riftwyn Manor were empty at this hour except for occasional patrolling guards. Jackson rounded a corner and nearly ran into Luke, who leaned casually against a pillar. The roguish traveler greeted him with a grin that made Jackson's cheeks warm.

"Late stroll?" Luke quipped. "You look winded. Also, kinda sparkly around the edges, if you catch my meaning."

Jackson gave him a warning look. "I'm not in the mood. Besides, I thought you went to rest."

"Sure, sure. I get it." Luke raised his hands with feigned innocence, then winked. "Nothing wrong with a little spark, my friend. I was on my way to rest, and I suggest you do the same."

Jackson would have replied, but he sensed movement farther down the hall. Riven stepped from the shadows, one brow raised. Her expression was hard to read. After a moment, she inclined her head. "There is more backbone in that human than I thought." Perhaps she referred to Elinora, or perhaps she'd simply observed the entire night's events from afar.

Jackson did not reply. The heat of the memory still burned in his chest. He brushed past them, cloak swishing, determined to return to his quarters before emotions, or demon-fire, surged beyond control. Behind him, he caught the echo of Luke's low chuckle. Riven simply watched him, silent as the dark.

He ascended the stairs alone, every step accompanied by echoes of that heated kiss and the knowledge that desire could be as perilous as any blade.

CHAPTER ELEVEN

A chill wind coursed through the ravine behind the old quarry, rustling sparse weeds that sprouted between jagged boulders. The moonlight hung pale and distant, revealing uneven ground littered with fragments of weathered stone.

Makeshift lanterns dangled from wooden poles, improvised beacons that cast shifting patches of sickly light over clusters of hooded figures. Their cloaks were stained with travel, and their hushed dealings spoke of danger. Beneath those weak lanterns, thick crates waited in stacked rows. The faint gleam of crystal shards peeked through the cracks of aged planks.

Luke wove through the gathering. He wore a ragged cloak that smelled of mildew, its tattered edges dragging over loose pebbles. His posture was deliberately stooped to appear harmless.

He paused near a cluster of merchants bargaining under their breath. Each time he edged closer, he flashed a glimpse of counterfeit trade tokens, letting them clink meaningfully in his palm. A few curious glances flicked his way, measuring the worth of the scruffy newcomer. He gave them a lazy grin.

Jackson stood in the shadows behind an uneven stack of cargo, one gauntlet resting lightly on the hilt of his sword. He kept Luke in sight, ready to intervene if anything looked suspicious. He listened to the hushed bartering, identical sums repeated in low tones, each payoff passed from trembling hand to eager fist.

Accented voices rattled about crates loaded with luminous crystals, the trade that fed Corgrave's black-market ring. Jackson's pulse beat faster. *If Corgrave is behind this, we will see proof tonight.* His scalp prickled at the memory of how easily these crystals could be used in twisted forging.

Riven crouched a short distance away. From her vantage point, she could see the entire ravine. The lanterns, the crowd of hooded buyers, and the small ring of bodyguards posted along the edges. Each time she inhaled, the old ache returned. She had fought scoundrels in many forms, bandits and cutthroats, all to keep dark commerce from spreading. The memory of war flickered across her body. She brushed those old fears aside. An arrow sat notched against her bowstring, half-drawn. In the gloom, her gaze flicked to each participant in turn, searching for any mark of Corgrave or other unwelcome presences.

High on a ridge, a lone silhouette kept watch. Lady Elinora, in a plain traveling cloak. Thin as the disguise was, she managed to blend with the shallow rocks. Her posture radiated tension. She pressed a spyglass to one eye to track the movements of each crate.

Although she had no direct vantage of Luke, she spotted the dull reflection of Jackson's gauntlet in the flickering lantern light. *No trouble yet.* She brushed away a stray lock of hair. *But it never stays quiet for long in these deals.* Her mind flashed to the merchant guilt on Riftwyn Manor's grounds, how tenuous all alliances were. Conspirators this brazen would not hesitate to shoot if threatened.

Down in the ravine, Luke sidled up to a bundle of contraband two men were haggling over. He clucked his tongue, muttering something about wanting a look. They scowled at him. One man had a scraggly beard. The other wore a bandage across his nose.

Luke's casual grin never wavered. He set a few tokens on the crate. "Heard you folks might have specialized crystals. The kind that glow real bright. Took me a bit of trouble to find you." One brow rose under the hood's shadow, and he allowed his voice to carry a hint of mock sincerity.

"Lower your voice," hissed Bandaged Nose, glancing around.

Luke offered him an apologetic shrug. "Sure," he whispered. "No point stirring up trouble." He flicked another token onto the crate.

Beard rubbed his chin, regarding Luke's soiled cloak. "Bounty hunters have roamed these paths lately," he murmured. "Fools poking around for easy coin. You're brave for coming here alone."

Luke's chuckle was soft. "Bravery, stupidity, same difference."

Jackson flexed his shoulders at that remark. He caught sight of movement on the quarry's far side. A second ring of watchers stood near the ravine entrance. *Not merchants,* he thought. They wore heavier cloaks. Instead of trade tokens, they carried weapons. The air around them crackled with tension. He exhaled slowly. *Everything about this smells like an ambush.*

Behind him, Riven eased forward, sensing the shift as well. The hush in the lantern-lit clearing took on a sharper edge. Moments later, the watchers near the entrance broke rank, advancing with rune-based firearms.

Their leader, a woman with stern features and a breastplate, stepped forward. She slammed a foot down, commanded attention, and raised her voice over the uncertain buyers. "In the name of House Corgrave, we claim these goods and brand anyone trading outside our authority as traitors," she snarled. "All your hush money is worthless unless we get our cut."

A ripple of alarm ran through the black-market crowd. Several men clutched the handles of crates, uncertain whether to fight or flee. Bandaged Nose shot Luke a wide-eyed look. Beard muttered a curse.

At once, a swirl of confusion tore through the gathering, people pushing and stumbling over each other.

Luke tilted his head. "And here I was hoping for peace." He laughed, stepping back from the crates.

The mercenaries unleashed warning shots. Bolts of arcane light spat from runic barrels, impact sparks dancing against the quarry stones. The shriek of the blasts rattled the entire ravine. Several buyers cried out and darted for cover. Others brandished short blades in desperation.

Jackson moved. His boots pounded over loose gravel as he rushed from his hiding spot. He let the demon-fire bloom beneath his collar. A faint red glow twined along his neck, enough to unsettle the nearest attacker.

Two of the bounty hunters, brandishing rifles with swirling glyphs, froze at the sight of him, panic tugging at their faces. One fired a scattering shot that whined past Jackson's shoulder, sparking against the rocky ground. Jackson's scuffed gauntlet flared. He lunged, sword striking the barrels aside before they could reload.

A few yards away, Riven snapped into motion. She raised her bow, sighting along an arrow fletched with runic etchings. She aimed toward the cluster of bounty hunters. Then she saw a tattoo on one man's forearm. An angular brand in black, the shape she remembered from the day her elven enclave was razed. Her breath caught with a ragged hitch. *They took everything from us.* The memory hissed through her chest, and her hand trembled with rage. She fired.

Her arrow flew in a blur and struck the tattooed man through his shoulder. He screamed, staggering behind a shattered crate. Blood darkened his sleeve, but he twisted to raise his runic rifle.

With trembling fury, Riven loosed another arrow so close that it nicked the weapon's grip, making it jerk. The shot went wide.

A sharp retort of arcs sizzled overhead. Riven's lips parted in a tight snarl. She pressed forward, ignoring the adrenaline that hammered her pulse.

Meanwhile, Luke ducked behind a stack of crates, the muzzle flash from a bounty hunter's rifle lighting the night everywhere he moved. "Unfriendly bunch, huh?" he muttered. He rummaged inside the bandit leader's satchel, having pilfered it earlier during the chaos. His fingers rubbed against parchment. *Looks promising.* He stuffed it under his cloak. A second shot blasted a crate over his head, sending splinters flying. Luke cursed and spun aside.

"Riven!" he called. "We're taking fire on the right!"

Riven dropped to a knee. In a smooth motion, she nocked another arrow, exhaled, and loosed. The spine of her arrow lodged into the thigh of a tall bounty hunter bracing himself behind an overturned trunk. He collapsed with a shriek.

Jackson spotted the opening and rushed in, demon-fire coiling along his collar. He thrust his sword, the steel glinting with a faint infernal light, and felled two of the men who tried to block his path. Neither had time to parry. One dropped to the ground, chest heaving. The other crumpled instantly.

Elinora, still perched atop the ravine, pressed her lips together at the sight of runic blasts ripping through the crowd. She scrambled down a slope of loose gravel, keeping to the shadows. She found an angle behind a tall boulder, ensuring no stray rifle shot could catch her off guard. Then, she rose slightly, scanning for a vantage.

Her gaze sought Jackson through the swirl of dust. *He is holding them back.* She whistled softly to get Riven's attention, then pointed to three bounty hunters bunched together near the largest crate. Riven gave an understanding nod, repositioning swiftly.

The air rippled with arcane residue. The runic firearms spat eerie flashes of green, each discharge accompanied by a piercing hum. Buyers scrambled for cover. A lantern toppled and shattered, partially extinguishing the garish light. Shouting and curses tore at the night. One shrill voice bellowed, "We will punish every traitor that dares cross Corgrave!" A second shot whined overhead.

Jackson advanced through the chaos. A swirl of demon-fire flickered around his left arm. He locked eyes with one bounty hunter, a tall, lean figure attempting to reload a rifle. Jackson's presence made the man hesitate.

Jackson clamped his gauntlet around the weapon's barrel and wrenched it aside. Sparks erupted. In a burst of reflex, Jackson slammed his elbow into the man's jaw. The bounty hunter sagged, groaning. Another rushed in with a blade, but Riven's arrow took him low in the side, dropping him in a coughing heap.

Within moments, the fighting began to subside. Of the seven bounty hunters, three lay still on the ground, weapons clattering away from limp hands. One had crawled behind a cargo stack, where Elinora held him at bay with a short blade. Another spat blood and curses, pinned under Jackson's boot. Riven glared at the one with the tattoo, her arrow still lodged in his shoulder.

Luke circled behind a mound of smashed crates, rummaging quickly. "Fancy ledger in here." His voice was taut with excitement. He lifted a half-burned parchment from the satchel. "Seems coded."

Jackson exhaled, the glow on his collar subsiding slightly. He pressed a knee into the pinned bounty hunter's ribcage. "You will answer to us."

The pinned man groaned, eyes wild. Sweat blurred the lines of filth caked on his face. "Shut up," he spat, though his voice wavered.

Riven stomped over, ignoring the pang in her shoulders. Her hands trembled with adrenaline. She looked down at the pinned man, then the one clutching his shot shoulder. "Who sent you?" Her arrow aimed at his head.

He swallowed, glancing nervously at Jackson's demon-fire. "We follow Corgrave's creed," he whispered. "He pays. He redeems those who aid him, grants them power. Anyone else is worthless."

Elinora approached, stepping around the crates. She flicked a glance at Luke, who tucked the ledger away. Her voice was steady. "What do you mean by redemption? Are you so desperate that you throw your lot in with a disgraced lord?"

The bounty hunter's lip curled. "He is not disgraced to us. He will reclaim Thornreach, then everything else."

"Where?" Jackson demanded. "Where are you taking these crystals?"

The pinned man coughed, blood flecking his chin. A sneer touched his lips. "Fortress near Thornreach Bluffs. All who stand in his path will be crushed."

Riven's eyes narrowed. The hatred in her expression flared again, recalling the brand on the man's arm. "You serve that cursed house. You have no idea the horror you've unleashed."

He only spat again, refusing to meet her gaze.

Luke stepped close. "That ledger might show us more. Look at him. He's not going to tell us anything else of value."

Jackson nodded. A faint tremor went through his fingers. *There is more ahead.* He released his hold on the bounty hunter, who slumped, moaning. The air smelled of gunpowder and scorched rock. Flickers of residual arcane energy clung to the broken crates. Buyers who had survived were scrambling away under cover of darkness, some limping, others carrying wounded.

Elinora released a shaky breath. She pressed her dagger to the side, still watchful. Indecision flickered in her eyes. Riven shook her bow arm to settle the ache, then shot a sharp glare at the man.

"He's worthless. Let him crawl off or deliver a message to his foul masters."

Jackson rose, scanning for bystanders or leftover dangers. Then, he spotted Luke holding the coded ledger. "We keep that hidden."

"Absolutely," Luke replied. "Might take a while to crack it, but it's definitely mentioning shipments of crystals. I saw some runic scribbles."

Elinora moved to Luke's side, her gaze shifting between the parchment in his grip and the mercenaries. "This is what we needed."

Riven turned away from the moaning men. She paused, trembling, anger still coursing through her veins. She pictured her destroyed enclave and forced it down, biting her lip until she tasted blood.

Jackson touched her shoulder lightly. "They are scattered now. Focus."

She jerked her head in a stiff nod, exhaling. "Yes," she whispered.

Dark clouds drifted over the moon, dimming the ravine further. The few unbroken lanterns cast a sputtering light across the scene of broken crates and fallen bounty hunters. Elinora wiped a smear of dust from her cheek and slung her dagger back under her cloak.

At last, Jackson lifted the ledger from Luke's hand. He skimmed the coded lines, though the strange symbols told him little. *We will find a way to read this.* A knot of worry formed in his gut. The bounty hunters had revealed enough. Mention of Thornreach Bluffs, talk of redemption, the promise of more infiltration. He clenched his jaw, still feeling the demon-fire roil under his skin.

Elinora's gaze flicked to a suspect who lay whimpering near an overturned crate. She watched dispassionately as he dragged himself across the gravel. "We have what we came for," she murmured. "There is no point in staying longer."

Jackson tucked the ledger under his cloak. Blood dripped from his sword's edge, marking the ground with small, dark spots.

They filed out of the ravine, climbing the slope back toward the plateau's track. At the top of the ridge, Elinora paused to survey the carnage below, her face set with grim focus. A gust of wind ruffled her cloak, blowing strands of hair across her cheek. Luke adjusted his stolen satchel, while Riven's bow string vibrated faintly as she calmed her breath. Jackson's knuckles were white around the ledger, a chill creeping through him.

He glanced at the cryptic text, and his heart pounded. *This is only a taste of what lies ahead.* Silently, the group turned and slipped into the shadows of the plateau, determined to uncover the secrets that would lead them closer to Corgrave's twisted ambitions.

CHAPTER TWELVE

Well before the sun rose over Riftcrown Plateau, Jackson leaned over a small writing table inside one of the manor's upper rooms. His gauntlet rested beside an inkpot. He flexed his fingers, still sore from the nighttime ambush. The glow of a single lamp revealed a thin piece of parchment, its edges curled from hasty handling.

He carefully dipped the quill and began drafting the letter to King Rodric. The scratch of pen against paper fit the hush that cloaked the manor. Outside, moonlight caught on shimmering spires of crystal.

My king,
We have uncovered new smuggling routes below the plateau. Corgrave's men were present at a black-market auction, brazenly enforcing his claim over stolen crystals. Evidence points to Thornreach Bluffs as their next base of operation.

He paused, glancing at the spidery lines of ink, then signed it with the simple flourish used by the King's Eye.

Elinora Riftwyn stood a few steps behind him, observing. Her expression remained poised, no sign of the heated tension she and Jackson had shared the night before. The only hint of lingering emotion was the soft rose color over her cheeks and the way she smoothed her hands over her mantle with more care than usual.

She finally spoke in a measured tone. "Are you sure those details suffice? You could emphasize how many mercenaries Corgrave has deployed."

Jackson rested the quill. "I've included enough specifics to show how urgent it is," he replied. "Any more risks giving away too much if the raven's intercepted." He folded the parchment and pressed a wax seal over the flap, stamping it with the small signet ring Cain had given him for official dispatches. "Rodric will understand the stakes."

Elinora nodded, her shoulders easing. "Then let it fly."

They crossed the corridor to a small balcony overlooking the plateau's edge. The predawn hush draped white mist across the manor grounds. A high spire of stone jutted up from where stable hands tended to early-morning tasks.

Jackson extended his arm, and a raven hopped forward from a perch near the balustrade. The bird's eyes shone with intelligence, reflecting the subtle sparkle in the walls of Riftcrown Plateau. Jackson tied the message to its slender leg while Elinora murmured a quiet instruction to guide it toward the capital.

The raven fixed them with a curious tilt of its head. Then, it launched upward, its wings eclipsing the last sliver of moonlight. Jackson watched until the bird vanished into the broadening sky. He and Elinora exchanged a brief glance. She pressed her lips into a thin line, as if steadying herself.

They left the balcony, descending toward a broad foyer. Hints of daybreak lit the high windows, catching on stray motes of dust. There, Luke and Riven awaited, the two standing on opposite sides of a table cluttered with new equipment. Luke fiddled with a faintly glowing map holder, rotating it under the lantern's glare, while Riven inspected a pair of grappling hooks etched with small runic sequences.

Luke offered a lopsided grin. "I tested these hooks an hour ago against the stable roof. They clamp to crystal like a barnacle on a dock post. Maybe they'll keep us from falling to our doom in Thornreach."

Riven narrowed her gaze. "They'll be useful, but watch your step, or you'll break your neck." She set the hooks aside and turned to Elinora. "So, you're accompanying us." It was neither question nor condemnation, but the edge in her voice made her skepticism clear.

Elinora dipped her head, ignoring the elf's withering tone. "My mother consented on condition that I bring a small guard detail. They'll remain out of sight, but House Riftwyn won't stand idle while Corgrave threatens to cripple these lands."

Luke returned the map holder to the table. "Your mother's a tough one. She'd probably have me hung if I said the wrong phrase at dinner." He winked, only half in jest.

A beat passed before Elinora spoke. "She simply wants to protect her legacy, and that includes me. To her mind, if agents of the King's Eye were lost on Riftwyn territory, it would cast suspicion. The barony's name matters more to her than any single person's feelings."

Riven folded her arms, features neutral. "Perhaps she wants to ensure House Riftwyn reaps the reward if we succeed. Influence in the capital can be more valuable than gold."

Luke's grin turned thoughtful. "Can't blame her for thinking about the future. People are always trying to come out ahead."

Jackson let the conversation settle before he cleared his throat. "We can't afford quarrels. If Thornreach Bluffs is as fortified as we suspect, we'll need every advantage. Maybe guards in the distance will keep bandits from picking us off. Or maybe they'll complicate things." He shot Elinora a meaningful look. "We'll adapt either way."

Her returning gaze was steady. "Then let me be clear. I'm joining this mission to ensure Corgrave doesn't use Riftcrown crystals to fuel his forging spree. If that aligns with the King's Eye's goals, all the better." Her gaze flicked to Riven. "I have no intention of discarding any ally who stands against Corgrave, we must move swiftly."

The elf's posture softened. Her quiet acceptance felt like a small truce.

Luke seized the lull and patted the glowing map holder. "Speaking of swift, we've got new toys. This holder reveals hidden runes. Should help if Corgrave's men set up illusions or wards." He flipped it open, revealing a gentle luminescence rippling across the interior lining. "We tested it on those leftover parchments from the smuggler's ledger. Some hidden scribbles popped right out. Like invisible daydreams or something."

A spark of interest lit Elinora's eyes. "That will be invaluable underground or in dim corridors. Thornreach might have old smuggler tunnels. I've heard rumors of hidden compartments in their coastal watchtowers."

Riven examined the map holder's hinge. "So long as it doesn't attract attention at the worst moment."

Luke shrugged. "Trust is a rare commodity these days," he murmured, echoing the remark he'd shared privately with Riven. "Better we bring the right gear than stumble blind."

Elinora drew closer, inspecting the runic grappling hooks. They gleamed with etched lines that pulsed faintly in response to the plateau's ambient crystal energy. "My mother's scout recommended these. The runes are intended to anchor themselves to stone or crystal with minimal slip."

Riven brushed a finger over one hook. "We'll see." She glanced at Jackson. "We depart soon?"

"Within the hour," Jackson replied. "I want to be on the road well before midday. We'll travel lightly."

A subdued bustle began as everyone split up to finalize preparations. Servants summoned by a brief chime scurried into the foyer with supplies. Luke rummaged through gear, carefully packing potions and small medical kits into a compact saddlebag. Riven tested the bowstring on her fine-limbed recurve bow, verifying tension and a fresh coat of wax.

Elinora stepped away to speak with her mother's steward, quietly relaying instructions for the guard detail's formation. Meanwhile, Jackson balanced his sword across a low bench, taking a moment to sharpen its edge. Each pass of the whetstone rasped in the hush.

He considered the letter to the king, riding the air currents aboard that raven. *Rodric will know soon enough,* he reflected. *I hope it spurs him to action.* Uncertainty tightened his jaw. He pushed it aside, focusing on the sparks dancing along the sword's metal whenever his infernal aura flickered. The runic lines across his gauntlet glowed.

Footsteps approached. Elinora, cloak draped over her arm, studied him with a calm expression. "We're nearly ready. Is your...power steady?" She nodded toward the faint red glow around his collar, avoiding passing servants' notice.

He sheathed the blade. "As steady as it can be."

She hesitated. Her voice softened. "Then let's do what must be done."

Their gazes locked for a heartbeat. Neither spoke of their fleeting closeness, as there was no time to dwell on it here. Yet Jackson felt the faint warmth behind her composure. He wished they could pause the world long enough for frank words. Still, the threat demanded urgency.

Out in Riftwyn Manor's courtyard, a handful of House Riftwyn guards waited astride sturdy mounts. Their commander was a tall woman in polished half-plate bearing the family crest.

She and Elinora exchanged salutes. Meanwhile, Luke and Riven loaded the last of their travel gear onto two horses. A third horse, black-coated and restless, stood apart for Jackson, who rubbed its flank in greeting.

Elinora's contingent consisted of half a dozen riders, each clad in chain and bearing a short spear. They kept a silent, respectful distance from the King's Eye agent. Slight tension hummed in the air. None wanted to cross the Hellspawned Knight, nor did they entirely trust him or Riven.

Jackson took the reins of his horse and swung up, scanning the yard.

Luke checked the new grappling hooks, ensuring they were snug in a saddle pouch. "So," he rumbled. "The plan is to ride down the southern switchbacks, skirt the low ridges, and make for Thornreach by the old trading road. That's the route, yeah?"

Jackson nodded. "We'll avoid the main highway. Too many watchful eyes. And word might have spread about last night's ambush."

Riven adjusted her quiver, scanning the manor's walls. "We'll see if these extra guards stir up more trouble than they prevent."

Elinora guided her horse alongside Jackson's. "My mother requested that I emphasize her caution is pragmatic, not personal."

Luke snorted softly. "Sure. Pragmatic as a rockslide." He caught Riven's sharp look and hushed.

Jackson directed his focus to the courtyard gate. A stable hand hurried to open it, the heavy iron rattling in protest. The sky had shifted from inky predawn to the first pastel glimmer of sunrise. The crystals embedded in the plateau's walls refracted the light, painting the courtyard in swirling colors.

The small column started forward. Elinora's guards formed a loose perimeter, letting the main party set the pace. Hoofbeats echoed against the stone as they wound past the manor's outer walls and onto a descending path carved into the mountainside.

The crisp air bit at cheeks, carrying a faint tang of pine. Below them, fog curled through ravines, obscuring the deeper valleys.

A few minutes later, Luke urged his horse closer to Riven so they could speak. Jackson and Elinora rode at the front, carefully picking their way over switchbacks. Occasional glances passed among them as they measured how silently the guards behind trotted. Tension coiled, yet adrenaline lingered from the night's confrontation.

Finally, Luke chuckled. "It'll be an interesting trip, that's for sure. If Thornreach is as pretty as its name, I'll buy you all a round of ale."

Riven's response was a raised brow. "You think a place called Thornreach is pretty?"

He shrugged. "I'm an optimist. Although, I guess brambles and cliffs might not be my dream vacation."

Elinora half-turned in her saddle. "Thornreach used to have scenic overlooks, until House Corgrave's sabotage forced the region into disrepair. Now, who knows?"

Jackson's gaze flicked across the rocky horizon. "We can worry about the view later. Right now, any vantage is an advantage if we encounter brigands."

They continued downward in a line, forging into a narrow pass leading away from the plateau's heart. The armor of Riftwyn's guards clinked softly. Otherwise, the group kept quiet. Nobody wanted to draw attention, even if the immediate threat had dispersed. The hush of dawn lent a strange calm.

Luke patted a saddlebag. "When we test the map holder, I bet we'll see hidden markings on the roads connecting to Thornreach. Corgrave's men love their coded scrawls."

Riven cast him a sideways glance. "First, let's actually survive the trip."

Elinora's horse sidestepped a loose patch of shale, prompting her to steady the reins. Once balanced, she addressed the group more loudly. "The route we're choosing isn't the usual trade path, so keep watch for old rockfall signs. If we pass any abandoned outposts, we should check for sabotage or secret supply stashes."

One of her guards, a sinewy man with short-cropped hair, spoke up. "My lady, we'll maintain distance as you instructed. Signal if you require aid or if anything emerges from the side ravines."

She nodded in acknowledgment. "We will."

They advanced steadily, the hooves of their horses stirring dust along the winding path. Heavy clouds gathered overhead. A breeze shivered across the plateau, carrying the promise of coming rain. The travelers' cloaks fluttered, and Jackson caught himself scanning each bend in the road, every ridge that might hide an ambush. *Corgrave must anticipate we'd strike soon.*

He considered the coded ledger tucked safely in Luke's pack. It bore references to hidden forging routes, unmarked convoys, and the dreaded mention of Thornreach Bluffs. *No telling how large Corgrave's network is.*

Behind them, Riftcrown Plateau's looming shape gradually shrank from view. The bright crystals in its walls still flickered, but distance dulled them to faint sparks. Soon, a stony silence fell over the company.

The slope flattened as the narrow pass opened onto rolling foothills. Stunted pine trees dotted the landscape, and boulders jutted from the earth in irregular clusters. A sense of transition seeped into the group as they left behind the sheltered domain of Riftwyn Manor for the uncertain roads toward Thornreach.

Jackson reined his horse beside Elinora. "If your mother's guards are discreet, hopefully Corgrave's scouts won't realize we have more numbers."

She inclined her head. "They'll keep back. House Riftwyn is determined not to tip the scales until necessary."

Riven slowed, letting Luke catch up. She looked at the horizon, where thunderclouds swelled. "If we get caught in a storm, it'll slow us down."

Luke exhaled. "At least it might hide us from prying eyes," he remarked, husky with faint optimism. "Rain can be friend or foe."

They continued at a steady pace, the hoofbeats merging into a single percussion. The swirl of clouds overhead cast shifting shadows across the foothills, painting the terrain in shades of silver and pale blue. An undercurrent of tension arced among them, as though the land itself anticipated the coming conflict.

Elinora raised her voice so all heard. "We'll make camp at midday in a sheltered area. After that, we push on. If all goes smoothly, we should reach Thornreach's outer boundaries by tomorrow."

Jackson responded with a grave nod. He caught Riven's alert expression, the unspoken watchfulness in her posture, and Luke's restless energy. Each carried their own motivations, but for now, unity was their shield against what loomed ahead.

House Riftwyn's banner swayed behind them, half-concealed, a subtle reminder that they traveled under a noble's watch, even as they carried out the King's Eye's directive. More than once, Jackson almost sensed the friction between that crest and the invisible brand blazing on his collar. Two loyalties, two opposite worlds.

Luke cleared his throat. "Elinora, I hope your mother's not aiming to brand me a troublemaker when this is over. I've got a knack for saying the wrong thing at dinners."

Elinora glanced back with a smile. "If you keep your wits, I'm sure you'll manage. She tolerates your humor in small doses."

Luke pressed a hand to his chest in an exaggerated gesture of relief. Riven looked away, hiding a smirk of her own.

A gust rattled a few scattered pines as they rode on, the path cutting across a ridge. Far behind them, Riftcrown Plateau rose like an impossible fortress of glimmering rock. Already, drifting clouds cloaked its highest peaks. Jackson slowed his horse enough to cast one final glance in that direction. *We leave a place of uneasy alliances, stepping into an even greater unknown.*

He sensed Elinora's attention. Their eyes met, though her features remained inscrutable. The small party and its distant guard contingent wound farther into rolling hills, the silhouettes of the plateau's spires receding behind the storm-laden sky.

None could say if the approaching storm would help cloak their journey or create new hazards. Still, they advanced, unsure whether the unity they clung to would become the shield they needed, or if it would fracture under the secrets ahead.

CHAPTER THIRTEEN

The wind whipped across the deck with unrelenting force, spattering salt spray onto every crevice of the creaking fishing vessel. Jackson stood near the mainmast with his hood drawn low, yet he could not stop the brine from stinging his eyes. A trio of deckhands, seasoned men with scarred forearms and sullen faces, sidled away from him whenever his infernal markings pulsed.

Their party had left the contingent of guards behind, with no room for so many on this ship.

Elinora had claimed a place at the prow, one hand gripping the worn railing as she surveyed the darkening horizon. Her traveling cloak snapped behind her in the gusts, but her stance never wavered. She kept silent for much of the voyage, though her gaze kept drifting toward the looming cliffs that jutted from the churning sea ahead. The flares of torchlight on distant heights unnerved her.

"These cliffs were abandoned after the war," she stated at last. "That fortress on the bluff should be silent and rotting. It hasn't been occupied for nearly four years. No watchtower fires have burned since House Corgrave lost their seat here. Until now."

Jackson followed her line of sight. Flickers of orange glimmered in the twilight, pinpoint beacons of unwelcome activity. "So they're re-arming the area." He sensed the faint hum of his demonic aura whenever he thought of Corgrave's ambitions. "If they have enough men to hold a fortress along these cliffs, they've dug in deeper than we expected."

Elinora exhaled. "We need to confirm how many. A direct assault would be unwise." She did not flinch at the cold sea spray that lashed her face. Her composure told Jackson how determined she could be, no matter the danger.

Behind them, Luke struggled to brace himself. He clutched a rope for balance as a fresh wave of freezing salt water hissed across the deck. He sputtered, his breath fogging in the chill air. "Someone remind me why I'm not at a cozy tavern table with a warm meal and a warming wench to soothe away this blasted cold?" he growled.

Jackson chuckled. "Careful, Luke. You're whining louder than the wind."

Luke shot him a narrow-eyed look. "I'd bet half the gold from our last job that you'd be face-down, begging for a blanket, if your demonic blood didn't run hot." He sneezed, then gripped the rope tighter as the boat lurched.

A passing deckhand, a grizzled sailor with a missing tooth, grunted at the exchange. The man muttered something about "hell-blighted knights" under his breath and gave the group a wide berth. Jackson ignored it. The stench of fish guts and wet timber hung in the air, mingling with the odor of fear among the superstitious crew.

Riven stood near the stern, arms crossed over her slim torso. She shifted her weight with each roll of the vessel, poised yet uneasy. Her silver-white hair had come loose from its usual binding, and strands whipped around her face. Her elf-keen senses scanned the ragged coastline ahead. Whenever the boat dipped, she angled her body to maintain perfect balance, a habit she'd refined long ago.

She caught fragments of conversation from two of the deckhands behind some crates. They whispered about "the elf lass with the bow" and shared hushed remarks about her figure. Riven stiffened. She cast them a cold glance that made them avert their eyes, but the brine-soaked wind quickly reclaimed her attention.

Luke rubbed his palms over his arms for warmth. "This is ridiculous," he muttered. "Feels like needles on my face. A thick cloak, a roaring fire, and a tavern stew, that's real comfort. This kind of cold can kill a man."

Jackson smirked, stepping around a coil of rope. "You're exaggerating. Enjoy the breeze, or learn to handle the cold like a real sailor."

"Funny." Luke snorted. "You mock me for wanting my body temperature above frostbite. If the jaws of some sea serpent swallow you whole, I'll be sure to—"

The vessel swayed again, forcing Luke to pause mid-sentence. He lurched sideways, nearly colliding with Riven, who steadied him with a firm grip on his leather vest. Despite the tension of the journey, a brief smile lightened her reserved features.

"Next time, hold on before insulting the sea," she rebuked.

Luke released a sheepish laugh and eased back. "I'll keep it in mind."

Near the prow, Elinora kept an iron focus on the cliffs ahead. Sharp-edged rocks thrust from the sea in jagged arcs, forming natural sea stacks. The swirling tide broke and frothed against them. The wind carried the squawk of gulls overhead. One bird swooped low, wings brushing the sails before it veered toward the coastline, which loomed closer with each passing minute.

Luke sidled up to Jackson, lowering his voice. "These sea stacks. I've heard dwarven salvage crews sometimes scour them for lost wrecks. They come out of nowhere and vanish just as quick, waiting for someone to pay them properly. Or they show up to salvage your sinking boat if you're unlucky. They don't pick sides, only coins."

Jackson remembered hearing rumors about King Ironbeard Stormdelve's stance. Dwarves this far from the mountains rarely swore loyalty to any barony. "I doubt they'd lend a hand, even if we saw them. They prefer neutrality."

Luke shrugged. "Or the highest bidder. I had a near run-in with a dwarven barge a few months back. Thought they'd help me navigate some hidden shoals. Instead, they demanded triple the usual rate, so I bailed. Ended up stuck on a sandy bar for two hours, cursing dwarves and my stupidity."

Riven joined them. "Keep your voices low," she insisted, though the wind already masked most conversation. "We're close to the cliffs. If Corgrave's men patrol with long-range glass scopes, they might spot us." She scanned the crags, scrutinizing every eddy of shadow.

Elinora, hearing her remark, nodded agreement. "A fortress was built at Thornreach Bluffs long before the civil war," she murmured. "House Corgrave once used it to watch for pirate vessels. It overlooked every approach from the sea. After their disgrace, the place was abandoned, but those torches mean it's back in use. My mother said no light would burn there unless it was a sign of Corgrave trying to reclaim their stronghold."

Jackson tightened his hold on the railing as the boat heaved under a fresh barrage of waves. *Let them gather,* he thought grimly. *We'll put a stop to this.* He forced his shoulders to relax, not wanting his demon sparks to glow brighter and scare the crew more. They needed all the focus they could keep.

As dusk approached, the sky above darkened into a bruise-hued twilight, swirling clouds hinting at oncoming rain. The fishing vessel's captain, a wiry man with skin rough as driftwood, cautiously guided them around a basalt outcrop to a small inlet. His voice rasped when he finally announced, "This is as far as I

THE HELLSPAWNED KNIGHT

go. Any closer, we'll catch the eye of whoever's skulking around those cliffs. I'll have my lads help you with the rowboat."

Elinora dipped her head in gratitude, then turned to Jackson and the others. "We should use the smaller craft. Slip ashore before full nightfall." Her breath formed a faint fog in the chilled air.

While the boat rocked, Luke and Riven hoisted a narrow skiff, barely more than a sturdy rowboat, over the side. The rowers among the fishing crew lowered it onto the churning water. Jackson climbed down first, bracing his stance. Elinora followed, passing her satchel to him before stepping expertly onto a wooden seat. Luke and Riven joined them, ignoring the crew's wary glances.

The oars creaked as Jackson and Luke paddled in unsteady unison, dipping the blades into the froth. Riven kept watch at the stern, scanning every flicker of movement along the shore.

The row toward the rocky beach felt interminable. Broken moonlight shimmered across the waves, revealing scattered seaweed strands. Gulls croaked overhead in restless arcs. Jackson couldn't help but feel their cries were a warning. *Turn back before it's too late. You should have never come here.*

Elinora peered toward a makeshift palisade near the waterline. Newly erected timbers jutted at an awkward angle, as if built in haste. "That's recent construction," she murmured. "They must be using a landing spot to move supplies to the fortress."

Luke grimaced at the brand scorched into one of the support beams. "Looks like the same black-market ring that's been smuggling crystals." He nodded at the coiled serpent etched in the wood. "We saw something like that in the ravine under Riftcrown Plateau."

Jackson rowed harder. *Corgrave is expanding fast.* A spark of anger flared behind his ribs. *So many brazen signs.* The chill wind bit at his cheeks, but he refused to let it distract him.

Waves slapped the skiff as they neared the shore. The tide left slick patches of kelp glistening under the moon. Luke hopped out first, boots sinking into frigid ankle-deep water. He shuddered and released a colorful curse about the "icebox sea." Elinora cast him a wry look, lifting her cloak to avoid drenching it as she followed onto the narrow beach.

Jackson pulled the skiff higher with Riven's assistance, mindful of the tugs from the receding surf. Damp sand clung to their soles. The brine in the air was almost overpowering here, thick with the tang of rotting kelp.

They crouched behind the palisade's outer piling. A small, hand-hewn gate stood half-open, a makeshift latch left undone. Within, they glimpsed two men hunched around a smoldering brazier, cradling half-empty tankards. Their ragged leathers and swords suggested local hires, not disciplined soldiers.

Luke pressed closer, peering through a gap. "They're hammered," he whispered. The stench of stale ale drifted on the breeze.

One guard swayed on his feet, took a swig, and swore about the cold. His partner laughed roughly, then nearly tripped over a stool. Neither seemed on high alert. They mumbled in low voices about shipments they expected soon and how "the boss better pay up."

Riven's lips curved. "We can slip past them."

Jackson glanced at Elinora. She nodded. "Better to avoid a scuffle. If they raise an alarm, the fortress might send reinforcements."

They synchronized their movements, hugging the fence line. The hammered guards barely glanced around. Luke led, stepped lightly until he found a gap in the wooden stakes. He lifted the lower edge of one plank, gesturing the others to follow. They eased under it in turn, careful not to snag their cloaks on splinters.

The night was cold, and the faint light from a waning moon cast shifting patterns over the makeshift outpost. Beyond a stack of crates, a path led inland. The crates bore the same coiled serpent brand, further confirming Corgrave's influence.

A swirl of tension coiled in Jackson's gut as he took the lead, guiding everyone deeper into the shadows. The distant fortress lights gleamed on the windy heights, an ominous beacon promising more trouble.

They found a darker patch of sand near an outcropping, and Jackson helped Elinora and Riven push the skiff off to one side, concealing it behind driftwood. They heaped loose seaweed and a net over the boat in hopes no passing patrol would spot it. The rolling surf provided a steady rhythm of crashing waves that muffled small movements.

"This is likely only the start," Elinora whispered. "But the fewer fights we pick tonight, the better."

Luke nodded, though he still stomped his feet to keep the numbness at bay. "A bedroll and a mug of mead would be a blessing right about now," he muttered. His voice softened at Riven's glare. "Fine, fine. I'll be quiet."

The wind off the sea gusted again, curling around them with a harsh whistle. Salty spray coated every surface, making armor and clothing slick. Jackson draped a strip of cloth around his collar to dampen any glow. The last thing they needed was to startle a drunken guard with demonic embers. He felt the roil of his power respond, as if eager for confrontation, but he forced it down. *Focus.*

He motioned for the others to follow. Step by careful step, they made their way past the crude palisade, always keeping to the edges. Flickers from the guards' brazier flared behind them, but no alarm was raised. The men remained too deep in their cups to notice a group of crouched figures slipping by.

They emerged onto the pebbled shore a safe distance from the outpost. After rounding a small dune strewn with driftwood, they quickly surveyed the coastline. Ahead, a broader track wound inland, leading uphill. The fortress crowned the bluffs above, torches dotting its ramparts and sending reflections winking across the dark sea. Thick clouds veiled the moon, casting an eerie, muted glow. Gulls keened in the distance.

Jackson nodded at Luke, Riven, and Elinora. The four huddled behind a fallen log to finalize their next move. They would seek higher ground soon, if luck stayed with them. For now, the crash of waves and the taste of brine on the wind reminded them how close they were to their foe's doorstep.

He exhaled once, scanning the lonely stretch of beach behind them. In the twilight, the faintly visible black-market brand on the palisade wood confirmed the enemy's foothold here. *We are close to unraveling Corgrave's new scheme.* The knowledge brought both tension and resolve.

They inched farther around the log, pressing inland under the night sky. The fortress at Thornreach Bluffs awaited them like a silent challenge, and the cold wind carried the promise of a trial yet to come.

CHAPTER FOURTEEN

The clash of salt-tinged wind and rising voices filled the makeshift camp along the rocky shore, where a circle of driftwood fires cast wavering silhouettes against a dark sky. The evening tide lapped and hissed at the pebbled beach, as though eager to swallow anyone foolish enough to stand too near the water.

A row of salvage-sloop hulls lay overturned to one side, each repurposed as reading tables or seats, illuminated by salvaged arcane lanterns that glowed faint turquoise. Clusters of coastal folk, weathered by brine and constant wind, had congregated under this flickering light. Their gazes shifted between the encroaching party of outsiders and the swirling shapes reflected on the water.

Jackson stood with shoulders tense. Even Riven, silent in her watchfulness, seemed more relaxed than the Hellspawned Knight. A few paces to his left, Luke hefted a small wooden crate onto a plank, revealing glimmering crystal shards. He set a folded wad of trade tokens beside them. An eager hush descended among the clans, broken only by the crackling fires and the distant cry of gulls.

Elinora approached the assembly with a measured sweep of her cloak, chin lifted. Strands of her hair caught the wind, but she maintained a calm expression. "We have come to bargain," she announced. "We need safe passage through your coastal caves, and we're prepared to pay a fair price in goods, along with the promise of House Riftwyn's wards, if you desire them."

Although some clanfolk listened intently, a few spat murky curses while fingering driftwood talismans. Others scowled at the mention of wards, wary of foreign magic.

Luke cleared his throat and rapped a knuckle on the wood. "This crate here. See these crystals? Fresh from the smugglers we snagged, so we can hand 'em right along. You could re-sell them if you like. Or use them to power your own arcane lamps, or, who knows, brighten a few corners of your huts."

He tried a disarming smile. A few haggard fisher-hunters squinted at him as though deciding whether to snap the scrawny traveler in half.

Riven hung back, scanning the crowd. Her hood shadowed most of her silver-white hair, but her eyes gleamed, keenly evaluating every stance, every muttered word. Many of the onlookers had driftwood charms or carved bone pendants slung around their necks, which they believed repelled "devil magic." A few older men, their cheeks lined with seafaring wrinkles, clutched harpoons. The rancid smell of seaweed and brine clung to the group.

At the forefront stood a wiry man with a ropy beard, perhaps one of their chieftains. He examined Luke's offering with a slow nod, as if tallying the possible profits.

Before he could speak, another voice rose from behind him, a woman's voice, steely and infuriated. "Ain't no devil-born bastard stepping through our seas unless we get something more than worthless tokens." Her tone carried enough edge to cut through any illusions of courtesy.

Heads turned. An older matriarch, hair wind-matted and

streaked gray, strode forward. She wore a tattered furred wrap above plain breeches. A resemblance of command glinted in her eyes. She planted her feet on the slick stones and glowered at Jackson. "You." She lifted a bony finger. "You reek of demon blood. I can taste your corruption in the brine." She spat on the ground. "You pay coin or blood. Your choice."

At that, murmurs spread among the clans. Some shrank back, unnerved by the savage authority in her voice. Others nodded as if her words had been overdue.

Jackson's gauntlet creaked as he curled a hand into a fist. His collar felt hot. Beneath the edge, faint, fiery sparks traced the infernal markings. *Keep it together.* Anger threaded through him, but he stayed silent, trying to bury his reaction beneath a stoic front. If he responded violently, it would spark a quick and bloody confrontation. That was the last thing they needed.

Elinora stepped closer, her gaze sweeping the matriarch's hardened face. "We honor your laws along this shore, but we will not stand for threats. We've brought trade tokens, crystals, and we offer your clan wards for protection against outside raids. Corgrave's men may twist these coastal routes for their smuggling operations. We can help you defend against them."

The matriarch barked a laugh so harsh it could have been the cry of a dying gull. "Fancy words. But you stand with the King's Eye, or so your man claims. Those eyes see only what suits them."

Luke drew a breath. He looked like he might try a witty aside but thought better of it. Instead, he shuffled forward. "We're not here to pry into your local affairs. We want to cross the labyrinth of sea caves, maybe glean a route past any of Corgrave's watchers. If you want payment, these crystals are worth a small fortune to the right buyers. We even have trade tokens from the black-market ring. The King's Eye won't chase you if you use them carefully. So, yes, we're paying. Let's keep the hostility to a minimum."

Her gaze flicked to the small crate again. Though she tried to appear unimpressed, the hunger was plain. Several younger clanfolk craned to glimpse the crystals better. The matriarch drew a slow breath. "You do know, if these tokens get traced back, we risk retribution?" She glowered.

Luke spread his hands. "All you need do is not wave them around the capital, and no one's the wiser. We recovered them from Corgrave's men. They won't be missed. They'll spend easily in a half-dozen black-market ports. Trust me, we tested them ourselves."

An uneasy ripple passed through the crowd. Someone asked, "What about the demon-born knight? Will the King's Eye punish us if he does something unnatural in our midst?"

Jackson's mouth tightened, but Elinora stepped forward, placing a calmly assuring hand against Jackson's armored shoulder. She made sure the matriarch and her kin could see. "Jackson answers to the Crown. He won't harm you unless you force his hand." Her voice was quiet but crystal-clear. "House Riftwyn has authority to share wards with allied clans. Those wards can shield you from any unnatural influences, hellspawned or otherwise."

She offered a small wooden token with the stylized crest of Riftcrown Plateau, an intricate swirl. "Accept our wards, and you have an extra measure of defense against Corgrave's meddling, if not total immunity."

The matriarch's lips twisted in distaste, but the mention of wards clearly interested others. Several clan members looked at one another, uncertain. The old woman eyed the wooden token as if it might bite her, then transferred her gaze to Jackson. "You keep your distances from our huts, demon knight." She stabbed a finger at him again. "If you cause trouble, I'll see you tied to driftwood at low tide, set out to sea for the gulls. Understood?"

Jackson remained silent, shadows dancing across his stone-set features. He gave a curt nod. The faint red glow around his collar sputtered like embers settling in a hearth.

The tension in the circle eased a fraction. The matriarch pulled her furred wrap closer, turning to Elinora. "Run your wards over by the far fire. My granddaughter is the best to test them. If they work like you say, maybe we can offer the guide you need. Someone who knows how to slip into the caves unseen."

A collective pause followed her words. Luke exhaled, his shoulders losing a measure of their rigidity. "We have a deal?" he asked tentatively, looking from one chieftain to another.

"We have an accord," growled a lean fisher-hunter who clutched a broken harpoon. "But betray us, and the clan..." He mimicked strangling the air with calloused fingers. "We know these shores, and no fancy knight or elf gets away."

Elinora inclined her head. "We understand. There is no betrayal here. We only seek passage."

Riven caught Jackson's eye, then tilted her head, indicating the clan's acceptance was tenuous at best. Jackson acknowledged her with a subtle nod. He could still feel the matriarch's hateful glare linger. *She'd see me drowned if she got half a chance.* The sensation of hostility curled in his belly, but he forced it down.

A group of clanfolk drifted forward to examine the crate. They fingered the crystals as if appraising fish at a market stall. Others took up the tokens, flipping them over in the lanternlight. Greed and gratitude warred on their faces.

Meanwhile, Elinora stepped away from the fires to demonstrate a small runic ward, an oval disk etched with House Riftwyn's seal. Two younger members of the clan, wearing hide vests, hovered close to watch her technique.

Luke lingered near Jackson and Riven. He cast them a sidelong look and mumbled under his breath, "I love it here. Absolutely friendly folks, yeah?"

Riven huffed. "Try not to comment too loudly on how friendly they are. They might sharpen their harpoons for us."

"Point taken. Let's keep it civil."

Two more clan elders approached from the side. One had a

scraggly fox pelt draped across his shoulders, the other wore a faded bandanna and reeked of fish oil. They eyed Jackson warily. "King's Eye punishes traitors, yeah?" the fox-pelt elder asked with a trembling voice. "You plan to track Corgrave soon?"

Jackson regarded the man, uncertain how much to reveal. "We have reasons to find him. If he's meddling in your territory, he's already moved against the Crown. Do you have reason to suspect you'll be targeted next?"

The elder tugged his pelt around him, glancing aside. "We see suspicious sails off the horizon sometimes. Strange rowboats plunder washed-up crates. Could be Corgrave's men, could be freebooters. Hard to say."

Riven's gaze narrowed. "When did you see them last?"

"Two days back, maybe three," the man replied. "They left quick when they realized we were watching."

A fresh wave of tension rippled as the matriarch returned. This time, she was accompanied by a petite woman wearing twin braids. The younger woman nodded to Elinora, trying to hide her awe at the demonstration of wards. "She showed me the glyph. Seems real enough." She turned to the others. "Might keep the half-wraith eels from creeping in our nets."

"Meaning you'll guide them?" someone else asked from the crowd.

A beat passed. The matriarch fixed Elinora with a stern eye. "We'll guide you as far as the first flood chamber. After that, you're on your own. Those caverns shift with the tide. If Corgrave's bastards lurk deeper in, that's your risk. We won't throw our lives away."

Elinora nodded. "Fair enough. We only need guidance to avoid the worst pitfalls. Our group can handle the rest."

That sealed it in a cautious way. The clanfolk resumed sifting through the crate of crystals, while a handful hovered around Elinora, asking hushed questions about wards, about ways to anchor them along driftwood huts.

Luke opened the trade tokens, counting enough for multiple families. Riven watched every exchange with hawk-like vigilance.

Jackson stood outside the ring of firelight, aware that many still shot him sideways glances. As the negotiations continued, the swirl of voices merged with the rolling surf behind him. He breathed in the tang of salt, scanning for any sign that the fragile bargain might shatter if he twitched the wrong way.

Coin or blood. The phrase stuck in his mind. His teeth clenched. *She'd have me pay in blood if I so much as blinked.* He exhaled, reminding himself that violence would sabotage everything. They needed these people's cooperation, no matter how fickle.

A short while later, the tension softened. The clan matriarch and her aides concluded their stern approvals, dividing the crystals among themselves with excitement. One younger fisherman grinned at a large shard's gleam. Others accepted trade tokens with guarded optimism. A few clan children, barefoot in the cold sand, peeked from behind an old boat hull. Whenever Jackson's gaze flicked their way, they ducked, uncertain whether to fear him or greet him.

Finally, the matriarch gestured with a gnarled hand that the main haggle was done. "We'll keep an eye out for you," she stated, then nodded at a tall, lean woman with net-laden shoulders "Come dawn, Orlittle here will take you as far as the cove entrance. That's all we'll risk. Don't owe you more than that."

Elinora thanked her. "We appreciate your willingness."

Luke shot Jackson and Riven a nervous grin. "I'd call that a rousing success," he whispered. "We're not skewered, at least."

"Yet," Riven murmured, returning her bow to her shoulder.

Before the crowd dispersed for the night, the matriarch offered a final warning. "If you cross us, or if your demon knight here tries messing with what's ours, we tie you to driftwood at low tide. Mark my words."

"We hear you," Elinora replied coolly, not quite looking at Jackson. She gave the woman a curt bow. "Have a safe watch."

The threat lingered like a bitter taste, but the group had no choice. They parted ways. Luke busied himself counting leftover crystals, ensuring they still held enough to bribe any other obstacles. Riven scouted the shadows along the beach, double-checking no one was creeping up with a spear. Jackson remained near the largest fire, the flames dancing in reflection off his dark armor.

Elinora soon finished explaining additional ward details to two clan members. When they left, she stepped away from the circle, scanning until her eyes found Jackson. She moved quietly toward him, cloak trailing over damp stones and paused at his side. "Walk with me?" she asked softly.

He inclined his head, and they strolled beyond the fires, heading for a stretch of shoreline littered with small shells. The ocean breeze cut across them with a biting chill. Occasional scattered torches behind them revealed the clanfolk dividing spoils. The hum of conversation tightened whenever Jackson's name or "demon" drifted on the air.

Elinora stopped near a half-buried log and folded her arms. "I saw your markings flare when she spat at you," she murmured. "You handled it well. Thank you for not letting anger control you."

He paused before responding. The minimal glow under his collar had faded almost entirely, leaving only the faintest red lines. "Your presence helped," he told her. "You reminded me our mission is bigger than any single insult."

She nodded, glancing at the surf. "The clans can be fierce defenders of their tiny realm. I don't condone their hatred, but we don't have the luxury of making enemies now."

He exhaled deeply. "I would have..." He stopped, shaking his head. "If she'd swung a blade, I might've answered in kind.

However, the rest of the negotiations went smoothly enough, thanks to you and Luke."

A smile curved Elinora's lips. "I'm relieved we still have a chance to pass the caves without a massacre." She hesitated, and her gaze lifted to his. "I came to tell you that I appreciate it. Holding back when your pride or safety was threatened isn't easy. Especially given how they singled you out."

He nearly laughed, a short sound devoid of humor. "They see me as something less than human. Or worse."

Elinora's expression softened. She settled her hand on his forearm. "They're afraid. Fear blinds them. But you proved them wrong tonight, giving them coin instead of blood." She squeezed gently. "Thank you for doing that. For me."

They stood quietly, drifting embers from a distant fire speckling the air like lazy fireflies. Elinora's eyes shone with gratitude and lingering worry. She exhaled in a hushed sigh, as though reminding herself tonight's fragile truce might hold. She kept her hand on his arm. "Without your restraint, this alliance would've died before dawn."

Jackson nodded, turning his gaze toward the swirling ocean. "We'll make it through those caves. Then, Corgrave can face something fiercer than gossip."

Elinora managed a small, earnest smile. The night air tasted of salt and tension, yet it also held hope. She knew how precarious everything was. She stepped closer, seeking a measure of warmth in the biting wind. "Again," she murmured. "Thank you."

CHAPTER FIFTEEN

Their torches hissed and flickered in the damp breeze, the flames casting a jittery glow along slick cavern walls draped in seaweed. Jackson led the way, boots sinking into a slurry of wet sand and kelp that clung to his ankles with every step.

Behind him, Elinora hugged her cloak against the clammy air. Luke, carrying a small lantern, squinted at the parchment they had traded a hefty sum of precious crystals for, scribbled charts hinting at hidden passages and safe routes. Riven brought up the rear, an arrow set along her bowstring aimed at the ground.

The passage descended at a stiff angle, forcing them to pick their footing carefully. Water dripped overhead in an irregular patter, forming shallow pools along the stone. Whenever a wave crashed outside, a faint rumble reverberated through the tunnel, as if the sea itself tried to swallow their intrusion. Even Luke lost interest in complaining about the cold when an occasional rush of water surged inland, drenching them from the knees down.

"Charming," Luke muttered, shaking brine from his hair. "One day, we'll do a job in bright sunshine, with a warm beach and friendly locals. Right?"

Jackson's cracked gauntlet squeaked when he flexed his hand. "If the tide gets any higher, we'll be swimming to Thornreach."

"And you'd be fine," Luke retorted, adopting an exaggeratedly gruff voice. "Hellspawn blood, all warm and toasty in these frigid waters. The rest of us might freeze or drown, though."

Riven only grunted, stopping to test the ground with her foot. Her elven senses alerted her to suspicious ridges under the silt. "Hold a moment," she whispered. She knelt and brushed aside strands of kelp, revealing a row of faint runic symbols etched into a long, submerged stone. "Trap or marker?"

Elinora crouched beside her. "Marker," she announced after a moment of study, the tips of her gloved fingers tracing the lines. "They're wards, probably set by smugglers to guide, or redirect, sea creatures. It's the same style I saw at the outpost above."

Riven nodded and straightened. "Makes sense they wouldn't want inquisitive crabs poking around their contraband. Or worse." She glanced pointedly at a deeper pool where a shape skittered beneath the surface.

Jackson exhaled sharply. "Let's keep an eye on the water. We don't need an ambush from anything lurking below."

They pressed on. A few paces later, the tunnel split in two directions. Luke tilted the bartered chart near his lantern. "Left branch," he stated, tapping a slanted line. "Faster path through the labyrinth, or so these scribbles claim." He lifted his gaze and squinted into the gloom. "But it also shows a symbol. A five-pointed star near an archway?"

Elinora stepped closer to confirm. The star symbol had been hastily scrawled. "Could be a landmark. We'll find out soon enough." Without waiting, she stepped into the left corridor, her breath puffing in the chilly air.

The deeper they went, the more meticulously carved pillars rose on either side, half-buried in centuries of silt and barnacles. Torn netting dangled from pillars, and shell fragments crunched underfoot. Shriveled starfish clung to walls. The reek of stale salt and rotted kelp thickened.

Suddenly, Luke yelped and jerked backward. A hidden pressure plate depressed with an audible *thunk*. Bone-white spikes erupted from the ground ahead of him, each nearly as tall as his waist, sharpened to cruel points. Arcane sparks danced across the spike tips, sizzling as they vanished.

Luke blanched. "That nearly cut me in half!" He gingerly poked a spike with his dagger to test if it was stable. A faint hiss of leftover arcane charge popped near the blade's tip.

Riven stepped around him, eyes narrowed. "Don't move." She scanned the floor for more triggers. A patch of older footprints suggested smugglers had navigated these tunnels regularly, likely armed with knowledge of each trap. She brushed aside grit to reveal another pressure plate. "There's a second plate. Keep close behind me, or you'll end up impaled."

As they maneuvered around deadly triggers, Jackson noticed the scattered remains of less fortunate souls, shell-encrusted bones slumped near corners, half-submerged in pools. Some wore tatters of old uniforms. Others were nameless silhouettes of the past, lost to the labyrinth's traps. Elinora's posture stiffened whenever her torchlight revealed another grim remnant. Still, she pushed on, her expression resolute.

A chittering noise echoed from the tunnel's far side, and Riven tensed. Something scuttled closer. In the wavering torchlight, they glimpsed crustacean monsters, large, spiny shells with multiple spidery legs, each creature nearly the size of a shield. Their pincers clicked with unnerving snaps. Pale, segmented antennae twitched at the newcomers, sensing movement in the darkness.

Luke's grip tightened on his lantern. "Of course. Oversized crabs. Why not?"

Elinora steadied her breath. "They're corralled by wards," she whispered. "Likely forced to dwell in the side tunnels to keep out curious explorers."

One crab scuttled forward, pincers raised, mandibles scraping in a hollow rasp. Riven drew an arrow smoothly, her posture lowering. With a soft *twang*, she fired. The arrow struck the creature's shell, glancing away in a shower of sparks. "Shell's too thick," she growled.

Jackson raised his sword, stepping in front of Elinora. "We handle them, or they'll ambush us later."

Two more crabs lunged. Jackson slashed at the first, metal scraping against the shell's jagged surface. The second creature lunged for Luke's legs. Luke jumped back, cursing, then swung the lantern at its face with a resounding *clang*. It recoiled, spitting foam.

Riven circled to the side, picking her target carefully. This time, she aimed for a gap beneath the shell's edge. Her arrow sliced through a joint, making the creature thrash. A wet hiss gurgled from beneath its shell, and it collapsed jerkily. "Better."

Elinora clutched a small piece of chalk in one hand. She pressed it against a nearby rune carved on the wall, adjusting lines with deft strokes. Another swirl of her hand set a shard of crystal into a groove. The faint hum of disrupted magic radiated outward. One crab, about to slash at Jackson's flank, froze mid-lurch. Confused, it scurried away from an invisible boundary, drawn back to the tunnel from which it emerged.

Luke whistled. "Handy trick," he noted, catching his breath. He pointed at the remaining monster that still menaced Jackson.

Jackson braced low, a flicker of infernal aura flashing along his neck. The crab lunged, pincers snapping with brutal force. Jackson met it head-on, driving his blade into a seam between armored plates. Demonic sparks danced along the steel, and the crab convulsed violently. With a harsh crunch, it sank to the ground, spewing brackish fluid.

Silence fell except for the drip of water and Luke's muted

cursing about crab guts on his boots. The rest of the creatures retreated into side cracks, likely nudged back by the newly altered ward. Elinora wiped her chalky fingers on a rag.

They advanced, forging deeper under the cliffs. Gradually, the corridor opened into a vast chamber. Pillars lined the walls at uneven intervals, many toppled or broken. Ancient runes coiled around the bases of those still upright.

Elinora paused to shine her torch on one particularly large inscription. "Corgrave's crest, but older," she murmured, running a finger over the faint lines of a stylized hawk. "His ancestors must have controlled these passages during some ancient conflict."

A swirl of briny wind gusted in from an unseen vent overhead, stirring the torch flames. Riven held up a hand. "There. Fallen arch." She pointed to a collapsed structure blocking part of the chamber. Stone blocks were covered by algae, but the hawk crest was unmistakable. Broken pieces of runic wards hung from chains, and water trickled between the stones, feeding a shallow pond at the base.

As they navigated around the rubble, the runic inscriptions on the walls grew more elaborate, spirals interwoven with cryptic symbols. Elinora's eyes shone. "It's older than the civil war. Possibly older than the founding of Kharadorn."

Luke edged closer, shining the lantern on a cluster of lettering carved in a semicircle. "Well, let's be quick about deciphering. Standing here gawking feels like an invitation for something nasty to jump us."

Jackson nodded grimly. "Agreed. Stay alert." He never fully relaxed his grip on his sword.

Water lapped at their ankles as the path dipped again. The temperature dropped, making their breath appear in faint white puffs.

Elinora knelt by another ward. "I can rework this one, like before. Might keep other creatures at bay."

Riven hovered protectively at her side, arrow nocked. "Do it fast."

Elinora carefully etched lines with her chalk, pressing a crystal shard into the ward's key groove. A faint glow pulsed. Then, in the watery gloom beyond, a deep rumble stirred. Subtle waves slapped the cavern floor.

Luke tensed. "That…didn't sound like a crab."

A shape emerged from the watery darkness, larger than the pillars. Gliding on sinuous fins, the amphibious beast reared its head above the surface. It sported a wide, lamprey-like mouth ringed with teeth. Its pale body glistened with barnacles, and stray patches of seaweed clung to its dorsal spines. The creature released a low, resonant hiss that rattled the bones piled along the cavern edges.

Jackson's demon markings flared as he stepped forward, sword raised. "Get back," he growled to the others. "This thing's not letting us pass."

The monster lunged, water cascading off its shoulders in a roaring surge. It snapped at Jackson's arm, but he parried with a jarring clang. Sparks of infernal energy crackled where blade met scaly hide. The creature jerked back, thrashing to the side, hitting a column with enough force to crack stone. Loose rubble rained around them.

Luke scrambled aside, dropping to a crouch. "I hate these fish-lizard abominations!" he shouted, fumbling for a throwing knife at his belt.

Elinora ducked behind a broken pillar, heart pounding. She clutched her chalk and crystal shards, uncertain if altering wards in the midst of combat might help or hinder. Meanwhile, Riven sized up the monster's hide. She fired an arrow at a gap near the creature's gills. It lodged briefly, then the beast whipped around and snapped the arrow with a reverberating snarl.

Jackson advanced, eyes narrowed. His infernal aura shimmered across his neck and shoulders. The creature coiled to strike again, teeth glinting in the flicker of torches. Jackson bunched his legs and sprang at its side, sword angled for a vicious overhead slash. His blade bit into thick flesh. A wash of brackish fluid sprayed the ground.

The monster roared, lurching, nearly dislodging Jackson. Its tail flailed, hitting Luke's lantern. Sparks vaulted into the air, rattling as the lantern flew. Luke cursed and dove after it, barely keeping the fragile glass from shattering against a rock.

Riven loosed another arrow, this time burying the tip in the creature's rubbery throat. The beast reeled, shrieking so loudly it made their ears ring. Jackson pressed his advantage. Demonic sparks raced along his sword's edge, fueled by his fierce will. With a heave, he wrenched the blade deeper.

Suddenly, the monster swiveled, thrashing its body in a final violent attempt. Jackson was flung off. He skidded across the slick floor. The beast lunged at him in a final burst of rage, jaws wide.

Elinora shouted, tossing aside her chalk to grab a splinter of luminous crystal. She hurled it at the creature's face. The shard flared on impact, creating a brief flash of searing light. The beast hesitated, disoriented by the radiance.

That hesitation was all Jackson needed. He shoved himself upright and brought his sword around in a swift arc. In one brutal stroke, he severed the beast's scaly throat.

Its jaws snapped uselessly in midair, then the creature collapsed, water sloshing in a frothing wake as it died. A ragged hiss escaped its mouth before silence returned, broken only by their ragged breathing.

Riven exhaled, lowering her bow. "That was larger than I expected." She flicked monster slime off her arrow hand, grimacing.

Luke approached, lantern trembling in his grip. "I was sure it'd swallow him whole." Relief shone in his eyes. "Jackson, you all right?"

Jackson nodded, brushing grime from his leathers. The infernal glow around his collar dimmed. "I'm fine."

Elinora retrieved her chalk, hands still shaking. "That was no ordinary sea creature. Someone or something made it thrive down here."

"We can blame Corgrave or his family," Luke remarked. "They apparently loved twisting these tunnels to protect their contraband."

They edged around the beast's massive corpse, careful not to slip on bloody water. The stench was thick enough to coat the back of their throats.

Soon the passage narrowed again. Trickling water rose halfway up their calves, but the tide seemed to recede for the moment, giving them a brief window to keep moving. A faint glow emanated from a crevice ahead, where the cave wall sagged inward, forming a small alcove. Riven signaled caution by raising her hand.

As they crept up, torchlight revealed a crumbling vault seal half-buried in rockfall. A chunk of carved granite bore the edges of a crest that looked suspiciously like Corgrave's hawk symbol. The seal had cracked in multiple spots, revealing a hidden nook within. Faint luminescence, likely from Riftcrown crystals, seeped through the gaps.

Luke's eyes lit with excitement. "Think that's the stash?"

Elinora bent, carefully brushing aside the rubble. "Looks like a smuggler's cache. The ward around it must have deteriorated." She tapped on a corner of dull runic etchings.

Jackson set his shoulder against a slab of rock, pushing it aside with a grunt of effort. A wave of cold, musty air spilled out. Inside, smaller lumps glimmered, pouches stacked behind a rotted crate. More lumps of luminous crystal nestled in damp cloth. A diffuse glow cast eerie shadows on the alcove's walls.

"Jackpot," Luke murmured, kneeling to rummage. He pulled back the cloth to confirm half a dozen crystals of decent size, enough to fetch a tidy price in the black market. "Corgrave's men must have hidden these while moving bigger shipments. Each one's got the same smuggler brand we saw along the palisade fence."

Elinora frowned, but she nodded. "Every little bit we gather is that much less for Corgrave's forging plans." She gestured for Luke to keep them.

Luke packed the crystals in his satchel, layering them with spare rags to soften any noise. Then he stood, shoulders set. "That helps. If nothing else, it slows Corgrave down."

A grim smile tugged at Jackson's lips. He looked from Luke to Elinora, then at Riven, who stood guard. "Shall we press on? We still have tunnels to cover before the tide changes."

Luke nodded. He gave the cache one last glance, then shifted his weight, satisfied. "At least we scored something. Let's keep going." He tightened the straps of his satchel, the stolen crystals clicking softly inside. "Corgrave won't be too happy losing these," he remarked, tapping the satchel. "Good."

They stepped into the next passage, leaving the alcove's broken seal behind. The water lapped higher at their ankles as they advanced, the torchlight throwing dancing reflections on the walls. Luke tightened his hold on the newly acquired crystals, grimly satisfied at slowing Corgrave's smuggling efforts.

CHAPTER SIXTEEN

A biting wind met them the moment they staggered out of the tidal caverns. They had survived the submerged tunnels, all four of them wet, splattered with kelp, and caked in a grit of crushed shells. Yet their relief at escaping with pockets of stolen crystals and their lives quickly soured. Baleful moonlight revealed sullen faces on a broad, rocky shelf a short distance ahead, figures standing with weapons raised.

Riven froze beside a craggy boulder, arrow already half-nocked. Her keen gaze flicked to the stand of hooded strangers perched above them. She recognized some of the outlines as members of the same coastal clans that had guided them this far. A clarion moment of suspicion surfaced in her mind, and her jaw clenched. *They whispered with outsiders more than once*, she remembered. *I should have pressed them harder.*

Before she could speak, a harsh voice echoed across the stones. "You think we'd risk our clans on a demon's promise?" The speaker stepped forward. One of the clan's fisher-hunters, nimble despite a pitted harpoon slung across his back. Scars lined his cheeks.

Beside him, two mercenaries pointed runic rifles at the group, the barrels shimmering eerily. "Corgrave pays better than any demon knight," spat the hunter, his distrust twisting into hatred. "We won't see our villages burned for your cause!"

Jackson's grip on his sword tightened. The glow around his collar flickered with the faint red pulse of infernal energy reawakening to danger. He scanned the huddled group of traitors. *We paid them. We offered them wards.* He ground his teeth. The tang of betrayal coiled in his chest.

"How about loyalty?" Elinora called, stepping forward enough for the moonlight to catch the side of her face. Her dripping cloak clung to her arms. She tried to keep her tone calm, but frustration seeped through. "We swore we wouldn't bring the king's wrath on your clans. We gave you crystals."

A bark of laughter came from a hooded mercenary behind the hunter. "Your crystals are worthless if Corgrave's forces burn every hut along the coast for helping you." His words drew a low murmur of agreement from the huddle. "Do yourselves a favor. Drop your blades, and we'll promise a quick end."

Luke sucked in a breath, water still dribbling from his hair. "Yeah," he muttered with a crooked grin. "I'm sure their definition of painless is a five-second decapitation." He patted the satchel at his hip, but the traitors strained forward, rifles raised. The barrels glowed with fresh arcs of magic. One wrong move, and they would unleash a volley of sizzling projectiles.

Riven pressed herself against a jagged outcrop, arrow nocked to her bowstring. She eyed a mercenary brand on the nearest man's gauntlet. It was a stylized claw mark, a familiar emblem. Her lip curled. *If they're the same sort who slaughtered my kin, they deserve no pity.* She exhaled slowly.

Jackson lowered his sword tip to the stone, not quite dropping his guard. The swirling lines at his collar reddened. "We had a deal," he insisted.

"There's no deal when Corgrave's coin says to kill you," snapped the clan hunter. "Enough talk."

They opened fire in the same breath, runic bursts streaking across the rocky shelf with searing arcs of orange. Jackson dove behind a clump of barnacle-laden rocks, raising his sword to block a second shot. Sparks danced off the blade, lighting the night with a flash.

Elinora threw up her hands, channeling the wards she had meticulously adjusted in the caverns. Tendrils of luminous script flared around her gloves, forming a glowing shield that deflected a third blast. She staggered from the impact, boots skidding on the wet stone, but held her ground. "Riven, flank left!" she yelled.

Riven gracefully sprang to the side. Her heart pounded as she recalled the brand's shape on the mercenaries' armor. *They helped butcher my people.* She loosed her arrow. It tore through the night, slamming into one mercenary's chest. He lurched backward, too stunned to scream before toppling onto the slick stones.

Luke, crouching behind a half-buried boulder, rummaged for anything that could serve as a weapon beyond his short blade. He seized a snub of driftwood. "Wish I had something sharper," he muttered. He angled himself around the stone, aiming to circle behind the nearest gunman. Another volley erupted, forcing him to duck as scorching lines of energy tore across the rocks. Salt spray and broken fragments of shell pelted his cheeks.

Jackson watched a pair of coastal fighters approach on the right, wielding short harpoons imbued with faint runic etchings. *They're serious.* The knight's infernal aura flared, molten fury welling in his chest. He lunged, sword sweeping in a tight arc.

One harpoon cracked against his blade with a blinding flash of runic discharge. The shock reverberated through Jackson's arms, but he forced his weight forward, driving the first attacker to the ground in a tangle of limbs.

The second fighter thrust a harpoon at Jackson's flank, grazing his ribs. He hissed, then seized the weapon's haft in a steel grip, demon-fire flaring across his collar. The fighter's eyes widened as a surge of hellish energy burst between them. The clan fighter's scream cut off abruptly when flames burst around his chest, scorching cloth and searing through salted leather. He collapsed in a haze of acrid smoke.

Jackson's breathing grew ragged. The stink of charred flesh slammed him with a wave of memory, smoke and burning men in a war-torn battlefield. *Not again.* His vision flickered. For a split second, he saw only the blazing ruins from years prior, the echo of shrieking voices. The demon-fire in his blood threatened to twist higher.

A shout from Elinora anchored him. "Jackson, behind you!" He whirled in time to meet another clan fighter's harpoon with a *clang*. They locked blades, and he forced the weapon aside, but the effort came with a cost. His shoulder pulsed with fresh pain. He shoved the fighter back, catching his breath.

Seeing his chance, Luke popped up behind a rifleman whose focus was pinned on Jackson's fight. He bashed the man's helmet with the driftwood. A dull *crack* echoing as the mercenary went down in a heap. "Stars above, that actually worked," Luke muttered. He spotted a folded parchment sticking out of the mercenary's belt. *A map?* He snatched it, then ducked as another runic shot whizzed overhead.

Elinora pressed her advantage on the left flank. She moved toward a robed caster among the traitors. Pale arcs of magic flared around the robed figure's fingertips, presumably aiming to counter her wards.

Elinora responded with a swirling glyph in midair. Ribbons of light encased the enemy's spell, forcing it to fizzle in a shower of harmless sparks. The robed caster reeled, stunned, and Elinora raised a hand. A final burst of her ward's glow knocked him onto his back with a grunt, where he lay motionless.

Meanwhile, Riven notched another arrow. Her eyes narrowed at two mercenaries crouching behind a low ridge. She exhaled, heart thundering. This time, she pulled back the bowstring with fury. The arrow soared in a graceful arc and found its mark, piercing the mercenary's throat. He slumped without a sound, leaving only one companion to scramble away in terror.

Despite the group's smaller numbers, the fury of an enraged Hellspawned knight, a ward-savvy noble, a deadly elf, and a cunning rogue was enough to tip the balance. The clan fighters' morale cracked. One by one, they faltered, realizing their advantage had slipped away. Bodies littered the rocks, some still breathing, most not. A few defenders hoisted themselves up the rocky slope in a panicked retreat.

The last enemy, a man with a helm, lunged at Jackson in a final, desperate push. His runic rifle had jammed, so he swung it like a club.

Jackson raised his sword, catching the improvised strike. Sparks danced along the blade's edge. With a snarl, Jackson knocked the rifle aside and drove his weapon forward. The tip found the mercenary's chest plate. For an instant, their eyes met in shared shock. Then, the last turncoat collapsed, the rifle clattering on the stones.

Silence reigned. The reek of singed flesh and lingering ozone weighed the air. Moonlight illuminated the fighters. Jackson's shoulders rose and fell in heavy breaths, Elinora's wards still shimmered faintly around her hands, Riven scanned the slope to ensure no more archers lurked above. Luke knelt by the downed mercenary he had clubbed, rummaging for anything else useful.

Luke stood with the folded parchment in hand. "Maps," he panted, tucking them into his satchel. He arched an eyebrow at Jackson. "Looks like a route toward the old lighthouse up the coast. Might be where Corgrave's men are massing."

Jackson nodded grimly, forcing the swirl of demon-fire to subside. The glow flickered once before easing to a dull red. He winced at the burn along his ribs. *I can breathe.* Another wave of dread threatened to clamp down on him. He closed his eyes, only to snap them open again when Elinora touched his arm.

"Come," she murmured gently, voice hoarse from the fight.

"We aren't safe out here." She scanned the carnage with a heaviness in her gaze. "There might be more."

Riven wiped a string of wet hair from her forehead. "The inlet beyond that ridge," she stated, gesturing to the west. "It's sheltered enough."

The four of them limped off the rocky shelf, stepping around bodies. No one spoke until they slogged their way to the inlet, half-ringed by towering stones that shielded it from prying eyes. The tide had come in enough to form a gentle pool in the alcove with a strip of wet sand near the stone wall. Moonlight splashed across the water in broken pieces, giving the place a faint glow.

Exhaustion pressed down on them. They sank against the rock face or crouched on the sand, trying to catch their breath. Luke pulled off his soaked cloak and wrung it out, muttering about worthless clan guides. Riven examined her quiver, counting arrows with methodical detachment.

Elinora knelt beside Jackson. Her gaze flicked over the red stains on his side, across the rips in his armor. "You're hurt worse than you're letting on," she murmured. She rummaged in a small pouch at her belt, withdrawing a roll of bandages and a slim vial of shimmering medicinal salve.

He tried to wave her off. "I'm fine."

She shook her head,. "You're not." Then she glanced aside, noticing how Luke and Riven were both keeping watch, giving them a semblance of privacy. She touched his arm lightly, guiding him to sit. "Let me see."

Jackson exhaled, nodding. He unfastened the clasp on his chest piece. Sweat beaded along his hairline, and the cut on his ribs bled through his shirt. Elinora pressed a strip of cloth against the wound, wincing at his muted hiss of pain.

They were close enough that he could smell the sea salt in her damp hair. Her eyes flicked up, meeting his. Subtle tension hung between them. His gaze fell on the faint bruise at her left temple from the earlier trap. *She's been risking her life for us, for me,* he thought, a pang of gratitude rising in his chest.

She dabbed her salve on the bandage. The faint glow made the darkness around them deepen in contrast. Then, she gently pressed the bandage to his ribs, her fingertips brushing his skin. He released a low breath. The ache ebbed a fraction. "Thank you," he muttered.

Elinora didn't answer. She reached up to adjust the torn edge of his shirt, her expression caught between worry and something else. Something warmer. That unspoken current surged when he covered her hand with his own. The day's brutality, the blood, the betrayal, seemed to push them closer.

She shifted against the stone wall so their bodies nearly touched. He glanced at her face, at the droplets of water along her cheeks. His heartbeat pounded louder in his ears than it had during the fight. She studied him, searching for a sign he was truly okay. Then, she pressed her lips together and hesitated.

In that flicker, Jackson realized how close their faces had become. He sensed the trembling tension in her shoulders. He lifted a hand to cradle the back of her head, tangling his fingers in the damp strands of her hair, and she exhaled in a sharp, silent gasp. Their eyes met, and he leaned in, capturing her mouth in a fervent, hungry kiss.

Elinora responded with equal intensity, pressing him back against the smooth rock. The lingering taste of adrenaline and fear made their closeness electrifying. She released a faint sound, something between a sigh and relief. He wrapped an arm around her waist, ignoring the sting in his side. The bandage was well-secured, but his pulse hammered. Her lips parted under his, an unspoken need passing between them.

After a few beats of shared breath, she eased back. Thin strands of hair clung to her brow. "We should…check on the others," she muttered. Heat colored her cheeks.

He nodded, chest heaving. They released each other as the

realization of what they had done crashed in like the next wave of the tide. For a heartbeat, he glimpsed shadows of guilt in her eyes. There was a war raging, betrayal all around them, yet they stole a moment of fierce connection. Their world might not forgive them, but they had needed it.

They gathered themselves, smoothing clothing and brushing away lingering touches. When they emerged from behind the rock, Luke was leaning near a burned piece of driftwood, raising his eyebrows but saying nothing. His subdued smirk betrayed his suspicions. Riven, standing a short distance away, kept her gaze angled on the dark water as if uninterested in the display.

Elinora cleared her throat. "Jackson's stable enough now."

Luke gave a slow nod. "Good," he returned evenly.

The night weighed heavy with the memory of ambush, and the rocky inlet offered only a fragile sense of safety. They all felt it, how easily their trust in the clans had been spurned, how quickly blood splashed the shoreline. Yet they drew closer together, forging unity in the aftermath of betrayal. Even Riven edged nearer, as if silently declaring she, too, understood that they stood as one.

No one spoke of regrets. They merely turned their faces away from the bodies left on the rocky shelf, letting the waves whisper a cold lullaby under the moon.

CHAPTER SEVENTEEN

As dawn broke, Jackson led the small band up a winding trail toward the decrepit lighthouse. Waves crashed far below, the thunder of water echoing against jagged cliffs. The half-burned scrap of parchment rescued from a traitor's pocket, had been enough to guide them here.

Each step brought them closer to the looming structure perched precariously on the bluff's crumbling edge. At that height, the wind roared with an almost feral intensity. Even Luke kept quiet, no doubt watching his footing where loose stones threatened to slip away into oblivion.

Elinora walked near the front, frowning up at the lighthouse. It stood taller than she had expected, shaped by centuries of savage coastal storms. Rusting metal plating wrapped around its lower walls like peeling scales, and an old crest, eroded beyond recognition, decorated a collapsed archway by the entrance.

Dim morning light revealed the building's top, where a fractured lens jutted out at a crooked angle, attached by a warren of warped scaffolding. The sight was enough to give Jackson pause.

He raised a hand to signal a halt. Riven, silent as always, touched the fletching of an arrow in acknowledgment. She scanned the upper balconies, searching for any sign of watchers. A swirling mass of black crows lifted from the parapets, cawing in harsh chorus as they disappeared amid the gusting winds.

"It screams 'no thanks,' does it not?" Luke ventured over the rush of the gale. His cloak whipped behind him, tangling around his legs. "We're either brave or stupid. Possibly both."

Jackson checked the page again. The ink had smeared, but the phrases "coil device, shift inland, scaf-," stood out in barely legible scrawl. "Corgrave's men tested something here," he stated. "We find it, we break it."

Riven lowered her bow. "No movement up top. Let's go before the weather shifts."

When they reached the lighthouse door, the hinges screeched in metallic protest. Inside, stale air hit them like an old tomb, thick with dust and the faint tang of ozone.

Jackson stepped in first, sword drawn low. Dappled sunlight sneaked through cracks in the walls, revealing piles of corroded debris. Strips of broken glass crunched underfoot. Above, precarious catwalks circled the inner chamber, anchored by columns that had begun to lean with age. Sheets of salt-stained metal clung to the rafters.

Luke nudged a fallen shard of the large lens with his boot. "I never thought an abandoned lighthouse could feel so…haunted."

Elinora raised a hand, eyes narrowing. She pointed to a row of half-finished runic symbols etched into the stone near the base of a spiraling staircase. The lines looked hastily drawn, partial circles and crossing geometric shapes reminiscent of half-formed wards. A low hum hung in the air, as if the runes wanted to come to life but lacked a final spark.

"Arcane contraptions," Elinora muttered. She ran a gloved fingertip over one symbol, leaving a streak of cleared dust. "Fragments. They were doing something big here."

Jackson bent to examine a piece of twisted scaffolding that had collapsed onto the floor. The metal was warped as though from a blast. "Probably tested too close to the storms," he guessed. "Or tried hooking the structure's lens to something it wasn't meant to power."

Riven snapped her fingers, calling them to a corner where a wooden chest lay half-submerged in damp rubble. She hauled it free with careful effort. Water damage marred the lid. Inside, they found old ledgers, pages stuck together in a pulp of ink and mold.

Riven flicked through them until she uncovered a small stack of readable entries near the bottom. "Shipments of crystals." Her brows furrowed. "Looks like House Riftwyn inscriptions on half these crates. That lines up with what we feared."

Elinora exhaled. She held a ledger up to a beam of dusty light to confirm the faint crest stamps. Her posture stiffened. "These were forcibly pulled from the plateau's mines. Corgrave's men must have dragged them here after forging some arrangement with local smugglers. This means they intend to retool the crystals for weapons." Sorrow flickered in her eyes. "He's turning my family's legacy into destructive technology."

Luke patted Elinora's shoulder. "We'll put a stop to it." He turned to rummage deeper in the crate, hoping for anything else of use. The rotted pages broke apart in his hands.

A sudden groan from above startled them. The ancient scaffolding shook, raining dust. With a swift glance, Jackson gestured for everyone to stay back. The wind battered the outside walls relentlessly, creating an eerie whistle through gaps in the stone. He stepped toward the staircase. "We check upstairs first. I want to see the lens access."

They ascended carefully. Each step creaked, and corroded banisters threatened to give way at a mere touch. At the top, the lens lay partially canted in a metal frame, black scorch marks etched around its perimeter. Wires with runic filaments dangled, swaying in the breeze.

Luke poked one with a dagger, wincing when a spark of

residual arcane energy snapped back. He sucked on his fingertip. "Still live. They sure tried to wring every drop of juice from the storms. A little close to blowing themselves to pieces, by the look of things."

Elinora tilted her head toward a tangle of metal rods sprouting from the lens assembly. She pressed two of them aside with her gauntlet and peered at the base. "They must have harnessed lightning directly through the lens. Look at those carved runes." She brushed debris away, revealing tight patterns that spiraled in half-finished arcs. "Someone was building or upgrading a runic amplifier."

Below them, the wind rose in a shrieking gust. The tower rattled, moaning like a wounded beast. Riven grabbed a crossbeam for balance, muttering something under her breath. When the tremor subsided, Jackson motioned them all back downstairs. Time was short. A single strong gust could bring the tower crashing down.

Upon returning to the ground level, they found a corroded hatch near the center of the floor. It had once been sealed with a thick iron padlock, but the lock now hung open, twisted as if struck with tremendous force. Jackson and Luke wedged crowbars against the metal ring and lifted. Hinges shrieked, releasing a musty gust of stale air. A narrow ladder led down into darkness.

Luke raised an unlit lantern. "Down the rabbit hole we go."

"Watch for wards," Riven warned, nocking an arrow regardless of the cramped space. "If they tried to rig anything lethal, it's likely here."

Jackson nodded. He began the descent first, steps slow and measured. The underground chamber radiated a chill that prickled his arms. At the bottom, his boots hit stone, and he held the lantern high. Dripping water echoed against the walls, accompanied by a low hiss of arcane static. Tangled wires and rods formed twisted shapes in the corners, and thick cables ran across the floor in a chaotic snarl.

Elinora came down next, sweeping her torch in an arc. She froze at the sight of half-assembled mechanical parts stacked against one wall. Metal rods with faint runic engravings jutted out from a wooden frame, and a large coil device, three rings interconnected by copper bands, sat in the center of the floor. A single chunk of luminous crystal glowed from the center ring, feeding faint arcs of energy along the coil's surface.

Luke whistled. "That is not your everyday contraption." He poked the coil with his dagger's hilt. Sparks danced, forcing him to yank his hand back. "Key amplifier for runic ballista beams, I'd wager. Corgrave's newest toy."

Elinora approached carefully, eyes dark with concern. "He's planning to shift heavy weaponry inland. If he can replicate large-scale ballista beams powered by these crystals, entire fortresses could be threatened. This is bigger than a petty smuggling scheme." She ran her fingers over a series of runic lines etched into the coil. "He must have tested prototypes here, tapping into the lighthouse's lens for storm energy."

Jackson exhaled, a weight settling in his chest. "We sabotage it now. If Corgrave doesn't have this place intact, his plans will slow."

Riven kept her bow ready, scanning the chamber for any living threat. "Then let's hurry. The ocean breeze sounded like it wanted to fling the lighthouse into the sea."

Working quickly, Elinora searched for the core crystal powering the coil. She traced the runes along each ring, nodding whenever she identified lines central to the device's function. Luke started prying off metal couplings, occasionally offering gleeful commentary about how certain pieces "definitely" looked essential to the contraption.

"Feel free to sabotage carefully," Jackson cautioned. "We don't want to blow ourselves into the next century."

Luke smirked. "Where's your sense of adventure?" He jiggled a coupling, then pried it loose with a grunt. "This might take the heart out of their doomsday gadget for a while."

Elinora located a cluster of runes near the center crystal. She pressed a small chisel into a curved groove, etching out a swath of crucial lines. The arcs of energy flickered. The crystal's glow faded, then pulsed again, as if resisting. "We need to scratch out more than a few lines," she muttered. "He might have backup arrays."

Jackson remembered the half-finished runes upstairs. His jaw set. "Corgrave can't repair everything quickly if we make a mess of the main power node."

Riven spotted movement in the corner. A flicker of greenish sparks crackled near a rusted tool bench. She raised her bow. After a tense moment, she let the arrow rest. Only loose wires flailing in an erratic flash of arcane discharge. She nodded at Jackson, who grabbed a crowbar and pinned down a thrashing length of wire.

Elinora inserted a narrow wedge of crystal between two plates, whispered a short incantation, and twisted. The coil rattled. A crackling flash flared from the core, forcing them all to shield their eyes. For a moment, the device hummed with unstable energy. Then, the glow subsided, leaving the coil inert. Elinora exhaled, beads of sweat forming at her brow.

Luke whistled quietly, rubbing the back of his neck. "We definitely knocked out its main spark." He walked around to confirm. The device lay motionless, faintly glowing in sporadic pulses, as if starved.

Satisfied, Jackson gestured upstairs. "Let's finish it by disabling the lens, too. That contraption is worthless if they can't feed it storm power."

They climbed back to the main floor, stepping over fallen beams and windblown debris. The fierce gusts outside slammed against the tower, tearing at its old bones. Jagged shards of lens glass littered the corners, remnants of previous experiments.

Elinora found the runic lines that tied the lens to the powering array. Some were carved into a ring of stone near the base. With careful motions, she scratched out entire sections of the circle, her gloved hand steady despite the howling wind. Jackson stood guard, sword in hand. The only response was a faint pop of residual magic, followed by a final hiss of escaping energy along the twisted cables overhead.

Luke gave a satisfied grin. "They'll need specialized forging knowledge to fix that. Which is exactly what we don't want them to have."

"Agreed." Jackson looked at Elinora. She slumped, exhaustion plain on her face. However, determination lit her eyes. He admired her resolve.

When they were sure the sabotage was complete, Riven motioned them toward the exit. "We should get out. The air tastes like a brewing storm."

They trudged outside, bracing themselves against the gale. The near-vertical drop at the cliff's edge churned vicious waves far below. Wind whipped salt spray into their faces. Broken boards and scraps of metal clattered around the lighthouse's perimeter.

Jackson led them a short distance inland, finding a shallow depression sheltered by boulders. The sun had climbed through a burdened sky of gray clouds, but it didn't offer much warmth.

They gathered around a lantern Luke produced from his pack, lighting it against the swirling wind. Elinora knelt to shield the flickering flame, gripping the lantern's handle as the others hunched near. The circle of light glowed against the dull rock, painting their expressions in a somber hue.

Luke cleared his throat. "We put quite a dent in Corgrave's operation. Still, it's disturbing how methodical he's been, seizing runic knowledge from the plateau and hooking it up to storm power."

"It means we must keep moving," Riven insisted. She plucked a stray hair from her face, gaze flicking toward the path they had climbed. "No telling how many more hidden labs he's got."

Elinora stared at the pages they had salvaged from the chest. "Every forced shipment leads him closer to mass production," she murmured. "He stole from my homeland, twisted our resources to empower dangerous devices. We found one. That means there are others."

Jackson placed a hand on her arm. "We will shut them down," he reassured her. He felt the swirl of old guilt in his chest, faint reminders of the war, the times when he was forced to do grim tasks. The vow that bound him now pressed him forward.

Riven nodded. "He'll be fuming when he realizes we sabotaged this site."

Luke smiled thinly, though it did not quite reach his eyes. "Good. Let him be angry. Better that than having him run wild."

A gust sent pebbles skittering across the stony ground. Elinora stood, lantern in hand, and surveyed the roiling sea in the distance. "At least we bought ourselves some time. Corgrave's path just got harder."

Jackson's shoulders tensed. The part of him that carried the demon scar sensed the tension on the wind, like an omen of deeper conflict ahead. For now, they had done what they came to do. The coil device lay gutted, the lens array crippled. This station would not feed Corgrave's ambitions any further.

They huddled tighter as the sky dimmed behind thickening clouds, too early in the day for nightfall. The sea's hollow roar formed a grim symphony, as if the cliffs, the wind, and the lighthouse sang a dirge for every doomed soul who once braved these rocks.

Elinora spoke softly. "We hold a war council here." She set the lantern on the ground. "We determine our route inland. Thornreach is vast."

Luke knelt, rummaging in his pack for a small, crinkled map. Riven and Jackson inched closer, scanning the rough lines Luke traced with a finger. The scribbled instructions from the half-burned page were useless now, but any detail might help find Corgrave's next hideout. They whispered tactics, hammered out possible ways through the harsh terrain, and debated what might await them beyond the horizon.

A solemn air hung over the makeshift meeting. Arcane sabotage was one victory, but countless unknowns remained. They could only plan with what meager clues they had.

They ended the discussion with no easy answers as the sun dipped, painting the sky in bruised purples. Along the broken trail, stones shifted underfoot in protest of their presence. The four stood in a half-circle around the lantern, exhaustion etched into lines of dust and sweat on each face. They had survived another day, yet the sense of dread loomed.

Together, they turned from the ruined lighthouse, stepping carefully away from the cliff's edge. Wind keened behind them, stirring the ancient structure into one final moan of defiance before night closed in.

CHAPTER EIGHTEEN

Jackson and his companions picked their way around a heap of damp crates near the mouth of Thornreach's craggy harbor. Blotches of algae stained the wooden planks underfoot, and a sharp wind off the water carried the smell of brine and ripe fish. The makeshift dock sat ahead, warped boards groaning with each wave. Closer in, figures on horseback waited under a low gray sky. Baroness Vesper Thornvein's patrol had arrived.

Well, shit. Jackson halted, gesturing for the others to keep pace behind him. His cracked gauntlet creaked around his sword's hilt. He spotted the baroness at the head of her line, a tall woman cinched in riding leathers. A short steel blade rested at her hip, but she projected more danger with her cool stare than any weapon could. Her posted guards, about a dozen riders, sat rigid as if expecting trouble.

Riven stepped up to Jackson's flank. She said nothing, but her gaze flicked across the riders' formation. Luke ambled alongside, hands stuffed in his cloak pockets, lips twisted in a wry half-smile. Elinora, wearing a travel-stained cloak over her stained velvet, moved closer on Jackson's left. The swirl of tension hung in the wind.

The baroness surveyed them with a single sweep of her eyes. "You are the King's Eye operatives?" She made it sound like a challenge rather than a question. Her voice carried over the crashing tide behind them, firm and unwavering.

Jackson nodded. "I am Jackson McCade." He reached inside his belt pouch and found the medallion bearing the King's Eye insignia. "We come with word from House Riftwyn, and from King Rodric himself."

Elinora stepped forward, producing a document sealed with the royal crest. "Baroness Thornvein," she began, her voice measured. "This writ bears the king's mark, confirming our mission to stop Lord Corgrave's sabotage. We believe he's funneling contraband through these shores."

Baroness Thornvein accepted the parchment from Elinora's outstretched hand. She removed a glove so she would not get the folded vellum wet. Her fingers were stiff as she opened it, then scanned its contents.

She lifted her gaze. "I've heard all manner of rumors. Corgrave's name stains these waters." She fixed her eyes on Jackson. "We have businesses failing, fishing routes sabotaged, and frightened merchants whispering of new horrors. I won't throw my domain behind a cause unless I'm convinced it's warranted." She extended the writ back and replaced her glove.

Riven cleared her throat, stepping forward. "Corgrave's men guard runic weapon caches along the coast. We encountered them further down shore." Her tone carried brusque confidence but no flourish. "He has necromantic guardians in the deeper tunnels, reanimated constructs fitted with crystals. This sabotage isn't rumor. It's real."

Luke nodded and scratched the back of his neck. "We've seen ambushes, sabotage, you name it. The last group we ran into tried to blow half a cave. They mentioned Thornreach Bluffs and alliances they'd forged. We suspect they're shifting stolen crystals right under your nose."

The baroness' gloved hand tightened on her reins. She studied Luke with narrowed eyes and turned back to Jackson. "I'll not accuse you all of lying, but let's say Thornreach has had visitors claiming authorization before." She paused. "Tell me, how can I be sure you won't wreak havoc here and leave me to pick up the pieces?"

Jackson lifted his chin. "We have no interest in harming your barony. We're hunting Corgrave's conspirators." He held up the medallion again. "This is our demonstration of trust. The King's Eye doesn't involve itself unless there's a serious threat. You have my word. We'll root out Corgrave's infiltration, not embroil Thornreach in new conflicts."

The baroness sniffed. She urged her horse forward a pace, scanning Elinora's refined garb, then flicking a glance at the swirling lines on Jackson's collar. "Very well," she stated at length. "If you speak truth, eliminating Corgrave's presence aligns with my own goals. But be warned, my domain has suffered enough from outside alliances. One misstep, and you'll face Thornvein justice." She glanced at her patrol. "Understood?"

Luke chuckled, though he tried to mask it with a cough. "We're not big on missteps."

Elinora dipped her head. "Mistakes cost lives. We aim to prevent that."

Baroness Thornvein studied them for several more seconds, then signaled to one of her mounted knights to dismount. "I'll lend what I can. That includes a unit of thirty crossbowmen and a handful of runic spearmen. They train daily along these cliffs, used to fighting on uneven ground." The baroness leaned forward in her saddle. "They won't hesitate to turn those weapons on you if you betray my trust."

"We don't plan to," Jackson replied. *We've plenty of betrayals in the past.* His mouth tasted of lingering salt air, but it felt bitter. "We appreciate your assistance. Corgrave's strongholds won't fall easily."

The baroness removed her riding gloves, tucking them under her belt. "I don't doubt it. My scouts will coordinate with House Riftwyn, as requested. Tonight, I'll send riders and scrying-lantern messages to confirm your credentials." Her jaw tightened. "My people deserve renewed prosperity, free from saboteurs. If you help ensure that, you'll find me an ally."

Her words carried a definitive finality. She turned her horse about, and her patrol followed. Before departing, she spared them one last hard stare. "I've enlisted a watch on this harbor. If you need anything, speak to my quartermaster in the main settlement. Fail me, and the consequences will be swift."

They watched the baroness and her patrol vanish into the swirling mists along the coastline, the rhythmic clop of hooves fading behind. Only the crash of ocean waves remained.

Luke snorted. "Nice lady. I like how she threatened to kill us about five different ways."

Elinora slid the royal writ back into her satchel. "She's allowed her skepticism. Corgrave's shadow still clings here." She cast a glance at Jackson. "You all right?"

He released a slow breath. "Yes." His gaze shifted to the swirling tide, then he turned to the trio. "We should find that quartermaster and gather what we need."

Riven clicked her tongue, relaxing her bow, though leaving the arrow nocked for quick use. "Let's go. The sooner we stock up, the less time we waste."

By late afternoon, they had reached Thornreach's small but busy center. Tents and wooden stalls straddled the uneven cobblestones. Vendors advertised salted fish and pumice-laced potions that allegedly cleared the lungs. A handful of blacksmiths hammered away, their forges fueled by driftwood and dried kelp. Above them all, a sea breeze whipped scraps of canvas overhead, revealing cracked signs, proof of the barony's recent decline.

They split up to resupply. Luke scouted for additional rations, whistling whenever a vendor tried to lure him with suspicious "miracle cures." Jackson, after meeting with the quartermaster to confirm the location of a suitable inn, secured a stack of new crossbow bolts as promised by Thornvein's men. After they concluded formalities, Riven and Elinora decided to check the local market on their own.

Elinora tugged her cloak tighter, stepping across a moss-slick step leading into a crooked row of stalls. Riven walked quietly, scanning the throngs with calm detachment. Lanterns bobbed overhead, their glass casings rattling in the wind. The smell of smoked fish and pungent spice drifted between them.

Elinora spotted a table piled with fresh produce. "We should gather some better supplies." Her voice carried a note of relief. "I'm tired of stale bread and rancid jerky."

Riven nodded, picking up a small bundle of radishes. "Agreed. Then we can rest."

Elinora paid for a few vegetables, tossing them in her satchel. She paused, brushing aside a stray lock of hair. Her cheeks flushed faintly. "Someone asked me earlier about traveling with a 'demon knight.' They must've heard rumors about Jackson." She hesitated, pressing her lips together.

Riven set a coin in the merchant's hand, retrieving an extra bundle of dried herbs. "I'm sure half this domain's heard stories. Thornvein's watch must gossip." She cocked her head. "That bother you?"

Elinora exhaled slowly. "Not exactly. It's just… I keep thinking about him." She glanced around, cautious of eavesdroppers. "He's so controlled, but under that calm is something else." Her next words emerged softly, confessional. "When I'm near him, I feel heated." Her free hand settled on her hip. "It's new. Unexpected."

Riven arched a slender brow and stepped closer, voice low. "You talk as though you're ready to melt in his arms." A flicker of an unreadable expression crossed her face. "I've seen how he looks at you. So, do what you must. Just don't get yourself killed if everything goes sideways."

Elinora released an uneasy laugh. "I know. We both carry responsibilities, but whenever he's nearby, I can't ignore the pull."

Riven nodded, busying herself with a jar of pickled roots. "I understand. Some men have that effect." She bit her lip, then spoke quietly. "You're lucky. He's a good man, even if he has that hellish spark in him." She shot Elinora a sidelong glance. Faint tension flickered in her eyes, as though she was turning something over in her mind. Then, she turned back to the jars, dropping two coins for the merchant. "Anyway, we should gather a few more supplies."

They walked deeper through the cramped stalls, weaving around roped nets hung to dry. Locals spoke in hushed tones about reduced fishing hauls, rumors of sabotage, and the possibility of a renewed conflict. Elinora purchased a small spool of linen bandages and a fresh water canteen. She rummaged through a basket of pungent-smelling poultices, testing their legitimacy with a glance.

Riven hovered near a stand displaying specialized arrowheads. One design etched with faint blue runes caught her eye, apparently intended for use against hardened scales or enchanted armor. She tapped a finger on the table, haggling with the booth's owner. After a few clipped exchanges, she walked away with a small, wrapped bundle and a ghost of a smile.

Elinora raised a brow. "Collecting more runic arrowheads?"

"Yes." Riven stowed the bundle. "Never know when we'll need them." She paused, scanning the thinning crowd. "Ready?"

"Let's head back. The day's almost gone, and we're up early tomorrow." She sighed. "I hope Jackson found what we need from Thornvein's quartermaster."

They returned through the winding path toward the designated inn, a two-story building pressed against a cluster of warehouses. The sign above the door read "Seabluff Lantern," paint chipping in the salt-laden wind. Inside, the air was stale with old smoke and spilled ale, but the straw pallets looked sturdy enough.

Luke was already waiting near the hearth, flipping a stale biscuit in the air. "You both look loaded up with goodies." He winked at Riven. "Find something fancy?"

Riven shrugged, dropping her new arrowheads onto the table. "Better than the worthless stock we had."

Elinora exhaled, pulling out the fresh vegetables. "We can at least cook something besides salted fish and old bread." She let the tension drain from her shoulders. "Where's Jackson?"

Luke jerked a thumb at the narrow staircase. "Securing an extra storage chest upstairs. Putting any final gear away. Don't worry, he's not running off to brood somewhere." His tone carried an undercurrent of humor along with a measure of genuine fondness.

Riven eased off her cloak and claimed a seat by the fire, pressing her hands to the warmth. The inn's few patrons appeared too exhausted to pay them any mind, hunched over their mugs or dozing in corners. Elinora joined her by the flames, stretching her cramped legs. "At least it's semi-comfortable here."

Luke rested his elbows on the table. "We head out first light, right?"

Riven nodded. "We'll meet Thornvein's soldiers near the road leading inland. Then we push on to find Corgrave's fortress." Her gaze flicked to Elinora. "No time to dawdle."

Elinora forced a chuckle. "We've dawdled enough." Her gaze briefly rested on the stairwell, imagining Jackson upstairs. *I can't stop picturing him.* Her cheeks heated before she turned away and cleared her throat. "Tomorrow, then."

They ate a simple meal of soup and bread, supplemented by the fresh vegetables Elinora had bought. Though the stew was meager, it was hot, and it chased away the chill from the ocean wind. Luke regaled them with a story about a traveling peddler who once tried to barter him a "cursed" fishing net, claiming it was guaranteed to trap any sea serpent. "I nearly believed him.

He had such *conviction*," Luke finished, drawing an eye roll from Riven.

As the night deepened, the common room emptied. One by one, they climbed the staircase to the cramped upper level. Jackson joined them halfway through, dropping a small pouch of crossbow bolts onto the table. He nodded an unspoken greeting to Elinora, his warm gaze lingering. She returned the look, then busied herself smoothing her cloak to hide the rush of heat.

Riven claimed a modest pallet against the wall, propping her bow within arm's reach. Luke set his pack near another straw mattress, muttering something about lumps in the bedding. Elinora took the pallet by the far corner, while Jackson stood near the flickering lantern, scanning the room for potential vulnerabilities. *He never stops checking for danger.*

Lamplight cast long shadows across the low beams overhead. The wind outside whistled, accompanied by the faint *clang* of ship rigging in the harbor. Slowly, the group slipped into an uneasy but necessary rest, mindful that dawn would bring fresh trials. For a while, the common room below bustled with a final round of drunken chatter.

At first light, they gathered their belongings, double-checked weapons, and stepped outside. Pale gold etched the sky near the horizon, though thick clouds loomed over the sea. Seagulls wheeled overhead, their cries echoing across the rocky harbor. In the distance was a small knot of Thornvein's soldiers, twenty or so crossbowmen, forming ranks in the early gloom.

Jackson's collar markings glinted with a muted red. He set his gaze inland. "Let's move," he stated. "We've come this far."

Elinora gave a firm nod. Past them, the baroness' patrol waited, scowling at the sky as if daring any storms to interfere. Horses stomped restlessly, and the harsh scent of morning sea air curled through the wharf. Riven hoisted her bow across her shoulder. Luke fastened a final strap on his satchel. Together, they pushed away from the inn and toward the gathered troops.

Betrayals might linger, but they would press on. The time for half-measures had ended.

CHAPTER NINETEEN

Jackson stood at the forefront of Baroness Vesper Thornvein's newly formed militia. The chill air stung his cheeks, and the salt-laced breeze carried the hiss of crashing waves far below. Rows of crossbow-bearing men and women fidgeted along the bluff, hands cramped with tension as they awaited the baroness' word.

He raised his chin when he sensed Thornvein approach. Her scarred riding leathers bore a short, deep-blue cloak pinned by a simple brooch. A plumed helm, its crest dyed in Thornreach's colors, lent her a severe silhouette.

Wordlessly, she extended a gloved hand for the sealed dispatch Jackson carried. Jackson withdrew a folded parchment pressed with the King's Eye sigil, still faintly damp from its hurried transport. Thornvein studied the document's contents, her expression shifting from wary skepticism to firm resolve.

"Looks authentic," she decided, flicking a glance at the official seal. She handed the parchment back, then scrutinized the militia. "All of you, pay attention. The King's Eye has endorsed our alliance. That means we are duty-bound." Her tone dripped practical authority.

A burly sergeant stepped out of line, an older man with a

pockmarked face and suspicious eyes. "Begging your pardon, my lady, but we have reason to distrust...well, a Hellspawned in Thornreach's affairs." His uneasy gaze slid toward Jackson. "Folks talk about him like he's part demon. Hardly good luck."

Jackson stiffened. He had grown accustomed to such accusations, but each one felt like a fresh needle in his spine. He said nothing. Instead, he placed a hand on the hilt of his sword.

Baroness Thornvein stood taller. "Sergeant, if you believe there is time for idle superstition while Corgrave's men threaten our trade routes, kindly step forward and volunteer to repel them yourself. Or do you think your crossbow is enough to shatter the heavily armed murderers gathering inland?"

The sergeant reddened. "No, my lady. I only meant..."

She cut him off. "He's come bearing the king's mandate. That is all we need to know."

A hush settled over the gathered troops. Some stared at Jackson as though expecting him to sprout horns at any moment. Others kept their gazes fixed on the baroness, determined not to let private doubts disrupt their mission. The tension rolled like banked coals, ready to flare if anyone said the wrong thing.

Jackson was relieved when Thornvein pivoted on her heel and addressed the group. "If Corgrave succeeds in reestablishing his power here, the entire coastline suffers. Our fisheries, our shipments, everything falls under his shadow. We strike first."

Beside him, Luke offered a half-smile from beneath the hood of his nondescript cloak. "Heartwarming speech," the rogue muttered. "Of course, I suppose that means I should keep a respectful silence. Or not." He snorted. Jackson shot Luke a look that said, *Behave or regret it.* Luke merely smirked.

At the rear, Elinora hustled between lines of spearmen. Two local scribes in loose-fitting robes assisted her, passing small shards of luminous crystals into her waiting hands.

The men she worked with looked exhausted but determined. They had spent the previous night hastily engraving partial runes near each spear's tip. Now, Elinora tapped a gloved fingertip to the final line of runic script, causing the crystal shards to glow with wavering light. In response, the nearest spear flickered with arcane energy.

Luke ambled over and watched the scene, though he kept a safe distance. "You realize you're letting a noble lady tinker with your best pointy sticks, right?" he teased a young militiaman. "That means double pay if they explode in your faces."

The lad offered a wary glance, then rolled his eyes.

Riven, leaning against a supply crate, eyed Luke with calm disapproval. "At least pretend you're part of a professional alliance," she chastised.

Elinora glanced up from the next spear with a faint smirk. "I am being very careful. If anything explodes, it will only take Luke's eyebrows. I promise."

Luke spread his hands in mock offense. "My eyebrows are my best feature." He winked at the militiaman, who looked ready to faint from secondhand embarrassment.

A short distance away, Jackson unrolled a stiff scrap of parchment. It had come from the traitors they had cornered in the tidal caverns after the betrayal, a captured map that depicted the approach to Blackrock Fort.

The markings were crude yet unmistakable. A few black lines indicated ramparts bristling with defenders. Jackson's gut churned. *Abandoned stronghold, indeed.* He pressed the parchment flat against an upturned crate so the baroness could study it.

Thornvein ran a finger over a bold stroke on the map, noting how it cut through thick forest before looping uphill. "This route offers partial cover. We can avoid direct confrontation."

Jackson nodded. "We suspect advanced runic rifles up there." His voice dropped, revealing a hint of the worry that gnawed at him. "Corgrave must be fortifying those walls with scorched iron or basalt. No easy approach."

Thornvein frowned. "We'll handle that when we arrive. For

now, we get these troops ready to march." She glanced around, expression grim. "The militia is fresh. Keep them focused. Morale is everything."

Luke sidled over to Riven as Thornvein walked off. "Morale might be shaky, but at least we've got pointy spears that might do fancy things in a fight. That has to count for something."

Riven exhaled. "Better than an unenchanted broomstick." She shot him a sideways look that could almost pass for humor.

Elinora finished with the last spear, patting the exhausted scribe on the shoulder in thanks. Her hair clung to her cheeks in the damp morning breeze, and she pressed a hand to her silver pendant. "They'll hold," she muttered as though convincing herself.

Jackson caught her comment. A wave of grateful warmth flooded him. *She never asks for thanks, yet she pours her energy into every step.* He forced himself not to dwell on that thought. Instead, he raised his voice so it carried to the clusters of militiamen. "We move soon, but first, we break for food. Fighting on empty stomachs leads to foolish mistakes."

At the mention of food, Luke perked up. "Now you're talking sense." He rubbed his hands together. "One near-death experience last week was enough for me."

"Only one?" Elinora teased. "I recall at least two."

Luke patted himself on the chest. "I must have blocked the rest out."

They gathered near a sprawl of supply crates and tents. A few hasty fires burned low, and militiamen bustled around, unwrapping travel rations from oilcloth. Jackson and his companions found a spot sheltered by a rocky outcrop. Despite the wind's chill, the crackling fire provided a small measure of warmth. Thornvein joined them, removing her helm to reveal cropped hair flecked with silver at the temples.

As they settled into a circle, the baroness accepted a strip of dried ration from Riven's outstretched hand. "We expected peace," Thornvein mentioned. She gazed across the camp at her small force, men and women who looked equally uncertain. "Thornreach's old baron never prepared for a conflict this size. Most of these recruits are fishers or dockworkers who lost their boats to sabotage. Corgrave's people have roamed these seas before, so they know how to choke our trade."

Jackson chewed a mouthful of salted fish, ignoring the burn of brine on his lip. "I've seen men fight fiercely when their livelihoods are threatened, but this is dangerous. Corgrave wants to do more than choke off the coast. He wants to reinstall himself as a power in Kharadorn."

Elinora shifted to sit closer to the fire. She balanced a piece of flatbread upon a small tin plate. "We are going to do all we can to stop him. We had glimpses of his contraptions at the lighthouse. If they were fully operational…" She trailed off.

Thornvein's jaw tightened. She took a measured bite of her rations and swallowed before speaking. "He has enough influence to recruit mercenaries, bribing them with stolen goods or false promises. My script-lamp signals from last night brought only minimal support from beyond Thornreach. The other barons are still licking their wounds from the old war. They do not want to risk an open campaign unless I feed them absolute proof of success."

Luke blew a frustrated breath. "Fascinating how certain barons stay cozy on their cushioned seats while the rest of us do the grunt work."

Elinora frowned at him, though not without sympathy. "They have their reasons. Political entanglements are complicated." She paused, glancing at Jackson. "However, ignoring Corgrave will only make everything worse. We might be the last line of defense here."

They finished the salted fish and stale bread in near silence, accompanied by the snap of flames. Riven occasionally scanned the horizon, watchful for any approaching scouts. Luke tried joking with another militiaman about how "at least we have better rations than we had at the tidal caves," but the man only managed a polite grunt. Tension pressed on everyone's nerves like a too-tight bandage.

After the last mouthful, Thornvein rose. The hush around the camp deepened. Even the wind seemed to hold its breath. "Form ranks. Crossbow units to the western flank, runic spearmen to the center, and the rest with me at the fore," she commanded. Her short cloak snapped in the breeze. "We travel inland. Only engage if challenged."

Sergeants called out instructions, rallying the militia into a semblance of orderly columns. Jackson stepped forward, passing between lines of anxious faces. Some nodded in greeting. Others averted their eyes. He exhaled slowly, letting the swirl of ominous tension settle across his shoulders. His infernal markings pulsed faintly.

Elinora approached him. "I checked each spear's rune. They will last long enough for a single battle. Any longer, and the script might destabilize." She swallowed, hesitating. "We'll need to strike quickly."

He nodded. "We'll do our best. Speed is key."

Nearby, Luke hoisted his pack, rummaging for a waterskin. "Better to save the jokes for after the fight, right?" He bore a crooked grin, glancing at Riven. She gave him the faintest hint of a smile, surprising everyone, then turned to scan the edges of the bluff.

Before long, Thornvein signaled to move, and the assembled forces began a measured march away from the crashing waves. Armor jostled, boots scuffed damp grass, and the low murmur of creaking leather rose from the ranks.

Jackson walked beside Thornvein at the head, the dispatch from King Rodric tucked in his belt pouch. Elinora kept pace near him, her polished gauntlet resting lightly on the hilt of a short sword, eyes alive with determined focus.

A smattering of sunlight broke through the cloud cover overhead. For the first time that morning, faint warmth spread across the path, illuminating the newly mustered militia. Their breath fogged in the cold air, hearts pounding toward the threat that lay beyond those distant hills.

Jackson lifted his gaze to the twisted outlines of wind-bent trees in the distance, and beyond them, the route that would carry them closer to Blackrock Fort. *No turning back now.*

Onward they went, step by measured step, guided by the knowledge that every hour of delay gave Corgrave more time to fortify his stronghold.

As the militia topped a small rise and descended into a wilder stretch of rolling hills, Jackson cast a glance toward the sea, half-hidden by the crest behind them. His breath crystallized in the morning air. *We have to succeed. We have no other choice.* He steadied himself, then pressed forward.

CHAPTER TWENTY

Nightfall enveloped Blackrock Fort in thick shadows, its towering basalt walls looming against a sky of bitter stars. Baroness Thornvein's militia crouched in the rocky scrub slightly out of arrow range, the soldiers eyeing the pale green glow atop the ramparts. Those eerie torches sputtered in the wind, revealing watchmen armed with runic rifles.

Whenever the guards shifted their grip, a flare of emerald light rippled across the weapon barrels. Several crossbow squads had already advanced along the fortress' secondary walls, drawing rifle fire to reduce the pressure at the main gate. Now, that meager distraction gave the infiltration team—Jackson, Elinora, Luke, and Riven—a chance to breach the portcullis.

Powdery dust clung to Jackson's cracked gauntlet. He flexed his hand against lingering tension from the day's forced march. Farther down the line, Luke knelt behind a boulder beside Riven, rummaging in a small satchel. Alchemical charges rattled inside. Riven cast a glance toward the fortress, then slipped her bow free of its wrap.

Elinora hovered close to Jackson. She touched a piece of chalk in her palm, and arcs of faintly glowing script danced across its surface. She exhaled. "I'll scramble the wards as quickly as I can, but if they catch me mid-rune, we're in trouble."

Jackson nodded once. "Make it swift. The fewer guards that see you working, the better."

He motioned for the group to move in. Thornvein's quartermasters had given Luke and Riven a cask of old alchemical charges, desperate relics of a war best left behind. According to the quartermaster's hushed promises, these charges still packed a punch. If the sabotage of the gate wards succeeded, a single blast might tear a hole in Corgrave's perimeter.

Luke ran a hand over the cask. "Surprising they kept these charges locked away. Smells like they mix saltpeter with a dash of arcane fun." He smirked at Riven. "Hope your aim's as good lighting a fuse as it is with arrows."

She gave him a sidelong look but said nothing. Her gaze flicked toward the walls, measuring distances from memory. Another volley of greenish tracers fired overhead, puncturing the darkness with sizzling arcs.

Thornvein's crossbow squads took cover behind tumbled stone at the fortress' flank. They returned sharp, disciplined fire, encouraging the defenders to fixate on that side. Meanwhile, Jackson led the infiltration party low along a half-crumbled ditch snaking toward the main gate. Cracked basalt blocks jutted from the ground, offering some cover. The hiss and clank of distant runic rifles signaled the defenders were fully occupied.

They crouched near the gate's shadow, close enough to feel the faint hum of wards carved into the black stone. Elinora edged forward. Pale script glimmered along the gate frame in tight, swirling lines, each stroke part of a well-crafted defensive barrier. If they triggered it, shrieking alarms or arcane flames would bring the entire fortress swarming down on them.

She held her chalk ready. "I can subvert the runes from here, but any slip, and we'll be pinned."

Jackson rose enough to glance over the low rock concealing

them. A solitary sentry paced above the gate. The soldier's runic rifle occasionally crackled as though anxious to unleash another barrage. Below, a smaller portcullis door sat worryingly intact, traces of faint green wards dancing around its edges.

"All right," Jackson whispered, turning to Luke. "You and Riven handle the charges. Wait for Elinora's signal." He glanced toward the top of the parapet. "If that sentry sees us, we're done."

Luke snorted. "He won't see a thing." Then, he rose half an inch and called out in a loud, sing-song voice, "Oi! Up there! Your mother ever teach you better posture, friend?"

The sentry jerked at the unexpected shout, leaning over the wall. "What in...who's there?"

Luke hopped upright behind the rock, grinning. "A humble traveler, friend, come to buy a runic rifle. Heard you were selling half-price to incompetent buffoons. Thought I'd snag a bargain."

"Blasted fool!" the guard barked, leaning further out, rifle at the ready. "Reveal yourself!"

Below in the shadows, Elinora hissed at Luke's improvisation. *He's distracting that watchman. Let's pray it works.* She dropped to her knees and pressed her chalk to the swirling wards. Sweat gathered at her temples as she revised the glyph lines. One by one, she overrode the gate's protective anchors with hasty, whispered incantations.

High above, the guard peered into the gloom, rifle muzzle dancing uncertainly. Luke continued his taunts. "I'll toss in a decent donkey if you can find your target in the dark. Or is that green glow in your face messing you up?"

The man growled, leaning out farther. "I see you! You'll regret this, you..."

A soft *twang* sliced through the air. Riven's arrow caught the sentry below the collar. His breath strangled. With a muted clatter, his rifle slipped from numb fingers, and he toppled out of sight behind the battlements.

Luke exhaled, adjusting his cloak. "Guess we're not negotiating donkey trades."

Meanwhile, Elinora etched the final lines. Sparks illuminated the recessed glyphs. A jolt of arcane backlash shot up her arm, forcing her to clench her teeth against the pain. "It's done," she gasped. "Wards are disrupted."

She barely moved away before Luke and Riven swung the small cask forward, lodging it against the iron bars. Jackson wedged a dagger under the cask to keep it steady on the uneven ground. Luke snatched a spark-light from his satchel, pressed its tip to the fuse, then jerked back as the fuse hissed and spat.

Luke began, "Fire in the—"

Riven clamped a hand over his mouth and dragged him behind the rock. She shot Jackson a pointed look. Jackson nodded and ducked low, motioning for Elinora to shield herself.

A tense heartbeat later, the explosives roared. A plume of sizzling orange flame belched through the gate, shaking the entire wall. Shattered bits of iron portcullis rained onto the stone.

The concussive blast reverberated across the fortress courtyard. Alchemical residue painted the air in a choking haze. Jackson gave Elinora a glance, confirming she was stable, then lunged through crumbling debris. Smoke billowed in hissing sheets, and faint tongues of leftover flame danced on the rubble.

From the far side of the courtyard, Thornvein's crossbow squads saw their opening. They sprang from cover, bolts singing across the gloom with lethal accuracy. The defenders reeled, momentarily disoriented by the explosion. Greenish rifle fire tried to respond, but the defenders' aim faltered amid swirling dust.

Jackson advanced into swirling chaos, gauntlet raised toward the first uniformed figure he spotted. The soldier stumbled in the smoke, rifle half-lowered. Jackson's sword lashed out, its edge sweeping the man from his feet. Another guard charged from the side, letting out a panicked cry, only to be cut down as well.

While crossbowmen riddled the walls with bolts, arcs of green runic blasts cut the air. Every volley from Corgrave's enforcers illuminated the courtyard in sickly flashes. Jackson's infernal markings burned along his neck, reacting to the tumult. Hellfire stirred behind his ribs, hungry for release.

A fresh wave of defenders surged from the far corner, rallying around a tall figure in partial plate. This warrior barked orders, his sword brandished in front of him. Jackson's eyes narrowed. *Some kind of officer.*

The ring of steel echoed as Jackson parried the first strike, then hammered back with a ferocious riposte. His gauntlet deflected a flaming bayonet that tried to pierce his side. Hellfire rimmed his sword, forceful enough to melt the rifle's muzzle as he drew in close.

Luke skidded behind a broken column, panting. He flashed a quick grin at Riven. "No saving the armor to be reused with him around, huh?"

Riven fired an arrow at a guard, her aim chillingly precise. "Hardly. Jackson spares no metal tonight."

Off to one side, Elinora ducked beneath a half-fallen archway to steady her breath. She caught sight of Jackson in the thick of the fight, wreathed in those uncanny embers. His sword glowed an ominous red as if stoked by the same dark flame that haunted him. She swallowed tight concern. *We need him to stay in control.* The courtyard filled with shouts and the clash of steel.

A sharp cry cut above the din. "Regroup! Seal the lower corridors!" The voice belonged to a rugged sellsword with a scarred jaw standing on a tall crate near the fortress' interior gate. *Alden.* Whispers among Thornvein's forces had named him as one of Corgrave's dedicated mercenary captains. He brandished a runic sword, motioning to the defenders. "Hold the alchemy labs at all costs! Push them back into the yard!"

Jackson stepped over scattered debris toward Alden, eyes flaring eerie red. Another soldier rushed him with a spear, hoping to bar his approach, but Jackson batted the weapon aside and slammed the man into the courtyard's stony floor. A crossbow bolt from Thornvein's ranks took the soldier down for good.

Luke snatched an extra dagger from the ground. "I swear these guys are breeding in the walls," he muttered, scanning the swirl of dust. Three more defenders sprinted from an open hall, rifles sparking, but Thornvein's crossbow volley pinned them down. The courtyard erupted in flashes of green and silver, bolts clanging off basalt.

Suddenly, a shriek sounded from above, the unmistakable call of reinforcements pouring onto the parapets. Torchlight flickered across a new line of soldiers. "More up top!" Riven barked, already loosing an arrow. She caught one foe in the shoulder. He spun, toppling with a ragged yell.

Thornvein's militia roared through the splintered gate. They had shaped into a disciplined wedge, led by a stout captain who bellowed for them to keep ranks. Bolts zipped in organized volleys toward the defenders clinging to the courtyard's perimeter. The fortress' walls shook under the combined assault.

Amid the hail of crossbow quarrels, Jackson pressed deeper. Each step left a trail of fleeing troops. His gauntlet pulsed with infernal energy, flickers of fire weaving around his sword. Near the gate's remains, Luke hustled behind Riven, ducking stray rifle blasts. Elinora hurried to keep pace, clutching the residual chalk in case they met more wards in the corridors.

Alden cursed from across the yard. He gestured wildly for defenders to retreat toward the fortress interior, shouting, "Fall back! Now!"

Corgrave's men, scattered and outflanked, began pulling back from the open courtyard. Some stumbled over broken stones or collapsed beams. Thornvein's crossbowmen advanced with systematic discipline, forcing the defenders to flee or be cut down. Flickering torchlight lit their determined faces, each soldier seizing their hard-won advantage.

With the portcullis shattered and the wards disabled, the once-formidable gateway lay in ruins. Files of militia poured into the courtyard, overwhelming any last pockets of resistance. Green runic rifle flashes dimmed under the relentless wave. Shouts of confusion and fear echoed from Corgrave's men as they scrambled toward safer ground deeper inside the fortress.

At last, the courtyard belonged to the invaders. Smoke curled from the wrecked gate, drifting above the basalt walls. Jackson stood near a toppled statue, sword still wreathed in faint fire. *We did it.* His breath came in sharp rasps. The defenders, unable to organize a final stand, peeled away to regroup in the twisting corridors beyond. Alden's angry bellows receded, the mercenary evidently resigning himself to a new fallback position.

A handful of Thornvein's crossbow squads halted, reloading their weapons, while others spread out across the courtyard to secure vantage points. Glittering shards of iron and basalt dust coated the stone underfoot, evidence of the alchemical onslaught.

Though the fight wasn't over, the fortress' mighty gate now stood wide open. The path had been carved for Thornvein's forces. Jackson stepped aside, letting the militia surge ahead in a coordinated formation. Through swirling torchlit haze, they pressed on, driving Corgrave's defenders ever inward.

CHAPTER TWENTY-ONE

Smoke lingered in the corridors of Blackrock Fort, drawing twisted shapes in the torchlight. The portcullis lay in jagged chunks at the courtyard entrance, and Thornvein's crossbow squads had already spread through the corridors and side halls, methodically rooting out the last pockets of resistance.

Jackson surveyed the aftermath with grave eyes. Rows of dust-coated rubble lined the stone floor, broken spears still crackling with leftover runic energy. The air smelled of scorched iron and fear.

He pivoted down a smaller hallway where the walls bore claw-like scrapes, courtesy of whatever twisted wards Corgrave had unleashed. A dull ache tugged at his arms. The battle had taken its toll.

Luke strode beside him, running a hand along his dusty cloak and coughing whenever a swirl of ash tickled his nose. "I'd kill for fresh air," he commented. "Remind me not to pick fights inside old fortresses again. At least not before a hearty meal."

Jackson considered replying with a wry remark, but the sight of a bruised mercenary slumped against a toppled crate drew his focus. The man pressed a hand to his side, blood seeping between calloused fingers. Metal shards from a shattered runic spear jutted from the toppled crate at awkward angles, luminous crystals scattered around him. The crystals' faint glow illuminated his pale, sweat-beaded face.

Luke lifted his crossbow, more for caution than aggression. "Guess we found one who didn't get the memo that surrender might be healthier."

The mercenary grunted, attempting to shift into a more upright position. "Could say the same for you." He spat a thick clot of blood. His gaze flicked from Luke to Jackson, then beyond to the flickering torches dancing along the corridor's wall. His breastplate bore Corgrave's colors in chipped paint, black and emerald. One buckle had snapped, leaving the armor crooked over his shoulder.

Jackson knelt a few paces away, sword angled low. "This fight's over. You can't stand."

The wounded man set his jaw, though his defiance flickered with pain. "Never said I could."

Elinora appeared at Jackson's side. Her silver pendant caught a stray beam of torchlight, reflecting specks of brilliance across the corridor. She didn't speak, but her lips pressed into a thin line as she watched the mercenary's ragged breathing.

Behind them, Riven's soft footsteps approached. The elf's bow angled downward, arrow readied with a loose tension. She kept half an eye on the corridor behind them, ensuring no one darted out from shadows.

Luke lowered his crossbow a fraction. "All right, friend," he drawled. "You're in no shape to keep fighting, so let's chat. Maybe you can tell us who's signing your paychecks these days."

A mirthless laugh escaped the wounded man's cracked lips. "We all know who. Corgrave." His brows knit together in frustration and pain. "But that bastard didn't pay enough. Man threatened my family if we deserted. Been a one-sided deal from the start."

Jackson nodded, remembering rumors of mercenaries strong-armed into service. *No wonder so many fought so viciously.* He set a hand on the hilt of his sword. "If you want out of that deal, we can help. Thornvein's no tyrant. She'll grant you safe passage if you talk."

Luke snorted. "Rumor is, free throats talk better than slit ones."

The mercenary captain, Jackson realized from the man's insignia, shifted against the crate, unleashing a hiss of pain. "Safe passage sounds sweet, but how do I know I can trust you?" He darted a glance at Jackson's sword.

"Elinora's got a knack for runic wards," Luke returned, amusement lacing his tone despite the tension. "If she decided we should torch you, you'd be so many sizzling pieces by now. We'd rather not, so let's keep it pleasant, yeah?"

Elinora's slight nod affirmed Luke's words. She knelt beside the crate, glancing at the luminous crystals. One shard glowed brighter with each breath the wounded man took, as if resonating with his faltering heartbeat.

"All right," the captain rasped, surrender in his eyes. He coughed, spattering dark flecks on the stone. "I'm done playing hero for that snake. If you can find me a medic, or at least keep me from bleeding out, I'll spill what I know."

Jackson hesitated, then pulled a ragged bandage from his belt pouch. He extended it wordlessly. The man eyed Jackson's infernal markings before accepting. The tension felt thick enough to cut with a dagger, but it was progress. The captain pressed the bandage to his side, pain contorting his features.

Luke tapped a booted foot in an impatient rhythm. "All right, pal. Let's start with the shipments. Or maybe you can confirm those runic rifles we saw. Didn't come from nowhere. Where's Corgrave sending them? We know there's a forging site somewhere beyond Thornreach's domain."

"Elinora, keep an eye on his injuries," Jackson suggested. "Let's not lose him before he spills the details."

She nodded, stepping closer, and rested a hand near the man's shoulder without quite touching him. "The shimmering of these crystals suggests some runic bleedover," she murmured. "You block a wound with that bandage, keep the pressure steady."

The mercenary captain released a shaky breath. "You're kinder than Corgrave's lot, that's for sure." He paused, jaw working as he fought dizziness. "He took some shipments inland, maybe two days' ride if you push it, near Wraithhollow Gorge. Some rickety town called Fellmarsh on the route. That's your best guess for the forging site, but there's another place deeper in the gorge. Could be holding the runeforger there. Don't know exactly. Word is Corgrave wants him to finish some doomsday piece by month's end."

Elinora's eyes narrowed. "Master Elarius? Is that who you mean?"

He nodded sluggishly. "The old scholar. Corgrave's been bragging that once the good Master completes his final runes, the rest of us will be unstoppable. Enforcers, monster constructs, the whole damned kit."

Behind Jackson, a few of Baroness Thornvein's sergeants advanced. One of them, the older, pockmarked sergeant from earlier, caught Jackson's eye and gave a curt nod. "We're rounding up survivors, sorting out the ones forced into service from the true loyalists. The baroness wants an update."

Luke gestured at the wounded captain. "Our friend here's about to do more explaining. Might want to get one of your medics or scribes."

The captain managed a bitter smirk, although he winced right after. "Corgrave has no reason to protect us now. He underpaid my whole crew, threatened to kill our kids. I'd have turned on him earlier if I'd known we had a chance to walk away alive."

Riven lowered her bow a fraction. "Better late than never."

The heat in her tone suggested she felt no pity for mercenaries who terrorized innocents, but she recognized the difference between coerced fighters and true zealots.

Jackson glanced up. "We'll keep our word. You help us locate Corgrave's strongholds, we'll see you get safe passage. You'll have to answer for any crimes, but Thornvein's command can sort out the details."

Elinora touched the wounded man's wrist, offering a faint note of reassurance. "If your family is truly under threat, we can pass word along."

The captain closed his eyes, pain carving lines on his face. "I appreciate it. What else do you want to know?"

Luke leaned in. "For starters, which route do they use from here to Wraithhollow? We saw maps, but they were incomplete scrawls. You got clearer directions?"

The man did his best to answer. He rattled off a half-familiar route through the hills, pointing out a place called Fellmarsh. "Used to be a trading spot, fell on hard times. Corgrave's men stock up on supplies there, then vanish toward the gorge. No idea what wards or traps they've set, but it's the road they patrol."

Riven exchanged a glance with Elinora. "We can cross-reference that with the documents we found in the courtyard. Might line up."

The conversation broke momentarily as the older Thornvein sergeant signaled from the corridor. "We've got the fortress mostly secured, sir. The baroness is in the central hall."

Jackson nodded. "We're nearly done here." He turned back to the captain. "You did well. Keep quiet until one of Thornvein's men can help you. She honors her word."

A strangled laugh escaped the mercenary. "Sure. Anything's better than continuing to bleed on these filthy stones."

As the group made to leave, Elinora noticed a creased scrap of parchment crumpled in the man's belt pouch, dark and stained. She knelt swiftly, asking permission with a glance. The mercenary shrugged. "Take it. Probably more runic scribbles from Corgrave's pet scribe." He coughed, spitting fresh blood onto the floor.

Elinora pocketed the parchment with a faint frown. Then, she rose and followed Jackson, Luke, and Riven deeper down the corridor.

Past an archway, they found Baroness Thornvein in a swirl of dust, hands on her hips, scanning the fortress' interior. The moans of wounded fighters echoed, mixing with the shouts of Thornvein's crossbowmen apprehending stragglers. Soot streaked Thornvein's dark cloak. One of her lieutenants relayed casualty reports in a hushed tone.

When she spotted Jackson and his companions, Thornvein approached, barking orders over her shoulder for two medics to check the southern corridor. "We'll keep a small garrison here," she told Jackson. "Can't leave it empty. Corgrave's men might try to retake it."

Luke arched an eyebrow. "No rest for the wicked, huh?"

She shot him a quick glare. "A small unit should hold the perimeter. The rest of us need to rally for what's next." She glanced between them. "You got what you came for, or do I need to ask more corpses?"

Riven shook her head. "We cornered a merc captain. He spilled enough details to confirm Corgrave's forging expansions. He's shipping crystals further inland, near Wraithhollow Gorge."

Thornvein exhaled sharply and clamped a gauntlet on the hilt of her sword. "We have word that Master Elarius might be stashed somewhere out there. Possibly forced to craft more of these cursed runic rifles." She looked at Jackson. "If that's so, we've no time to waste. But my men are drained. We can't push on immediately."

Jackson's shoulders tensed. "Understood. Rally who you can. We'll do the same."

Thornvein motioned to a messenger who stood near a

collapsed wooden pillar. "We're sending riders to the capital for reinforcements. Might be days before they arrive." She planted a hand on Jackson's shoulder. Whether she ignored the flicker of infernal lines across his neck or didn't care, he couldn't tell. "You've done well. For now, we hold here."

Luke rested his crossbow against his thigh and gave Jackson a sideways grin. "You hear that? Recognition from a baroness. We'll be invited to fancy banquets next."

Thornvein glanced around at the broken walls and snorted. "If we manage to hold this ruin long enough to see a banquet, I'll send invitations by runner pigeon." She gestured for them to follow her into a wide foyer that served as the fortress' central hall.

They passed rows of unconscious or wounded mercenaries. The baroness' troops herded others into side rooms for questioning. Occasional flashes from damaged runic weaponry crackled in the air. A few unlucky loyalists to Corgrave had been senseless in the final rush. They were thrown roughly onto the stone, swords kicked aside.

Thornvein's brow furrowed at the sight. "Sort out the coerced from the die-hards. We can't waste time on mass executions, but we can't let them slip away, either."

One of her sergeants saluted. "Yes, my lady."

Jackson half-expected an argument or bitterness from the mercenaries, but only subdued acceptance filled the hall. *They know they're beaten,* he realized, stepping over a fallen shield. *This fortress is ours now.*

Elinora cleared her throat and eased the crumpled parchment from her pocket. "Baroness, we found…something." She opened the note, scanning it. "It's half-coded, but the runic scrawl is almost corrupted. Could be designs related to forging. Possibly necromantic forging." A chill settled over her tone. "Master Elarius' forced research might go beyond rifles."

A flicker of alarm crossed Thornvein's face. "Worse than we feared. We'll get the best scribes on it."

Luke peered over Elinora's shoulder, frowning at the spindly runes. "I see too many lines for a normal ward. This is something advanced, yeah?"

Elinora glanced his way. "Yes. Possibly a blueprint for some new weapon. All the more reason to rescue the runeforger."

Outside, the clang of armor signaled the arrival of more militia. Riven patted dust from her cloak, evidently uneasy. She stepped forward, arrow in hand, as though longing for a target to release tension upon. "We need to move on Corgrave before he finishes whatever this is."

Thornvein drew a breath. "We can't. Not yet. We're low on men, and reinforcements won't magic themselves here in a day." She gripped her sword tighter. "But we also can't let Corgrave vanish into Wraithhollow. So, a partial force must press on as soon as possible. The rest of us secure this fort and regroup."

Jackson exchanged glances with Luke, Riven, and Elinora. He saw the same conflict in their eyes. They wanted to storm out now, but logic demanded caution. The captain's intel about Fellmarsh and the savage route near the gorge hovered in Jackson's mind. *No sense riding to certain death.* Still, he couldn't deny the urgency.

Thornvein's gaze flicked to them. "Any help you can muster, gather it. If you've allies in the area, call them. We'll dispatch messengers. The blow we struck here matters, but it's not enough to topple Corgrave. Not yet."

Luke exhaled, resting a hand on his belt. "I expect some folks owe me favors. Not all of them want to see me again, some might prefer my head on a spike, but maybe we can twist arms." He grinned.

Elinora stared at the runic scrawl again. "We can't attempt decoding it alone. If I funnel these notes to the right scribes, we might glean how advanced Corgrave's forging is, and how close he might be to finishing. That buys us a chance to sabotage it or at least prepare."

Riven's ears twitched as more footsteps sounded near the hall entrance. A few mercenaries, hands pressed behind their heads in a sign of surrender, were herded through by two crossbow-wielding militia.

At length, Thornvein released a ragged breath. "We'll fortify the gates. Post watchers on every corridor. No sense being surprised." She met Jackson's gaze. "The cost of retaking this fort was high, but we have good intel. That has to be worth something."

Jackson nodded. "It is. We found evidence pointing to Wraithhollow as the next step. We won't let Corgrave vanish." He couldn't help wishing for a moment's rest, but he set his jaw. "We'll do what we must."

Elinora tucked the cryptic parchment away. "House Riftwyn can be called upon. My mother's favor is cautious, but these revelations might convince her we have no choice but to unify."

"Same for me," Riven added. "My presence can ease tensions with certain elven scouts. We'll see who else might join."

"Then we press on." Thornvein pivoted, her cloak brushing the dusty ground. "You four, gather supplies, rest, what little rest we can afford, and get ready for the next stage."

No time for respite. The realm depends on us. Jackson caught Elinora's gaze, the determined glint in her eyes. She clutched the scrap of parchment as though it weighed more than steel.

"I'd offer a round of celebratory ale, but the fort's cellar is probably a smoking ruin." Luke shrugged with forced levity. "Guess we'll settle for stale water rations."

In the corridor behind them, distant flames snapped and hissed in the debris. Another mild explosion of leftover alchemical powder echoed from somewhere deeper in the fortress. Thornvein nodded to her sergeants, who peeled off to organize the newly captured mercenaries. Some, forcibly conscripted, might switch sides now.

She angled a final look at Jackson. "Valuable intel, indeed. Wraithhollow is no easy ground, but at least we know where to strike. Corgrave's forging sites must be dismantled. And if Master Elarius is truly there, we must rescue him before that new weapon sees completion."

She stepped aside to consult with a cluster of her crossbow sergeants, leaving the small group with a moment's reprieve.

Jackson inhaled the acrid smoke. "Let's gather what we can. If we're heading out soon…"

Elinora straightened. "We'll get scribes on deciphering these runes. Meanwhile, you and Luke can talk to the Thornvein quartermasters about supplies."

Riven swung her bow across her back. "I'll see if any of the mercenaries can guide us or at least confirm the path around Fellmarsh. Might glean more details."

Luke tipped an imaginary hat. "Then we regroup. Maybe get a handful of hours to rest before we head for that gorge."

Jackson nodded. "Corgrave's corruption has spread far enough. We rally everyone we can. We don't have the luxury of letting him regroup."

Nobody disagreed. They stood for a moment longer, the flickering flames casting their silhouettes against the stone. Then, they split off to do what needed doing.

Though the cost in blood pressed heavily upon every soldier, the path ahead pointed inexorably toward Wraithhollow Gorge, and the twisted secrets waiting in Corgrave's sidelong ambitions. One blow was struck here, but the finishing blow lay farther ahead. Their only choice was to unite or see the kingdom devoured by one man's lust for power.

CHAPTER TWENTY-TWO

The evening sky stretched violet and gold above the neutral clearing, soft light dimming against the tall pines that flanked both sides of the winding road. Jackson tore his eyes from the horizon. As much as he would have liked to admire the colors, he had to pay attention.

Baroness Thornvein's crossbowmen, still scuffed from the previous battles, lingered near a cluster of supply wagons. Their plate-and-leather armor clicked whenever they shifted weight, as though bracing for the next confrontation.

At the center of the clearing, a trio of mage-lamps glimmered on tall iron poles, their pale blue radiance reflecting off the damp grass. Baroness Morrivale's scouts loomed there, wrapped in dark cloaks, watchful and tense.

Morrivale herself arrived moments later, emerging from the shadows in sleek riding leathers. Her garments bore embossed designs of her house crest, a subtle swirl of vines and daggers. The emblem seemed to catch the mage-lamps' glow. Her hair, braided close to the scalp and threaded with metallic beads, accentuated high cheekbones and a regal poise. She surveyed Thornvein's forces without a smile.

Elinora stood near a small wooden post hammered into the ground, its purpose unclear. She wore a hooded traveling cloak, the edges damp from earlier mist. Though she had shed most trappings of her noble estate, she kept her silver pendant visible above her tunic. Pale runes glimmered on its surface in the mage-lamp light.

She kept her chin raised, acknowledging Morrivale with a cool nod. Beside her, Baroness Vesper Thornvein cut a more militant figure, arms folded over a short, fur-lined coat. Thornvein's expression held neither welcome nor hostility, only a coarse readiness for business.

Riven was stationed at the clearing's perimeter, hidden behind a half-fallen log. From afar, one might not notice her shadow among the logs, but Jackson knew exactly where to glance. He caught sight of the slender silhouette trembling with each controlled breath. Riven was prepared to sink an arrow into any throat at the merest sign of trickery.

Jackson stood a few strides from Elinora. He rested a hand lightly on the hilt of his sword. Though he did not draw it, the air around him felt impatient. Luke, for once, managed to keep quiet, but his eyes were bright with curiosity as he hovered near Jackson's elbow.

"Baroness Morrivale." Thornvein's voice was a crisp salutation. She inclined her head enough to be courteous. "I see your scouts have been thorough."

Morrivale returned the inclination with equal restraint. "We keep them on every road leading to Wraithhollow Gorge. Recent rumors demand vigilance." She swung her gaze across Thornvein's crossbow line, then to Elinora. "I trust House Riftwyn had no trouble completing its business, Baroness Thornvein? Lady Elinora?"

Elinora pressed her lips together. "The fort we seized was more than a handful." She raised an arm to indicate the weary soldiers. "But the problems run deeper than any single stronghold. Corgrave's forging circles pose a threat to us all."

Morrivale's sculpted features twitched. Her attention fell on the coded ledgers Elinora clutched against her hip. "I hear you carry interesting evidence."

One of Morrivale's scouts, a tall woman in a charcoal cloak, approached with cautious steps. The scout's gaze traveled to Jackson, pausing at the glow around his collar. Morrivale raised a hand, silently granting permission for the scout to speak, but the woman hesitated. At last, she turned away, gliding back into the darkness. In the hush that followed, the baroness' gaze settled on Jackson.

He stepped forward, his boots sinking into the damp ground. The swirl of faint demonic light flickered at his neck. "We learned Corgrave has accelerated the forging of a new war machine. He's using stolen Riftcrown crystals, twisted necromancy, and volcanic steel to power it." He spoke calmly, keeping his tone measured despite the swirl of frustration inside him.

Morrivale regarded him without blinking. "So, the rumors ring true. A near-finished monstrosity, fueled by your luminous crystals, threatens to escalate beyond petty baronial feuds."

Elinora exhaled, rummaging in her pouch to retrieve a small, folded parchment. "These ledgers detail shipments to Wraithhollow. Each route is coded, but I've deciphered enough to confirm Corgrave's next stronghold. He's not merely stockpiling supplies. He's refining them into something more."

Baroness Thornvein moved a half-step closer to Morrivale. "We're preparing to tackle Corgrave's lines near Wraithhollow Gorge. We require cavalry, or we risk being flanked along those roads." She gestured to her crossbowmen. "Mine are excellent at ranged support, but we'll face trouble if Corgrave deploys mounted brigades or vile constructs in open terrain. We can't rely on foot soldiers alone."

An uneasy silence settled over the clearing as Morrivale

weighed Thornvein's words. The baroness took in Jackson's infernal markings, then Elinora's anxious face, and finally the worn expressions of the crossbow squads. "I'll grant you a squadron of my cavalry and a handful of my house mages, if needed. But I have conditions."

"The name of the game," Luke murmured under his breath. "Always conditions."

Jackson pretended not to hear.

Morrivale's voice remained flat. "First, I demand a written pledge from King Rodric that House Morrivale's neutrality will be respected. I won't have my troops or war mages partaking in a conflict, only to become scapegoats for some palace faction. Let him confirm it via a messenger or a sending mirror, two days at most. Without that formal pledge, my large-scale deployment remains off the table."

Elinora nodded. "We expected as much. The King's Eye can deliver the request." She glanced at Jackson, then studied Morrivale's stance. The baroness had paced forward enough to loom within arm's reach of Elinora.

Morrivale took advantage of the proximity. "Second, all forging secrets gleaned from Corgrave's labs and caches must be shared with loyal baronies. That includes trade secrets involving volcanic steel and Riftcrown crystals. We can't allow House Riftwyn or Thornreach to hoard knowledge that could shift power balances."

A flicker of tension flashed across Elinora's face, but she held her composure. "Do you suspect us of wanting to replicate Corgrave's abominations?"

"Does it matter what I suspect?" Morrivale returned dryly. "The point is, we distribute knowledge responsibly among baronies that remain loyal to King Rodric, to ensure none can exploit it."

Elinora bit down a terse reply as the itch of frustration filled the air. Thornvein cleared her throat. "A fair requirement," she stated. "We can arrange scribes from the King's Eye to copy or lock away anything that's too dangerous. None of us want another civil war."

"Then it's settled," Morrivale declared. "For now, consider it an interim pact. You'll have my cavalry support in the next engagement. Deploy them as you see fit, but I'll expect updates and caution."

Jackson shifted uneasily. *Politics,* he thought. *The one thing that sets my teeth on edge.* He hated these measured barbs. "Unless you mistreat it, your sword will always keep the faith," he muttered under his breath. Thornvein heard him and briefly smiled, acknowledging she shared the sentiment.

Morrivale heard as well. She angled her head with a faint smirk. "Certainly more reliable than any treaty on parchment. Swords do not lie, do they?"

Elinora stepped into the tension like a well-practiced diplomat. "We appreciate your cooperation, Baroness. You're right. We do need more than words. We're all here because Corgrave's threat endangers everyone. Let's stand together."

Morrivale's posture eased a fraction. "I can't deny we're on the same path. If Corgrave completes some monstrous weapon, we all suffer." She glanced again at Jackson, as though reevaluating his presence. "Your aura suggests strife in every muscle, knight. I assume you'll lead the first thrust?"

Jackson dipped his head. "Yes. Thornvein's crossbow lines will give us a flank advantage, and your cavalry can sweep in, draw enemy fire. Meanwhile, Elinora's runic enhancements should disrupt any wards or ephemeral guardians."

Thornvein studied Morrivale's face. "We move soon. Perhaps in two days, after we've confirmed your pledge with the king. If the official response is delayed, we'll deploy a scouting force anyway, but keep your cavalry at minimal risk."

Morrivale's brows arched. "Pragmatic enough. My life would be easier if we weren't forced to pounce on illusions in the dark, but so be it. I'd rather join forces than wait for Corgrave to pound at my gates."

Elinora's eyes brightened, a tiny spark of hope that the combined might of Thornvein, Morrivale, and any other allies would be enough to crack Corgrave's defenses. She touched her pendant, the subtle swirl of House Riftwyn's crest reflecting in the faint glow of a mage-lamp.

"Then we have what we came for." Thornvein stepped back. "Will you remain with us the night or return to your keep?"

Morrivale's lips curved. "I'll keep my camp here. My scouts will patrol the perimeter. Perhaps we can share a meal and finalize the details." She gestured toward a small corner of the clearing where two canopies had been erected.

Jackson was grateful for the subdued courtesy. He turned, scanning the silhouettes of the trees and the occasional shifting soldier. Riven was still at her vantage spot, silent. She lifted her arrow in a slight salute before easing the bowstring slack. No immediate threats glinted, only watchful calm as the last colors of daylight bled into the sky.

While Thornvein moved to coordinate ration distribution and map overlays, Luke meandered closer to Jackson. "You think she'll really hold to her word about that pledge?" he asked in a low voice.

Jackson studied Morrivale in the distance. "She's too proud to lie. She'll keep her promise if the king issues s neutrality vow. If he balks, we'll face new friction."

Luke rolled his shoulders. "Round and round the politics goes."

They parted ways, each man drifting to different tasks. Thornvein's crossbow squads hammered in a few stakes to tether the horses. Morrivale's scouts arranged chest-high barricades in a semicircle, marking territory for a possible watch post. Lady Elinora joined them, inscribing small runes in the soil, temporary wards to keep out less conventional threats. Occasionally, she paused to speak with an attendant, apparently checking for updated intelligence.

Over an hour passed. A cluster of smaller mage-lamps lined the edges of the improvised joint encampment. Their pale glow illuminated wandering shapes. Foot soldiers checking on supplies, a cavalry officer walking rigidly around the perimeter, Luke tying up a restless horse, and one of Morrivale's mages conjuring a faint flicker of flame to boil water. Soft murmurs replaced the earlier tension, each faction keeping a wary eye on the other but abiding by a fragile truce.

Elinora finished her runic inscriptions. Jackson joined her, stepping over a coil of rope. "All quiet so far," he remarked.

She nodded. "Morrivale's more open than I expected. Guess the looming danger is bigger than our differences."

Jackson's infernal marks glowed again, an involuntary flicker responding to a surge of adrenaline. "We'll see how open she remains after the next skirmish. The minute her cavalry takes a blow, she'll want reassurance."

Elinora set a hand on his gauntlet. "Maybe, but we must try. Corgrave thrives if we stay divided."

He exhaled. "Agreed."

A commotion rippled near the north edge of the clearing, frantic shapes pushing past the low barricades. Crossbow carriers from Thornvein's side perked up, raising weapons, while Morrivale's scouts parted.

Through the gloom strode two elves, lean, long-limbed figures with braided hair and traveling cloaks. They appeared out of breath from a hard ride, though no horses were in sight. Possibly, they'd dismounted beyond the clearing. Grassland elves, by their attire. Jackson recognized the leaf-stitched pattern along the sleeves, typical of tribes wandering the wide prairies.

Their arrival drew immediate attention. Thornvein pivoted, hand resting on her sword hilt. Morrivale stepped forward, exchanging a quick word with one of her scouts. Riven left her vantage in a swift movement. Luke sidled closer, curiosity gleaming on his face. Elinora stood straighter.

The two Grassland elves halted under the mage-lamps, chests heaving. One dropped to a knee, pressing a palm to the ground as if steeling himself. The other raised a trembling hand to address Morrivale. The makeshift camp froze, breath collectively held.

Jackson's heart thumped. *What news do they bring?*

CHAPTER TWENTY-THREE

Baroness Morrivale stood at the edge of the clearing, shoulders squared beneath a leather cloak emblazoned with her house crest. She listened to the elves with her arms folded, her polished gauntlets glinting in the eerie glow of mage-lamps. Around her, the strike force comprised of Thornvein crossbowmen, Morrivale scouts, and a handful of volunteers from Riftcrown, gathered in tense semicircles.

Jackson watched from a few paces away. He noticed how Baroness Morrivale's expression tightened each time the elves mentioned sightings of wagons laden with luminous crystals. Beside Jackson, Elinora drew a measured breath. She looked poised as always, though a subtle tremor in her hand suggested how worried she was about the stolen cargo.

Luke edged closer, his patched cloak snagging on a nearby bramble. He huffed. "We barely took the fort, and now we're being herded straight to the next snake pit. I'd hoped for a better break than this."

Jackson inclined his head toward the baroness. "We do what we can. Corgrave's not slowing down."

After a final round of tense questions, Baroness Morrivale dismissed the elves to rest, then beckoned Jackson, Elinora, and Thornvein to stand nearer. The baroness' solemn glance flicked across them all. "My scouts confirmed movement along Wraithhollow Gorge, two or three convoys a day. Each loaded with volcanic steel and luminous crystals." Her mouth formed a thin line. "It can't be good. No one hauls that much forging material for a casual experiment."

Thornvein nodded stiffly. "A full forging site, no doubt. Possibly where they're holding Master Elarius." She glanced at Elinora. "If he's forced to refine all that steel and crystal, we're looking at advanced weaponry, maybe worse."

Elinora's eyes darkened. "We can't let Corgrave's men vanish into that canyon. If he's weaving necromancy into forging, the damage could unravel half the kingdom."

Morrivale's armor creaked as she shifted. "I'll dispatch more scouts, but I'll send you my cavalry, too. Our best chance is to press on by day, when we can pick off Corgrave's outriders. By night…" She frowned. "Well, we've heard the rumors."

They needed no further explanation. Rumors of runic rifles powered by twisted rituals had circulated for weeks.

Jackson forced a calm nod. "We'll brace for those enforcers."

"Then gather your people," Morrivale replied. "We begin at dawn."

They set out at first light, an unwieldy column of crossbow carriers, cavalry scouts, and a handful of runic spearmen. The path led them over craggy ridges and through shadow-hung groves, the air steadily growing sharper as they neared Wraithhollow Gorge. By midday, Jackson noticed stray shapes darting among distant rocks. Forward scouts of Corgrave, no doubt.

Thornvein's cavalry did their part, riding across the slopes in small detachments. More than once, the sudden pop of crossbow strings or the rattle of steel sounded as they scattered enemy outriders. The group pressed onward, morale buoyed each time they found a dead or captured scout. Elinora scanned the fallen foe, her brows knit, searching for runic clues or signs that Master Elarius might be nearby.

By dusk, they crested a final ridge overlooking Wraithhollow's entrance. A cold wind hissed through the gorge, carrying an uncanny whistle that seemed like voices taunting from beyond the cliffs. One of Baroness Morrivale's lieutenants, a short, hard-faced woman, pointed out faint tracks curving down toward the canyon's depths, where stolen goods likely traveled.

Amid the rocky foothills, they made camp. Luke busied himself distributing the last of their serviceable rations, encouraging everyone to eat enough for strength but not so much that they depleted reserves.

Thornvein's sergeants grumbled about dwindling supplies, but Luke reassured them, stepping in with a plan to have Morrivale's quartermasters run quick supply caravans whenever the path was clear. He even had a short chat with a cavalry captain, something about setting up drop points near the ridge. Despite the tension, folks seemed optimistic.

However, night brought new terrors. Jackson had barely finished a perimeter check when a distant, panicked shout echoed. He sprinted toward the noise and found a group of Thornvein soldiers pinned behind jagged stones, runic rifle beams scything overhead in sizzling arcs of raw energy. Gray shapes lurched in the gloom, a half-dozen monstrous constructs. Even in the faint moonlight, the bony frames glistened with embedded shards.

"Elinora," Jackson called. "Those are the twisted skeletons the scouts mentioned."

Her voice was urgent. "Yes. The runes are etched on the bones. They're channeling necromantic spirit anchors."

Jackson glimpsed her stooping closer to a fallen creature as the fight raged. Her voice was hushed, almost academic. "Crystals embedded along the spine." She pointed with a gloved finger. "Dark script along the femurs, see? That's how they animate. Forbidden warlock practice. The spirits get tethered inside."

Luke cursed from behind a broken boulder. "Foul. And here I was complaining about normal undead. This is definitely worse."

A sudden crackle ended further talk as a freshly conjured rifle shot slashed across the stones. Jackson lunged forward, sword in hand, the infernal lines on his neck flaring with heat. A monstrous skeleton advanced, jaws wide in an unearthly grin. Jackson smashed it aside, feeling demonic sparks course up his arm. Two crossbowmen fired to cover his flank.

Riven emerged from behind a narrow ledge, her bow drawn taut. She loosed a single arrow etched with runes. It pierced one construct square in the sternum. With a shudder, the undead form collapsed in on itself.

Luke huffed, his voice echoing over the wind. "Remind me to find a holy balm. My nerves might be shot forever."

Within moments, the enforcers broke away, scurrying down into the deeper ravines. All that remained were rattling piles of bone fragments. Thornvein's guards released shaking breaths, then set about clearing debris.

Jackson knelt by a fractal spine. *They're forging an army of abominations.* Smoldering anger flickered through his veins.

Elinora crouched at his side. She brushed aside a bit of stone, glancing over the embedded shards. "They're definitely funneling stolen crystals into necromantic sockets. If Master Elarius is forced to refine them…"

She trailed off, and he understood. *Corgrave is escalating.* Jackson placed a hand over the cracked gauntlet on his sword hand, as though reminding himself to keep his demon-fire in check.

Over the following days, the column threaded deeper into Wraithhollow. Tall cliffs loomed on either side, their surfaces carved with ancient grooves. The echoes of the wind at times resembled whispers or faint moans. At midday, the cavalry roamed ahead, picking off small squads of Corgrave's watchers. Yet every night, a fresh wave of horrors emerged. Skeletal beasts, dark shapes swirling with runic force, or rifle-wielding enforcers who harried the perimeter.

Rations ran low. Thornvein's sergeants muttered openly about hunger. The baroness did what she could, urging patience until another supply run arrived. Luke took the lead, coordinating with Morrivale's quartermasters to push quick supply caravans at dusk, then slip away before the larger undead patrols took note.

One evening, the troops stumbled upon an abandoned encampment strewn with discarded crates and half-eaten meals. Jackson ordered a quick search. They found signs of volcanic steel scraps and a few crystals, possibly left behind in haste, but no Elarius. As they pressed on, the gorge tightened, the walls so steep that the sky above formed only a thin strip of fading light.

As Jackson led the advance through a narrow defile, he sensed a pulse beneath his skin. Demon-fire, smoldering in response to the oppressive tension. *Something big is near.* He couldn't blot out the thought that each step brought them closer to a forging site of unspeakable scale, and Master Elarius' predicament might be dire.

Jackson's one consolation was that Elinora stayed close. At times, they exchanged glances of determination and concern. She'd mutter scraps of runic knowledge or point out fresh wagon ruts in the track, guiding them deeper. Whenever she noticed Jackson's aura flicker, she rested a hand on his arm in support, not speaking but offering silent reassurance.

Riven's ever-watchful eye was another assurance, though she spoke fewer words each day. Luke jested less, and when he did, he could no longer bring amusement to Riven's eyes. Jackson appreciated Luke's leadership over the supplies and felt the weight of the journey on everyone. *Where would I be without them?* he wondered.

On the fifth night, a chill mist settled in, swirling across a rocky plateau where the troops made camp. Shadows danced along the ridge. Word drifted among them that a major clash might be only a day away. They were nearing Corgrave's final stronghold in the gorge. Weary soldiers took what rest they could, though tension gnawed at everyone's nerves. Even Luke was subdued.

When a crisp wind picked up, they huddled in a natural alcove, a shallow cave formed by a collapsed overhang. Flickering torches lit the cavern's jagged walls. Thornvein's sergeants spread out bedrolls in the back corner while Luke rummaged for anything that could burn for warmth. Riven stood sentry at the entrance.

Despite the gloom, Luke's voice carried an odd cheer. He had gathered a small circle of militiamen, telling them a wild story about a misguided romantic escapade. Jackson caught the tail end of Luke's anecdote, something about him "tangling in the bedsheets with a buxom lass," only to be interrupted by two men, one at the door and one at the window.

Laughter rippled through the cave as Luke described trading places with a startled local until he finally jumped out the window to safety. A few of the militiamen nearly fell over, howling with amusement.

"'Told myself that was the last time I'd trust a sweet smile in a shady tavern,'" Luke finished with a dramatic sigh. "Of course, I lied."

A startled giggle came from a young crossbow woman, then she tried to hide her grin. Briefly, the air in the cave felt less oppressive, like they could pretend they weren't about to face more undead horrors at dawn.

In a separate corner, Elinora knelt near a makeshift brazier, fiddling with runic chalk. Jackson joined her. She pressed a palm to the small metal bowl at the brazier's center. Only faint embers glowed from earlier attempts to ignite it. When Jackson crouched at her side, she glanced up.

She whispered, "I still have basic flint, but we need stronger heat for these crystals." She paused. "Could you…"

Jackson inhaled. *Use the demon-fire.* He steadied himself, raising a hand above the brazier. A tingling pulse ran along his neck as faint flames licked at his fingertips. Elinora carefully added a shard of crystal. The combined heat and arcane synergy made the shard flare with a brilliant teal glow. A dull warmth spread around them.

"That's it," she murmured. She studied the swirl of color, her eyes shining with worried intensity. "Jackson, I'm afraid of what Corgrave's forging. Every day we see more broken wards, more runic nightmares. If this is a fraction of what Master Elarius can craft, we might be unleashing something we can't contain."

"We can't let fear stop us, but I understand."

Elinora shivered. "The brutality we've witnessed, reanimated bones, runic rifles, unspeakable constructs. It chips away at everyone's hope. I worry it might taint us if we fight darkness with darker means." She gestured at his hand, where the infernal sparks had finally subsided.

He closed his fingers around the last trickle of flame. "What else can we do? If we stand by, Corgrave wins. I'd rather risk my own soul than watch him tear the kingdom apart."

Her gaze flicked to his face, and she reached out, resting her fingertips below his jaw where a faint red line glimmered. She didn't speak, but the gesture settled something in both of them. The distant clamor of Luke's story and the soldiers' chuckles seemed to fade, leaving only the hush of the brazier's crackle.

They shared a moment in silence. Elinora's cheeks warmed from the fire's glow. Jackson exhaled, releasing a tension he had barely realized he was holding. *We stand on a precipice. We can't falter now.*

She shifted, leaning nearer. "Whatever happens tomorrow, I know that I trust you. More than I ever thought possible."

His hand closed over hers in acknowledgment. The air felt charged with unspoken hopes and fears. No further words passed their lips, only a silent promise sealed by the flickering light of what they might save.

Riven cleared her throat from the cave's entrance. "Movement outside. Might be the wind." Her voice carried more gently than usual. She must have seen them close, recognized the fleeting tenderness.

Luke ambled over, grin askew, but respect lit his eyes when he noticed their posture. He didn't comment. Instead, he dropped a small bundle of dried meat near the brazier. "Energy for tomorrow," he stated. His tone was subdued. "We'll need it."

Elinora stood slowly. Jackson rose beside her, letting the renewed warmth kindle in his chest, fortifying him for the battles ahead. In the back of the cave, Thornvein's sergeants lapsed into slumber. The echo of Luke's story receded, replaced by the distant moan of wind skirting the canyon walls.

Outside, clouds skimmed across the moon, casting twisted shapes on the gorge floor. Even from this sheltered spot, Jackson could sense how close they were. Every bone-littered skirmish, every rumor of half-finished weapons, every scrap of intel pointed to a single heart of darkness. They would find Corgrave's fortress soon, and with it, Master Elarius.

Elinora gave Jackson's hand a final squeeze before stepping away. "We'll break camp at dawn. Morrivale's scouts expect a rough approach."

"We're ready," Jackson replied.

Their eyes met once more. Outside, the gorge beckoned with silent malice, but they would press on and face whatever twisted abominations waited.

CHAPTER TWENTY-FOUR

The next evening, the combined forces gathered around a broken tower clinging to the face of the crags. Mage-lamps offered only sparse blue light, leaving most of the jagged rocks in ominous shadow.

Morrivale's cavalry formed a defensive crescent in the ravine below, while Baroness Thornvein's men crouched behind rubble, crossbows at the ready. The distant cry of monstrous birds echoed, but the cavalry's presence kept those flying threats from swooping in. A fine mist curled around the stones, as if the land itself dreaded what lay within the tower's depths.

Jackson stood at the edge of a small outcropping, rolling his shoulders to dispel tension. The infernal marks on his neck had begun to prickle with a low heat. He drew a measured breath and surveyed the defenders around him.

Thornvein's spearmen huddled in undergrowth nearby, each soldier well aware they followed a knight said to have demon-fire running in his veins. He was used to others avoiding him. Only a handful met his gaze, nodding with grim respect. Those who did had encouragement from Riven, Luke, and Elinora, who showed no issue interacting with him. If not for the people he'd come to consider as friends, he'd had felt an outsider in this group.

From the gloom emerged Morrivale's lieutenant, a stout woman clad in worn leather and half-plate. She extended a small cylinder etched with delicate runic lines. "Sir McCade," she murmured. "Baroness Morrivale says if you find yourselves overrun, activate this flare. It will burst above the tower, and we will storm in."

He took the cylinder and weighed it in his palm. "Appreciate the precaution." He slipped the device into a pouch at his belt. The runes glimmered as though sensing his latent power. He offered a curt nod, then turned to find the others.

Luke, perched beside a mossy boulder, clutched the runic compass that pulsed with frantic flickers of pale light every time he edged closer to the tower's door. His patched cloak shifted, making him look more like a haggard traveler than ever. "This thing's going half-mad," he whispered to Jackson, tapping the face of the compass. "It's pointing us into the worst possible place, I'd wager."

Riven appeared behind them, moving with uncanny silence. "We knew that already." Her keen elven gaze swept the tower's broken battlements overhead. Electricity flashed along the turrets, arcs of bright energy that spat sparks onto the rocky ledges. "Corgrave's tampering has turned this ruin into something foul."

Elinora approached next, silver pendant glinting. Something about it seemed magnetic to Jackson, for it always drew his eye when she appeared. That was Elinora as a whole, though. He couldn't help but feel drawn to her. Her expression was stiff and resolute. When she finally spoke, her voice carried a thin thread of calm. "Jackson, I'll handle the wards if they appear. I can't promise I'll have the strength for more than a few twists of necromantic script."

He placed a gauntleted hand on her shoulder, feeling the

ripple of tension beneath. "We do what we need to do. Nothing more."

They parted with no further words. While a group of Thornvein's spearmen formed a wedge near the collapsed entry, Jackson, Luke, Riven, and Elinora slipped through a narrow cleft in the tower's craggy foundation. The crag floor sloped downward into darkness. At once, the stench of ozone and layered dust closed in.

Lightning slashed overhead again, accompanied by the crack of runic rifles. Shouts followed as Thornvein's soldiers engaged Corgrave's outer sentries. The corridor beyond the hidden crevice glowed from the intermittent flashes above.

Luke held the compass out front, swallowing audibly. "If I get shot again, I want hazard pay," he muttered.

A crackle erupted from the gloom as two of Corgrave's enforcers appeared, brandishing rifles that spat sizzling arcs of volcanic energy. They wore breastplates marked with Corgrave's crest and had the wild look of men pushed to desperation. Jackson lunged, sword drawn, as his infernal markings lit his collarbones in a dim red glow. The first enforcer fired a close-range blast that hissed past Jackson's shoulder, scorching a chunk of stone.

A spear hurtled through the narrow opening behind Jackson, courtesy of Thornvein's nearest squad, forcing the second enforcer to duck. Riven used the moment to draw her bow. Her rune-carved arrow caught one marksman beneath the chin. He collapsed instantly, weapon clattering on the floor. The second enforcer tried to scramble away, but her follow-up shot struck him in the throat. He crumbled in a heap.

Luke huffed. "That was efficient," he whispered, shoulder pressed to the damp wall.

Jackson waved Thornvein's men to hold position near the crevice. "Keep watch here. We'll push deeper." One of the spearmen nodded, stepping aside so Jackson's group could slip further in.

Beyond the first bend, the corridor opened into an antechamber large enough to have once been a storeroom or workshop. Broken crates lined the edges, stenciled with cryptic runic symbols. The walls bore scorched patterns, likely from misfired weapon tests. A half-toppled iron brazier lay on its side, still faintly smoking.

Elinora crouched beside a crate. Her pendant flickered as she brushed soot away from an inscription. "They are refining the crystals onsite," she whispered. "That means Master Elarius can't be far." She winced, pressing a hand briefly to her temple. "I sense wards deeper in. They feel…twisted."

Riven scanned the room. "Then we move, quietly as we can. If they're forging abominations here, the monstrous half-living guardians won't be far." She rummaged for a fresh arrow.

They slipped through another passage, soon confronted by gradually descending steps. The temperature rose with each level, as if something smoldered deep below. Sparks danced along the corridor's ceiling, an effect of the runic wards crackling in the air like invisible netting.

The hair on Jackson's neck prickled with each step. *Steady*, he told himself. He let Luke lead with the compass' faint glow, resisting the hungry pull of the infernal flame in his bones. He recognized that gnawing urge to lash out but channeled it into single-minded resolve. *Not now.*

A swirling bolt of energy streaked past Luke's head. Startled, he flung himself toward Jackson, nearly dropping the compass. Ahead stood another group of Corgrave's enforcers, their rifles humming with power. One of them barked an order. Gunfire erupted, scorching the walls with sizzling lines. Riven dove behind a fallen column, and Elinora flattened herself behind a wooden crate.

"Stay behind cover!" Jackson roared, brandishing his sword.

Another blast scorched a jagged hole in the crate. Splinters rained onto Elinora's hood. Luke cursed under his breath, fumbling for a throwing dagger. He lobbed it with questionable aim. It clattered across the enforcers' boots, at least distracting them briefly.

Riven popped up from her cover and released two arrows in quick succession. One enforcer was struck in the chest, staggering back with a sharp cry. The second arrow grazed another foe, who staggered but did not fall.

Jackson lunged forward, the infernal glow brightening around his neck. Sparks of eldritch flame licked around his sword's edge. He parried an incoming bayonet lunge, then with a savage slash, ripped aside the rifle. The enforcer gasped and collapsed under the blow. Another whir of projectiles flew overhead, but Luke sprang into action, tackling a wounded man to the ground.

At last, the corridor fell quiet except for ragged breathing. Luke groaned, hauling himself upright. "I think I'll bruise in new places after that tackle," he muttered, wincing.

Elinora rose with a trembling exhale. Her cheeks were ashen in the flickering light. "We have to keep going." Her gaze darting to the far archway. "I sense more wards below. They're distorting the normal flow of magic."

"Lead on. We're close." Jackson squeezed her arm gently, though his rough voice implied urgency.

They descended another flight of stairs. A pungent odor of molten metal rolled up at them, mingled with the reek of singed flesh. Muffled screams reverberated through the walls. Luke's face tightened. "Master Elarius must be close," he remarked in a disquieted whisper.

The corridors expanded into a labyrinth of branching halls lit by sparks from runic arrays hammered into the stone. Twisted runes crawled along the walls, some in thick, scrawling script that radiated necromantic presence. Elinora shuddered each time she passed near one, her silver pendant flaring in protest. She came upon a heavy black door braced with rivets, where a scribble of glowing lines spelled out the foul brand of Corgrave's forging circle.

"I have to disrupt these wards," she breathed. "They'll rip us apart if we pass unprotected." She knelt and produced a small piece of chalk from her pouch. Her fingers shook. She began a delicate process of rewriting certain key glyphs.

With the corridor so cramped, Jackson and Riven kept watch, tense as coiled springs. The ward lines sparked, and each time Elinora's chalk made contact, a new jolt lashed at her mind. She gave a quiet cry of pain on the fourth attempt, bracing herself against the doorframe. "It's fighting back," she hissed. "This is necromantic forging. It's not a normal ward."

Luke touched her shoulder. "Take your time." The runic compass in his grip flickered and dimmed, as though overshadowed by the malevolence in the scripts.

Elinora pressed her hand to her pendant. "I can do this," she whispered, then forced herself to continue. The wards crackled and spat tiny arcs at her fingers. After a final scrawl of chalk, the door's runes fizzled with a hiss. The barrier clicked ajar. Elinora swayed, eyes fluttering shut as she tried to steady her breathing.

Jackson caught her before she collapsed. "Easy," he murmured, supporting her with one arm. *She's at her limit.*

She stared up at him, fear flickering in her gaze. "I can't keep unraveling them. This ward was almost too much."

He nodded. "There is no give in, no give up. We survive for tomorrow." She cracked a small, weary smile at that, the faintest glimmer of hope in her eyes.

Riven carefully eased the damaged door open and peered inside. Flickers of red light danced against the walls of a narrower corridor. "It leads to some deeper chamber," she whispered. "I hear forging hammers or something like that."

They pressed on. The deeper they ventured, the more the

labyrinth seemed alive with hateful whispers. Odd runic lines glowed within the stone, pulsing in time with the drip of molten metal from overhead pipes. Smoke billowed at every turn, stinging the eyes and choking the throat.

Within that gloom, they passed more signs of forced labor. Broken shackles pinned under scraps of twisted steel, half-carved chunks of luminous crystal, and the faint moans of imprisoned souls somewhere beyond.

At one intersection, a swirling vortex of magical residue flickered across the passage, likely a byproduct of the forging spells. Elinora avoided it, leaning heavily on Jackson. Luke frowned at another corridor that spiraled off into darkness. "Feels like a place that wants to swallow us alive."

Down the main corridor, two double doors loomed beneath an arch hammered with Corgrave's personal crest. The lines of the crest glowed with an eerie red luminescence that pulsed like a living heartbeat. Necromantic wards webbed every inch of the metal, fusing forging runes with vile conjurations. The air hummed with malevolent tension.

Jackson exhaled, letting the demon-fire simmer in his chest. "This is it." The door rattled from within, something monstrous paced or howled behind it. He felt Elinora's slight weight on his arm.

Luke swallowed. "Well," he muttered. "I guess we find out if we can't handle ugly, or if ugly can't handle us."

Jackson allowed himself a brief, grim smile. He summoned the flickering flames from his infernal markings, letting the red glow course down his arms. "Elinora, can you break those wards from out here?"

She scanned the twisted script and shook her head. "It's too tightly woven. I would need hours to rewrite them. Hours we can't spare."

A tremor ran through the floor, sending loose stones rolling. Above them, echoing blasts hinted that Morrivale's cavalry still hammered at distant turrets, keeping avian beasts or runic artillery pinned. Time was short. Jackson nodded for everyone to step back from the door.

"We do it the direct way." He raising his sword. Heat pulsed around his gauntlet, the infernal flame intensifying. The wards flared as if sensing his intent. Sparks danced across the metal surface.

In a fluid motion, Elinora pressed her trembling palm to a cluster of runes, channeling every shred of her will. The wards flickered in protest, lashing out with smoky ribbons of necromantic force. Her pendant flared bright. Jackson roared a wordless cry, focusing demon-fire into the sword's edge. The wards hissed, sizzling under the assault.

Bit by bit, the script peeled away, leaving stinging shadows. Elinora nearly collapsed again, but Luke grabbed her around the waist, steadying her. Riven flattened herself against the wall, arrow aimed at the seam of the door.

A final wave of heat rippled through Jackson's gauntlet, scorching the decaying wards. The door hinge groaned, half-melted by conjured flame.

Jackson lowered his shoulder, driving forward with raw strength. The door buckled. A surge of horrifying aura spilled from the gap, thick with the stench of rot and molten metal. Something huge roared on the other side, a guttural bellow so forceful it rattled the walls.

The final wards collapsed in a shower of dying sparks. Jackson exhaled a determined breath and held Elinora's gaze. "We break this darkness," he stated.

He kicked the door inward. The rusted metal split wide.

From the darkness within came a bestial roar that shook the corridor.

CHAPTER TWENTY-FIVE

Jackson's boot was still pressed to the shattered remains of the iron door when two hulking shapes lunged through the swirling dust. Their tall, sinewy bodies were covered in coarse fur. With eyes that glowed a hateful gold, the lycanthropes snarled, clawed hands reaching for the intruders as if starved for blood.

Elinora shouted a warning. "They're cursed beyond normal lycan-kind. Look at those eyes!"

Jackson didn't need another hint. He swung his sword up to meet the first lunge. Steel impacted thick fur, sending a jarring shock up his arms. The monster staggered sideways, baring a set of slavering fangs before hurling itself at him again.

Riven was already moving behind a fallen archway of damp stone. She slid an arrow from her quiver, her gaze flicking between the two lycan creatures. "I'll distract the second one," she stated. Her bow hummed. A rune-infused arrow shot across the corridor, striking the second beast high in the shoulder. It roared in anger and spun with surprising speed.

Luke, who was still fumbling with the runic compass, blanched at the sight of the beast's clawed hand swiping toward him. "I could've used a second more of warning!" he yelped, diving behind a broken chunk of rubble. The lycan's slash scraped sparks from the stone.

Elinora, pressed against the left wall, gripped a small runic rod. She focused on the swirling lines etched into its surface and channeled a flicker of magic through her fingertips. A faint gleam raced along the floor. Runic shapes took form around the beast's ankles, slowing its movements as it lunged again. "They regenerate quickly," she called. "We need to strike hard, keep them from re-forming if they go down!"

Jackson gritted his teeth, meeting the first were-creature again. Its snarl echoed in the narrow corridor. The air smelled rank, a mixture of damp fur and bitter copper. Another slash of his blade traced sparks along its ribs, drawing a hiss of pain. Yet the wound barely slowed it.

The lycan turned, gold eyes blazing with madness, and hammered a heavy paw across Jackson's torso. He staggered, catching himself against a slime-coated wall. The wolfish monster advanced, claws curling. Jackson peeled himself away from the wall, bracing for a savage follow-up strike.

Riven's second arrow soared. The shaft buried itself in the monster's thigh, but with a jerk of muscle and a snarl, the beast ripped it out, flinging it aside in a spray of dark blood. "Persistent," Riven muttered, reaching for another shot.

Meanwhile, Luke crawled behind the chunk of fallen masonry. He hissed, "I'll distract the hungry one!" He rummaged in his satchel, producing a small, half-broken flask. He hurled it over the rock without looking, hoping for the best. It smashed on the ground, releasing a patch of acrid fumes that stung the monster's nostrils. The lycan reeled, momentarily disoriented. "That's it, you big flea-ridden…"

The beast whipped around, glowering through the haze. "Uh, Jackson?" Luke blurted, heart pounding.

Jackson was already locked in a vicious exchange with the first lycan. The demon-fire in his veins burned. He channeled the dark energy into a savage slash, aiming lower. The ring of steel against bone sent shockwaves up his arms.

The creature barked a rasping snarl and pitched forward, one leg turned to ragged flesh. Jackson saw an opening and thrust his blade, catching it in the torso. The beast snarled again, ignoring what should have been a crippling wound.

Across the corridor, Elinora darted behind the second werecreature. With careful footwork, she etched a new glyph in the slimy floor using her runic rod, arcs of pale light dancing around her hand. "Back away, Luke! I'm going to set off a tracer ward."

Luke gasped and ducked as Elinora released a flash of azure energy. The magic flared beneath the lycan's feet, staggering it. Riven used that moment to loose two arrows in rapid succession. One struck the beast's torso, the other caught its upper arm, pinning it against the pitted wall. The creature roared, but momentum slammed it into a tangle of rotted chains draped across the corridor.

"Got it!" Riven yelled. "Jackson, how's yours?"

Jackson put his shoulder into the first lycan's chest, driving it back a few paces. He sidestepped a slash of its claws, then answered with another heavy strike. The sharpened steel bit deep. The monster's snarl erupted into a guttural shriek as sticky blood splattered onto the stone.

The corridor's cramped space forced them nearly shoulder to shoulder, the filthy stench of the beast's breath choking Jackson's nostrils. He fought through his revulsion and slashed again, the demon-fire fueling his arms with preternatural strength.

A final blow crippled the first lycan's left flank. It sank to one knee, panting raggedly, but still snapped its jaws, refusing to fall. With a savage effort, Jackson thrust his blade along the creature's collarbone. Bone cracked.

The lycan slipped sideways. Only then did it slump, eyes rolling back into its skull. The faint torchlight flickered across matted fur, gleaming with fresh blood. Jackson exhaled, pressing a hand to his throbbing chest. The infernal markings on his neck pulsed like a second heartbeat.

He turned to see the other beast straining against the pinned arrows. Its corded muscles flexed as it yanked one arrow free with a spatter of blood, letting out a roar that echoed through the gloom. "We're not done," Jackson called hoarsely.

The creature lunged, ignoring a fresh wave of magical sparks from Elinora's tracer ward. It tore across the corridor, throwing itself forward despite the arrow buried in its shoulder. Riven cursed, diving aside as the beast barreled toward her. She scrambled up, flattening her back to the wall. The lycan's gaze flared with rage, and its jaws snapped inches from her face.

Luke rushed forward, brandishing his dagger. "Over here, you drooling hairball!" He feinted, jabbing at the creature's flank. It rounded on him instead, giving Riven a precious moment to regroup. Luke's courage wavered as the lycan batted his blade aside and advanced with shocking speed. "I regret all my life choices," he breathed.

Jackson, still wincing from bruises, planted himself behind the monster. He hacked at its leg, forcing the lycan to pivot. Elinora raised her rod, lips moving in a quick incantation. A sphere of shimmering energy formed around the beast's head, squeezing shut its snapping jaws for a fraction of a second. The monster howled, muffled by Elinora's spell, and staggered.

Riven took advantage, firing another arrow that sank deep into the lycan's lower back. It arched in pain, half-turning. Luke seized the opening to slash across its exposed ribs. The beast yowled, flesh ripping beneath Luke's blade. Blood dripped to the floor in dark rivulets.

They hammered it from three sides, each strike chipping away at its savage stamina. Jackson landed a brutal blow across its spine. Riven, ducking a flailing claw, lodged another arrow in its chest. Elinora's tracer ward sent sparks up its legs. Luke jumped in again, dagger flashing with uncharacteristic boldness.

Finally, with a guttural snarl, the beast collapsed, bleeding.

The corridor fell quiet save for ragged breathing and the drip of blood onto cold stone. The stench of gore hung thick in the air. They stared at the downed lycans, bodies glistening under the wavering glow of the torches. Neither beast moved, but Jackson saw a faint twitch in the second creature's hind leg.

Elinora raised a trembling hand. "We have to keep the heads. If these things reattach, they'll regenerate."

Luke coughed, looking queasy. "Keep the heads attached but isolated? Oh, that's lovely."

She nodded. "We can't remove them entirely, or we risk unleashing some heightened curse. We sever only enough to ensure they can't re-form. Leave them partly attached so the curse doesn't spread uncontrollably."

Riven approached cautiously. She looked as though she'd prefer to burn both corpses to ash, but she deferred to Elinora's knowledge.

Under Elinora's guidance, the group pinned each creature's jaw half-askew using leftover scrap metal from the fallen door, making sure the heads remained attached to the torsos only by a narrow strip of sinew. A series of gory cracks and wet rips later, the lycans lay pinned, their savage forms inert.

Jackson exhaled. "At least they're quiet now."

Riven slipped a cloth over her mouth, nose wrinkling. "We'll have done a favor for whoever cursed them. I doubt they had any sanity left."

"Agreed," Elinora remarked softly. "They were far gone."

They took a moment to catch their breath. The corridor continued deeper, a yawning blackness ahead. Faint moans and the flicker of greenish witch-lights underscored the tower's ominous hush. Chiseled runes glowed faintly on the walls, some half-scorched, others rippling with raw necromantic force. Several times, the floor beneath them gave a foreboding rattle as if the stone might collapse at any moment.

Luke wiped sweat from his brow and hoisted the runic compass. "Better keep going, right? Or do we flee back the way we came?"

Jackson pressed a hand to his bruised ribs and shook his head. "We push on."

They stepped around the lifeless lycans, crossing into the next section of the corridor. Broken shackles hung from the walls, and slick pools of water mirrored the dancing lights above. The corridor branched left and right, both directions equally shadowed. Low groans drifted from somewhere ahead, perhaps from more twisted creations of Corgrave's forging.

Riven raised her bow. "We stick close," she murmured.

Luke advanced, holding out the runic compass. The needle whirled, as if uncertain, then settled to point partially left. "This way," he announced. He moved carefully, searching for tripwires or pressure plates. Twice, he motioned for everyone to halt. They stepped over rusted iron cables and the skeleton of a shattered trap.

At one turn, Luke froze at the sight of a faint glyph scrawled in dripping greenish ooze. "That's got necromantic forging vibes," he whispered.

Elinora studied it, then used her runic erasure device on the smaller glyph. She carefully placed a swirl of chalk across the lines. The glyph fizzled, sputtering out. "That should sever its link."

When they pushed farther, the corridor opened into a half-collapsed antechamber. Mold-encrusted pillars leaned at precarious angles, and the floor sloped with scattered debris. A series of runic guardians loomed along the walls, carved figures of winged warriors embedded with luminous crystal shards.

Jackson's demon marks prickled. "They might wake if we disturb the wrong symbol."

Riven nodded. "We'll keep wide arcs. One wrong foot, and we'll have a horde of living statues."

They navigated carefully, stepping over toppled stone blocks. Drops of water echoed in the gloom, a steady plip-plip. Luke brandished the tattered ledger page. "These bloodstains match up with the tunnel we want," he observed, rising from a crouch. "See how it's torn? I think whoever wrote it was fleeing deeper."

He led them to another corridor. The path curved, narrowing until the walls nearly brushed their shoulders. Patches of algae and wormy growth clung to slick stone. The stench of rot made each breath a chore.

They paused at a battered iron door. Scratches marred its surface, as though something large had tried to claw its way through. Elinora pressed her ear to the door, listening. When she pulled back, she shook her head. "Quiet. But that might mean something nastier is lurking."

Riven nocked an arrow. "Better I lead." She nudged the door open gently, revealing a cramped chamber with a sagging ceiling. The greenish haze of witch-lights reflected on half-collapsed shelves crowded with rotted tomes and shattered glass. Everything reeked of foul magic.

At the far side, a skeletal construct slumped against the wall, fractured spine fused with a single, pulsating crystal shard. As soon as Riven's foot touched the threshold, the shard flashed. The skeleton stirred with a rattling hiss.

Jackson stepped in, sword raised. "We do this quick. No sense letting it get the jump on us."

It jerked upright, bones scraping. Near the clavicle, twisted runes glowed a dull red. The skeleton reached for an abandoned scythe handle. Riven loosed an arrow, snapping through its ribcage. The creature shook, an unholy gleam in its empty sockets.

Luke grunted. "Great. Another abomination." He skirted left, searching for more threats.

At a nod from Jackson, Elinora etched a counter-sigil on the floor. She had discovered this method earlier to disrupt necromantic forging runes. With quick strokes, she scrawled a circle. But the skeleton was already rising, scythe raised.

Jackson sprang in, bashing a shield he'd pried off a dead guard to knock the creature's arms aside. Riven's arrow pinned it to the wall once more, a direct hit through the spine's embedded crystal. The skeleton quivered, then collapsed into a heap of bone.

Elinora finished the last line. A sizzling pulse wiped out the runic glow around the bones. "There," she stated, breathing hard. "That should sever it for good."

Luke peered at the remains. "This place is downright heartwarming," he quipped, voice shaking slightly. "Wonder what vile contraption the next corridor holds."

"We press on," Jackson repeated, stepping over the scattered ribs. The tension in the air hardly lessened. Though they'd battled monstrous lycans and reanimated abominations, the catacombs stretched deeper, promising even darker horrors. The walls themselves felt alive, thrumming with leftover forging magic.

Riven collected her spent arrows as best she could, wiping them on a scrap of cloth. "I'm nearly out of specialized heads." She glanced at Elinora.

Elinora grimaced. "We need to be mindful. I'm almost drained, too."

Luke exhaled. "That means no showy heroics from me," he joked. "Let's be sure not to set off any more war-golem armies."

Jackson set his jaw. "Let's move carefully." He stepped through the half-collapsed doorway into the next stretch of corridor. The darkness teemed with foreboding. Somewhere in the distance came another low moan, or perhaps it was the wind coursing through the broken vaults above. Corgrave's twisted forging had tainted every stone.

Luke eyed the tattered ledger again, matching spattered blood patterns on the wall to the scribbled notes in the margin. "We're getting closer to something. I just don't know if it's the main site or another nasty side project."

Jackson's demon marks still burned, as though resonating with necromantic energy. He inhaled, ignoring the ache in his ribs. "We handle it either way."

They crept forward, the corridor narrowing again, the distant flicker of green witch-lights reflecting off the damp walls. Dripping condensation trickled in tiny rivulets, pattering onto their shoulders. A faint whir of arcane energy thrummed beneath the stone, making the hair on the back of Riven's neck stand on end.

Luke caught sight of a metal wire crossing the floor. "Tripwire," he muttered, kneeling down. "I'll deal with it." He worked carefully, snipping it free of a hidden mechanism. A small runic device, shaped like a box with etched lines, clicked off. "Better not leave that behind," he growled. "I don't fancy a fiery explosion at our backs."

He stowed the device and rose gingerly. "All done."

Jackson gave him a nod. "Thank you."

They paused at another intersection, the walls branching left and right again. The air felt closer than ever.

"This isn't all of it," Jackson told Luke, lowering his sword for a moment. "Feels like this place wants to swallow us alive." There would be no easy exit until they uncovered the next twisted horror hidden in these catacombs.

CHAPTER TWENTY-SIX

A low hum echoed through the labyrinth's narrow corridors, a sound that set every nerve in Jackson's body on edge. He and his companions pressed deeper, their footsteps echoing on damp rock. Shadows danced across their faces, cast by feeble witchlights cemented into half-broken sconces. The air clung to them with a murky heaviness.

Elinora paused at an intersection, breathing hard. She ran two fingers along a faint line of runes scrawled across the wall. A shifting swirl of necromantic script glowed beneath her touch. "They're twisting these wards," she murmured. "It's forcing us down a choke point."

Jackson flexed his hands, the infernal scars along his neck prickling in warning. "The deeper we go, the worse it feels." He flicked a glance at Riven, whose eyes darted over the darkness.

Riven's voice held a cool undertone. "We have to keep pushing. Master Elarius must be down here."

Luke hefted a small mirror wrapped with wire filaments. "At least I'm consistent in wanting to get out of these claustrophobic halls. This place smells like a rotted mushroom pit."

A hollow boom echoed through the corridor, cutting short

any response. Jackson motioned for them to stay close. They followed the narrow passage until all four emerged into a wide, gloom-filled chamber.

The stench of molten metal hit first, rank and metallic, sharp enough to sting nostrils and eyes. At the chamber's heart stood a makeshift workshop, canopied by twisted iron bars and half-collapsed scaffolding. Strange apparatuses cluttered the edges, lumps of volcanic steel glowing with sullen heat beside jagged chunks of Riftcrown crystal. Greenish wards shimmered around the forging station, arcs of corrupted magic dancing along severed rods and hammered plates.

On the far wall, a hunched figure was bound to a stone anvil. The man's wrists were chained apart, forcing him to slump forward at an uncomfortable angle. Runic inscriptions ringed the anvil, some half-etched, others incomplete.

Even in the chamber's dim glow, Jackson recognized Master Elarius from the man's gaunt frame and the weary intelligence in his eyes. Wrinkles of exhaustion, bruises, and a haunted terror marred his features. His fingertips were scorched and blistered, showing how relentlessly Corgrave's minions had forced him to labor.

Elarius' head rose at the sight of approaching figures. For an instant, disbelief flickered across his face. Then, recognition flared. "S-Stop," he croaked. "The wards here are primed to detonate the forging station."

Elinora inhaled sharply. She took a wary step inside, scanning the runic inscriptions. "They set up a feedback trap," she murmured, noting the arcs of sputtering magic along the station's rods. "If anything jostles them too hard, it could blow."

Luke cursed under his breath, holding the sending mirror in one hand. "I'd planned to call for backup, but that's not looking like an option here. Let's do it carefully. Maybe we can reach Elarius first?"

Elinora bit her lip and crept forward. She withdrew a small

piece of luminescent chalk from a pouch at her belt. Jackson followed, sword in hand, though he kept it low to avoid scraping any unstable surface. Riven sank into a half-crouch, scanning the corners for hidden guards.

Broken lumps of volcanic steel littered the floor near the forging station. Hissing wards flickered across the lumps, as if channeling twisted necromantic power. Their combined glow painted bizarre patterns of light on the walls. Jackson felt a tug in his chest, the sensation of the demon-fire stirring within him. *Steady*, he thought. *We'll free Elarius.*

A ragged groan came from the bound scholar. He tugged at his chains. "You shouldn't have come," he rasped. "Corgrave left these wards to kill anyone who tries to rescue me."

Elinora reached the anvil's edge. She surveyed the runic circle etched in the floor. "Hold still," she whispered. Then, she swiped the chalk across a cluster of sigils, her hand steady despite the tension in her voice. "I can invert them." She beckoned for Riven. "Help me break his chains, but not yet. I need control of the circuit first."

Riven slipped forward. "Say the word."

Off to the left, Luke repositioned the sending mirror on a rusted bench. "If I can get this to connect, we can signal the outside," he muttered, fiddling with the wires. "C'mon, you fancy chunk of arcane glass. Do your job."

At the forging station, a swirl of noxious steam rose from a vat half-filled with melted slag. Tiny shards of Riftcrown crystal floated in it. Thin lines of runic script crawled up the vat's sides, sizzling whenever the goop inside bubbled. The mixture smelled like burned hair and sulfur.

Elinora knelt by the largest cluster of wards, chalk in hand. She singled out a crucial runic pivot, a naming glyph that anchored the feedback loop. Sparks danced along the glyph each time she pressed the chalk closer. She exhaled through her teeth.

"If I misalign this, the entire station might blow." She glanced at Jackson. "Be ready."

Jackson's infernal marks glowed in response. He stepped to her side and spoke gently. "Keep calm. You know what to do."

She steadied her breathing and drew a single line with the chalk, bridging two half-etched sigils. The arc of greenish energy flared, spitting embers at her hand. She winced but held firm. Then, she lifted a carefully cut piece of crystal wedge from a leather pouch. She slotted it against a metal rod thrumming with power. The rod's hum changed pitch. The entire forging station crackled.

"Everything all right?" Riven whispered, inching closer to Elarius' chains.

Elinora swallowed. "One more stroke." She pressed the wedge further, forcing the loop's energy to reroute. Sparks erupted from the rod, and she quickly traced another line with her chalk. The final glyph hissed, a searing wave scorching the dust at her feet. One breath, then another. The wards stabilized, their glow substantially dimmer. Small arcs of leftover power danced harmlessly along the station's edges.

"That should break the meltdown cycle," Elinora announced, pushing damp hair off her forehead. Relief warred with lingering fear in her eyes. "Now, the chains."

Riven and Jackson approached the anvil from each side. Elarius shivered, eyes glistening with confusion and hope. His cheeks were sunken, bearing the exhaustion of days without rest. "We have to hurry," he managed. "Corgrave forced me to forge something. The Dreadblade. It's almost complete."

Jackson nodded. "We'll get you out." He stepped to the thick shackles that bound Elarius' wrists. Each was latched to an iron ring anchored by runic bolts. Riven pressed a hand lightly against Elarius' shoulder, a silent gesture of reassurance while she lifted her dagger to wedge into the iron ring.

Luke, a few steps away, twirled a copper dial on the sending mirror. "I'm getting static," he muttered. "Something's jamming the connection. We can't call for reinforcements from here."

"Corgrave buried this place in necromantic wards." Elinora touched the floor, eyes narrowed in frustration. "We'd need to break half of them to open a signal."

"Which we don't have time for." Riven half-turned to Jackson. "Your turn with those infernal muscles, if you please."

He pressed his gauntlet to the chain's lock, letting a sliver of demon-fire simmer in his palm. The steel hissed, protesting the unnatural heat. *Careful*, he thought, controlling the flow. The chain weakened, then seconds, the links snapped with a dull *clank*.

Elarius sagged against the anvil, half free but still pinned by the other shackle. Riven sawed at that one with her dagger, but the metal was thick. Her blade skittered off its surface. Frowning, Jackson laid a glowing hand there. The demon-fire flared, severing the chain.

Elarius toppled forward, knees buckling beneath him.

Luke stepped around them, scanning the perimeter of the messy workspace. Soft arcs of leftover energy still glowed on the floor, but the meltdown threat seemed contained. "We need to move. I don't want to chance this place deciding to blow us to pieces, after all."

Elinora bent down and grasped Elarius' arm. She flinched at the bruises and faint scorch marks near his elbow. "Can you walk?"

Slowly, the runeforger nodded. "Yes, but it hurts." His voice cracked. "I've been forging day and night. Corgrave threatened to kill me if I refused." Another spasm of pain twisted his features. Then, he coughed. "He wants a doomsday blade. The thing is meant to harness the synergy between Riftcrown crystals and volcanic steel. He forced me to combine that with necromantic forging processes, so the blade would feed on living energy."

A flicker of dread crossed Jackson's face. "Living energy?"

"Yes," Elarius confirmed, trembling. "I tried to sabotage it, but Corgrave made me rewrite certain runes. He's close to finishing the final step. When the Dreadblade is fully awakened, it could drain entire ranks of soldiers in a matter of heartbeats. Every drop of life essence fuels its strikes."

Elinora's eyes burned with horror. "That is monstrous." She closed her grip more firmly on his arm. "We're getting you out of here."

Riven glanced over her shoulder. "Luke, any sign of reinforcements behind us? Or anything?"

Luke raised the mirror again. It sparked with faint reflections in the swirling gloom. He released a bark of disgust. "No such luck. We're on our own. I can't get a signal past these wards."

Jackson glanced toward the corridor they had come through. The hush of the hidden workshop only amplified the tension. He offered Master Elarius a canteen from his belt. The older man gulped the water in shaky relief. "Without reinforcements, we'll have to stop Corgrave ourselves," Jackson muttered. "How far along is he?"

Elarius' gaze flicked anxiously to the forging station. "Not far. If what I overheard is correct, he's likely in a hidden forging circle somewhere above, finalizing the runes that will anchor the blade's necromantic matrix. Then, the Dreadblade's thirst for living energy will be unstoppable."

Elinora steadied the trembling runeforger. "We have to deny him that final step." She surveyed the still-glowing leftover lumps of volcanic steel. "Any idea how to slow him?"

Elarius shook his head. "Time is all that matters. If we wait even an hour, Corgrave will finish. The forging circle is specialized, a twisted adaptation of artifacts stolen from older wars. It channels the combined force of the crystals and the steel. The blade's essence effectively regenerates itself by siphoning life. It could tear through baronies. My work was forced, but please believe me…I tried to hamper him."

Riven gently rested a hand on his shoulder. "We believe you. Your sabotage probably bought us the chance to get here."

"We can't stay." Luke stuffed the worthless sending mirror into his satchel. "We'll find him and shatter that forging circle. If we hang around waiting for cavalry, we might as well gift-wrap this Dreadblade for Corgrave."

Jackson gritted his teeth. "Elarius, you'll come with us. I won't risk leaving you behind in this nest of wards."

The runeforger nodded. His arms shook, but he stood with Elinora's help. Another wash of molten metal smell wafted through the chamber, as if even the leftover husks of forging were rotting from misuse.

Jackson peered around, ensuring no uninvited guests lurked in the corners. A table lay overturned near the door, covered in scribbled notes. They were splashed with dried ink and flecks of blood, presumably Elarius' frantic scrawls. Broken runic rods littered the floor, scuffed by boots that had retreated in haste.

Riven slid Elarius' arm around her shoulders. "Let's get out of here."

They turned, stepping away from the anvil. Elinora pressed a palm to the forging station's nearest rod, verifying it would remain inert. The remains of runic power subsided beneath her chalk lines. "That should keep it from overloading. At least we won't blow ourselves up on the way out."

Luke threw her a tense smile. "Counting that in the column of small victories, yeah?" He shot a glance at Elarius' tired face. "You sure you can manage, old man?"

Elarius drew a quivering breath. "I have to. I'd rather collapse doing something meaningful than stay down here to die waiting for Corgrave's triumph."

Jackson reached the corridor first. The walls still vibrated with the leftover hum of powerful wards. He slowly led them past the threshold, guiding Elarius so he wouldn't stumble over the jagged stones. Elinora hovered in case another wave of energy rippled through the chamber, but the wards had collapsed into exhausted flickers.

As they stepped fully out, Elarius' foot caught on a loose fragment of basalt. Luke steadied him. The older man managed a shaky nod of thanks. "We can't give Corgrave any more time," he whispered. "He's almost completed the final runes. After the last lines of script are placed, the Dreadblade…"

Riven flexed her hands around her bow. "We've dealt with abominations before."

Elarius shook his head. "This is different. He's binding the steel to a necromantic anchor. If the blade's runes converge, it will siphon living auras for power. He wanted me to create a weapon that can spread terror across the kingdom. I stalled him as best I could, but he's too close now."

Elinora rested a supportive hand against Elarius' back. "We're not letting him succeed," she insisted, her voice low but fierce.

Luke frowned. "We can't call for backup, and we can't wait. That's a fine combination. Remind me to quit the hero business after this."

Jackson huffed, setting his jaw. "We don't have a choice." He glanced at Elarius. "Tell us exactly how it works, the Dreadblade. We need to understand."

Elarius closed his eyes, then spoke in a trembling voice. "He used volcanic steel from Ashenfold Dales, fusing it with Riftcrown crystals. The crystals act like amplifiers, taking raw magical potential and intensifying it. Then, the forging circle saturates that energy with necromantic essence.

"Normally, forging with these crystals is delicate, but Corgrave forced me to warp their properties. That means the Dreadblade can regrow its power by draining whoever it wounds. If a warrior so much as blocks its strike, the blade feasts on their life force. It can spark undead reavers in its wake if the forging runes are completed." His voice shook. "And Corgrave is hours, perhaps less than an hour, from finishing it."

Luke muttered a curse. Riven's mouth tightened with grim disgust.

Elarius' eyes glistened with desperation. "You reached me in time, but you must stop him. I can't fight, but I know he's in the upper halls. Please, whatever you do, don't let him finalize that blade."

Elinora nodded, voice trembling with emotion. "We won't."

Luke exhaled, pushing the useless mirror into his bag with a frustrated shove. "No cavalry. No time. We still have enough fight left. Let's move."

Jackson pressed a hand against Elarius' arm in silent reassurance. *We arrived in time*, he told himself, determined. *We'll do what must be done.* Yet the roiling energy in the fortress walls reminded him that too many dangers still lurked.

The necromantic wards might be only half of Corgrave's arsenal.

CHAPTER TWENTY-SEVEN

Jackson led the way up the crumbling steps, muscles burning. Elinora supported the runeforger's weary arm. Riven and Luke followed close behind, scanning the corridor for threats. Damp air clung to them, thick with the stench of abandoned magic gone sour. Their boots scraped over loose chunks of rubble. Small flakes of odd green moss dusted their ankles at every misstep.

At the final landing, the steps curved into a broad antechamber that smelled of old incense and candle wax. The floor was scattered with shattered candelabras, their metal frames bent and useless. Threads of thick, swirling energy, blue one moment, then an oily black the next, shimmered across the cracked tiles.

Elinora kept an arm around Elarius, helping him ascend the last step. The runeforger paused, sweat beading on his forehead, dread etched into every line of his face.

"We have to stop him," Elarius managed in a ragged whisper.

Elinora nodded, her expression set. "We'll handle him." She regarded Jackson with a flicker of determined steel in her gaze. "Let's end this."

Jackson felt a grim resonance in his chest. The infernal markings hidden beneath his collar ignited a faint warmth as if prodding him forward. He tightened his grip on his sword. "Everyone, stay together," he muttered.

The antechamber opened into a wide platform ringed by tall arches that must have once been glorious. Now, each arch was marred by fresh runic scrawl, twisted inscriptions pulsing with stolen crystal energy. At the platform's center stood a raised altar, the stone carved into swirling patterns that gleamed with malicious light.

A figure stood behind the altar, half-shrouded in drifting motes of arcane haze. Lord Arvest Corgrave. He turned slowly, revealing a face contorted with triumph and bitterness. He was clad in tattered finery bearing the faded crest of his disgraced house. Between his gloved hands, a curved sword caught the ambient glow. The steel's surface seemed alive, rippling in subtle waves. Runes along its length pulsed in a sinister pattern.

Luke froze in the doorway. He heaved an exaggerated sigh, sweeping an arm wide. "Of course we couldn't have made it in time," he grumbled, voice dripping sarcasm. "Show up, Dreadblade hasn't quite been finished, lop off Corgrave's head, we spin some tall tale about a valiant fight, and next thing you know, minstrels are singing about my heroic feats. Which obviously results in me being laid in every new town I visit."

He flashed a lopsided grin. "Little Lukes popping up across the continent. Life would've been grand. Did I say that out loud?"

Even Elinora paused, tears of tension mixing with a startled smirk. Jackson blinked, speechless. Riven turned and stared at Luke as if he'd announced a plan to tame a rabid dragon with a teacup.

Corgrave's gaze flicked to Luke curiously, and the corners of his mouth twitched in brief confusion. Then, his mouth settled into a disdainful curl.

He cut a hand through the air. "You wretches stole everything from me. My birthright, my lands, and my future. Now you add insult by slinking into my domain?" His voice cracked with emotion. He raised the curved blade in a slow, deliberate gesture. "You stand in the presence of the Dreadblade," he hissed. "Forged from volcanic steel and Riftcrown crystals, tempered in runic spells that kings feared centuries ago. This should have been my family's legacy."

Elinora stepped around a shattered candelabra, steadying Elarius against her side. "You used an innocent man's talents to create a monstrous weapon. You twisted forging rites until they're barely recognizable."

"Spare me the lecture, Lady Riftwyn," Corgrave spat. "Your mother should have understood that one cannot maintain power by kneeling to a false king. Look at Kharadorn's sorry state. Barely stable, fragile alliances, crippling fear of another rebellion. The throne spat on my house when we surrendered, let rodents pick my home apart, and called it justice. This kingdom never cared for the rightful families who built it!"

His voice trembled with resentment. So much hatred poured from him that the swirling runic inscriptions on the altar brightened with fresh malevolence. "I will tear down the illusions of peace. I will end this farce of a stable realm. Then, when Kharadorn collapses, they'll remember who truly had the will to shape destiny."

Corgrave's knuckles whitened around the Dreadblade's hilt. Arcane runes danced along the steel, each symbol bristling with stolen energy. Luke's cheek twitched at the sight. "He's definitely monologuing," he muttered. "That sword's about to do something nasty."

Riven readied an arrow, her keen gaze locked on Corgrave. She angled closer to the far side of the platform, making a slow attempt to flank. "We could try hitting him from two directions," she whispered to Luke.

Corgrave's dark glare flicked across them. "Try it." He

sneered. "That blade devours magic and repels lesser strikes. My wards are woven into every inch of steel. If you think your cheap parlor tricks can breach it, be my guest."

Luke exchanged an uncertain look with Riven. She decided to test his bravado anyway. She replaced her ready arrow in her quiver and withdrew a runic arrow etched with bright ward-piercing lines, the best she had left. Luke dipped into his satchel and produced a small flash grenade, swirling with faint runic wisps. They nodded in unspoken agreement.

They sprang apart, Luke pivoting right to pitch the flash grenade, Riven darting left to draw aim. Corgrave snarled under his breath. The Dreadblade's aura distorted the air around him, warping the geometry of the platform as if reality itself were bending. The grenade soared in, but the swirling, inky tendrils that shrouded Corgrave's presence batted it aside. The device clattered to the floor and detonated in a burst of wasted brilliance.

Riven loosed her arrow at the same instant. It soared true until Corgrave raised the blade. The arrow's velocity sputtered, then fizzled, dropping like a stone at his feet. A faint spark of dispelled magic crackled along the shaft before it broke in two.

Riven hissed in frustration, stepping back to assess her next move.

Corgrave twisted the blade, and a creeping wave of blackish power surged outward, forcing Luke and Riven to lurch back. They nearly lost their footing. The air tasted metallic, and a subtle beehive buzz slithered against the walls.

Jackson advanced, scowling at the nauseating vibes rolling off the weapon.

Elinora urged Elarius to stay behind a broken pillar, then tried to channel her father's forging talisman, a polished artifact shaped like an elongated diamond. She aimed it at the swirling runes, her whispers full of desperate flickers of magic. But a shriek of feedback tore through the air, and she nearly dropped the talisman as dark arcs leaped from the Dreadblade to her device.

She hissed in pain and stumbled back, her forearm scorched by black sparks. "That blade's corruption is unimaginably dense."

Jackson's demonic fire stirred with a violent jolt, as if something in that blade spoke the same foul language. The skin on his throat prickled. He reached deep into the infernal power he typically tried to subdue. The red sigils coiled around his neck flared, feeding off his anger at Corgrave's spiteful arrogance. Heat raced along his arms.

He exhaled and summoned the Hell-Forged armor, letting its chaotic energies swirl through him. A moment later, blood-red glyphs shimmered around his torso, congealing into plates of blackened metal that pulsed with malevolent runes. The armor's surface rippled like it was alive. Gazing upon Jackson was akin to staring into some fiendish war champion from a demon-fueled nightmare.

Corgrave's grin twisted. "So, the rumors were true. The King's Eye had a demon dog on their leash. How fitting."

Jackson advanced without retort, steps resonating with raw power. The aura radiating off Corgrave's blade met the hellish glow of Jackson's armor in midair, forming jagged sparks that flared across the platform.

Riven flattened herself behind a piece of debris, forcibly shielding her face from the crackling arcs. Luke crouched beside her, eyes wide.

"Where do we even aim now?" Luke stammered.

Riven's expression was grim, but her voice did not waver. "We wait for an opening. That's all we can do."

Elinora hovered by Elarius, pressing a waterskin to his lips, then offering him a worried glance.

He shook his head. "The failsafe is rigged to the forging circle. If Corgrave's lost control or if the blade suffers catastrophic disruption, the runic meltdown might breach everything."

Elinora's lips tightened. She prepared another attempt with her forging talisman, but it was clear halting the meltdown would require far more than a single stroke of magic.

At the center of the platform, Corgrave lifted the Dreadblade in both hands. "You speak of monstrous weapons," he growled. "Yet I see only hypocrisy. Kharadorn's dear champion stands by using demonic might, and you dare condemn what I forged for my own survival? The kingdom turned its back on me first. Let it reap the consequences."

Jackson lunged forward. Corgrave lashed out, and their weapons sparked in a thunderous collision that reverberated through the stone. The shockwave rippled outward, rattling the walls, echoing in a low, deafening rumble. Spiderweb fractures danced across the floor.

Jackson's blade caught an arc of pale necromantic energy that shot across his Hell-Forged armor, scraping it with a teeth-rattling force. Heat climbed his throat as if a furnace roared under his skin, but he held fast. His eyes narrowed behind the glowing visor of infernal metal.

Corgrave pressed, unleashing a vicious cyclone of strikes fueled by bitterness. Jackson met each blow, his demon-fire flaring. Sparks of greenish-black lit the platform with every clash. The swirling runes on the floor flickered ominously, and an eerie tension built in the air. Stones ground on stones. Somewhere behind a fractured arch, Luke ducked away from flying debris.

Riven risked another shot, but the swirling aura shoved her arrow aside again. "Pointless," she muttered, lips curling in frustration. She gestured for Luke to hold tight. Perhaps Corgrave would slip. Perhaps Jackson could create a fleeting gap in that tide of malevolence.

Jackson and Corgrave slammed swords again, flinging arcs of sizzling magic across the stones. Corgrave snarled, his eyes glinting with mania. "I was cast aside by your precious monarch. You know nothing of my losses!" His voice echoed in a rising pitch. "Now, I hold a key to rewriting Kharadorn's future. The Dreadblade devours your meddling illusions. It's unstoppable."

Shrieking energy laced the next strike. Jackson gritted his teeth, forced to yield half a step. The demon-fire in his veins crackled angrily. He pivoted, forcing a counterattack that smashed the Dreadblade's flank. Sparks flew, painting the dais in a sickly glow. The strain in Corgrave's face deepened. He roared, fierce and ragged. Their locked weapons dripped with arcs of chaotic light.

Luke bolted from his cover and tried to circle behind Corgrave. Riven followed, ready to diagram a possible shot. But dark pulses spewed in all directions from the blade, forming a net of roiling energy. They both had to spring back. The stone at the platform's edge cracked and crumbled away into the darkness below, leaving dust swirling in a gaping hole.

Elinora struggled to find a stable vantage, forging talisman at the ready, but every time she approached, waves of hateful magic lashed out, pushing her back with gut-wrenching force. She braced herself against a chunk of broken pillar, glancing to the runic altar. The swirling mass of etched runes on the floor was growing more and more agitated. Each clash fed it like an overfilled flask trembling on the verge of explosion.

"Jackson!" she cried. "We're fueling the meltdown by letting this fight escalate."

He heard her, but his attention remained locked on Corgrave's hateful scream. The lord hammered another blow down, brute force spiked with arcane might. Jackson's sword braced it, but the floor cracked under him. *Not good*, he thought. *I can't let him walk away with that blade.* He let the demon-fire churn, reinforcing his stance, driving the Dreadblade's assault back an inch at a time.

The Dreadblade pulsed with renewed fervor. A swirl of black lines burned along its length, and an unholy shriek tore through the air. The swirling runes beneath them flared a harsh, sickly green, radiating out in jagged lines. The entire tower seemed to quiver. Small stones tumbled from the ceiling, and the dais trembled with building energy, resonating with the thunder of their final clash.

Luke flinched. "Uh, that can't be good," he yelled over the clamor, shading his eyes against the brightening glare. Riven grabbed his shoulder, struggling to maintain balance on the shaking floor. Elinora covered Elarius protectively.

Jackson planted his feet, pushing one last time against Corgrave's blade. For a heartbeat, they locked gazes, one consumed by vengeance, the other driven by a vow to protect. Then, a colossal discharge erupted between them, a wave of runic backlash that seared the air with screaming force. Both men lurched back, separated by surging arcs of molten light. Corgrave stumbled, eyes wide, the Dreadblade still twitching in his hands.

In that instant, the forging circle on the floor exploded with brilliance, arcs dancing wildly. Elarius' voice rose in alarm. "The failsafe. He's awakened it!"

From the center of the dais, runic lines swarmed outward in unstoppable fractal patterns. Half-living energy coalesced around the Dreadblade's tip, an electric storm of doom swirling faster than any of them could contain. Elinora's forging talisman sparked in her hand, powerless to quell it. Luke and Riven shouted over the roar, though their words drowned in the ear-splitting crescendo. Jackson's armor flickered with demonic flames, bracing for whatever cataclysm was about to break loose.

With a single, shrill keening, the meltdown sequence activated.

CHAPTER TWENTY-EIGHT

Jackson's boots skidded on stone shards as Corgrave staggered back, clutching the Dreadblade with trembling hands. A savage glint of triumph burned in the disgraced lord's eyes even as his lip curled in pain. Above him, arcs of twisted energy leaped from the sword's blade to the vaulted ceiling in venomous green streaks. The tower shuddered as if some invisible net had been thrown around it and was now tightening with each frantic heartbeat.

Corgrave's hoarse, taunting voice cut through the haze. "My dear rescuers. You think you've won?" His free hand pressed over his ribcage, where fresh bruises bloomed from Jackson's last strike. "If I lose this sword..." He gave a rasping cough that turned into a crooked smile. "Everyone pays."

A swirl of sickly aura intensified around the weapon, blotting out the sputtering torches with flashes of nauseating green. Elinora, crouched behind a cracked pillar with Master Elarius, inhaled sharply. Beneath her pale gaze, the floor glowed with necromantic sigils.

She traced them with one finger, her body tense. "This sequence is tapping the Riftcrown crystals," she told Elarius, voice trembling at the edges. "And feeding off the volcanic steel's heat. We have to sever the runic circuit."

Elarius' face was gaunt and slick with sweat, his breath hitching in ragged gasps. "Corgrave forced me to design a chain reaction. If the meltdown isn't stopped, the backlash will blow, not only here, but possibly the entire gorge." His knuckles whitened against the heaps of broken crystal rods piled around him. "Gods help us, it could bury us all."

Meanwhile, half of Corgrave's assembled mercenaries, seeing the violent arcs overhead, wavered and began backing away. Some looked downright terrified, gazes darting from the blade to the trembling stone walls.

A burly sergeant shoved them forward. "He'll kill us if we disobey. Push forward!" The man's armor rattled as he advanced, runic rifle at the ready. His mouth curled in fear, but desperation fueled his next scream. "We hold them off or burn either way!"

Jackson's infernal markings flared in response to the twisted aura. Heat prickled along his throat and collar, forcing him to swallow hard. *We stop Corgrave, or we die here.* That singular truth thrummed in his mind.

He stood near the center of the platform, sword angled low, demon-fire twitching around him in faint red flickers. Corgrave lifted the Dreadblade again, arcs of crackling necromantic light curving through the air to slam against Jackson's waiting blade.

Their weapons crashed with a jarring shockwave that made Luke, crouching near a toppled statue, shout a frantic curse. Chips of masonry rained down, spattering off Luke's cloak. He patted frantically at small embers clinging to the leg of his pants.

"I swear," he yelled. "Flames keep finding my crotch like they've got personal vendettas!" He rolled behind the statue, an old effigy of some forgotten knight, and tried to aim a hastily gathered throwing knife at the mercenaries pressing in from the left.

Riven dropped to a knee on a chunk of collapsed archway.

Without hesitation, she nocked an arrow etched with her last remaining ward-piercing script and loosed it. The arrow soared across the chamber in a silver streak. It punched through a mercenary's pauldron and sent him sprawling with a ragged scream. Sparks sizzled as his rifle misfired, the shot ricocheting off the wall in a vivid burst of green flame.

Elinora clenched her teeth, pressing a hand against the stone, and called over her shoulder, "Master Elarius, guide me!" Her other hand traced the complex runes carved into the floor, warding circles that Corgrave had twisted into triggers. The loops brimmed with frantic arcs of magic, enough to sear flesh if touched incorrectly. Elinora's silver pendant gleamed, the only steady light in the storm of chaos.

Elarius forced a steady breath. "Find the anchor glyph near the perimeter," he urged. "Use a chalk wedge. We invert the route of mana along those lines..." His words caught as more debris crashed behind them.

"War-hammering scum!" a mercenary roared, lunging from behind a broken column. He swung a short sword at Elinora, eyes wild with panic.

Before the blade could hit, a dagger whizzed through the air and embedded itself in the attacker's shoulder, courtesy of Luke. The mercenary reeled, cursing in agony. Luke risked a quick grin at Elinora. "Letting them kill you would ruin all our fun," he panted.

Elinora nodded briskly and refocused. She drew a half-circle onto the floor in pale luminescent chalk, trying to connect it with the existing lines. The second her chalk touched the runes, a jolt of sickening green energy spat sparks at her wrist. She hissed, ignoring the sting. A swirl of runic text hissed around her ankles, resisting her efforts, but she pressed the wedge against a portion of the design. "Elarius, line up now!" she shouted.

They worked in tandem, Elarius trembling but resolute, guiding her with short, precise commands. Each swirl of chalk shifted the meltdown's flow, attempting to reroute the lethal surge. If they succeeded, it might buy them enough time to contain, or at least delay, the chain reaction. If they failed...no chance to reevaluate that.

At the platform's center, Jackson and Corgrave exchanged furious blows. Their blades locked in a storm of sparks, illuminating Jackson's drawn features. Every clang rang in time with the meltdown's rising pulse. Cracks snaked along the walls, and the entire chamber groaned under the building pressure.

A fresh wave of mana arcs flared around the Dreadblade, scorching black lines across Jackson's Hell-Forged armor. He released a ragged breath, forcing more of his demon-fire up through his arms. Their weapons sparked with a hellish brilliance, red colliding with sickly green. "You've lost," Jackson rasped.

Corgrave's eyes were ringed with madness. "No," he managed, a wicked sneer twisting his lips. "This sword devours everything. Your precious king will watch his realm collapse to ashes!"

With a guttural roar, Jackson slid a foot forward and slammed his shoulder into Corgrave, forcing him back. The two nearly slipped on broken shards of basalt, sparks dancing around them like angry hornets. A chunk of the ceiling groaned ominously overhead.

Riven gasped and sprang aside as a slab of stone crashed down, sending shockwaves through the floor. Dust choked the air. One of Corgrave's riflemen tripped in panic and fell screaming into a jagged chasm opening near the platform's edge.

In the swirling haze, Luke released a startled yelp when a spray of green flame hissed along the ground. He leaped over it, face contorted. "Closest shave since that time with the mayor's daughter," he wheezed, patting out glowing embers on his boot. "I cannot catch a break today!"

Riven ignored him. She fired another arrow, crippling the last rifleman who had been stubbornly taking aim at Elinora. The man's rifle sputtered and died. She advanced, face grim, scanning the chamber for more threats. The quiver at her hip was nearly spent, but she kept her posture steady. "Luke, if you can move, push the mercenaries back," she shouted. "I'll guard Elinora and Elarius."

Luke gave a frantic salute, snatched another knife from a belt sheath, and darted around the toppled statue. The mercenaries who refused to retreat were pinned between the meltdown's swirling arcs and Jackson's frenzied group. Some had dropped their weapons altogether and were cowering behind half-collapsed columns, but a pair remained, barking curses as they tried to corner Jackson from behind.

They never got the chance. Jackson pivoted with lethal grace, sword striking out in a flare of demon-fire. The wave of heat that followed sent the two mercenaries staggering. One collapsed, clutching a charred wound, while the other tumbled off a crumbling ledge with a final, panicked wail that cut short in echoing darkness.

Corgrave howled in frustration. Blood streaked his chin, and his breath rasped like a man on the brink of madness. The Dreadblade's aura flared to a blinding intensity. "You think wiping out a few hired swords can stop me?" he spat. "I will bury every last one of you under these ruins!"

Elarius jerked in alarm as a deep tremor rocked the tower. "The meltdown is cascading faster! We're not inverting it quickly enough," he croaked.

Elinora's voice wavered. "We need an anchor to drain the malignant energy. Something big enough to funnel the overload…" She looked desperately at the chalk lines. Her hair stuck to her damp forehead. "I can redirect part of the current, but I need more time."

They had none. Another hail of debris thundered down. Riven threw herself in front of Elarius, blocking chunks of falling stone with a snapped-off piece of broken wooden scaffolding. She exhaled in relief when the debris tumbled aside.

Across the platform, Jackson used the momentary lull to unleash his own desperation. His infernal markings seared with unnatural light. He lunged forward with unbridled force, blade singing as it cut through the noxious aura around Corgrave.

Sparks from the Dreadblade lashed out in furious arcs, scorching Jackson's gauntlet. Ignoring the pain, he pressed his advantage, fueling each strike with the maddening fire that roiled within him. Their swords locked again, shrieking, the entire dais pulsing with deadly rhythm.

Corgrave released a strangled laugh. "You're a puppet for that king," he snarled. "My house was cast out, yet I stand here with the power to reshape everything. You? You're merely a tool."

Jackson's answer was another brutal slash, forcing Corgrave back toward the massive, half-fractured runic altar. The exiled lord's shoulders shook, but the arcs only grew in intensity, as if feeding on his twisted determination.

Luke fended off dislodged rubble and slid closer to Elinora, yelling over the roar of collapsing stone, "Any chance we can, you know, skip all these steps and switch this thing off?"

Elinora's eyes blazed with frustration. "The wards are fused to that blade. We have to break its link or subdue it long enough to neutralize the runes." She braced a trembling hand against the floor, checking the half-finished lines she was trying to carve with chalk. "Elarius, push the last pivot. Do it now!"

Clutching the wedge with shaking fingers, Elarius pressed it against a set of pulsing glyphs. The runes spat arcs of green flame up his arm, searing his tattered sleeve. He choked back a cry but jammed the wedge firmly. A sputter sounded in the runic circle, and part of the field dimmed. For a brief moment, the air felt less suffocating.

That was all the opening Jackson needed. With a final surge, he pushed aside Corgrave's guard and slammed his pommel into the exiled lord's ribs, sending him reeling to one side. Corgrave coughed, nearly colliding with a half-toppled sconce. For an instant, the Dreadblade wobbled in his grasp, almost slipping free. A flash of raw panic crossed his face.

Then, a twisted grin returned.

"Fool. I can still end this on my terms," Corgrave hissed. He gripped the hilt tighter. The meltdown runes flared again, brighter than before, forcing everyone to shield their eyes. Deafening pops of mana blasted overhead. It felt like the air itself was tearing apart at the seams.

Chunks of masonry broke from the walls, smashing into the ground in bursts of dust. One chunk tore past Luke, who dove onto his belly with a squeak of terror. He scrambled behind an overturned workbench. "This is insane!" he shouted. "I'd rather be telling tall tales of heroics to peasants in a cozy tavern than risk getting flattened!"

Riven's next arrow whistled past Corgrave's shoulder, narrowly missing a chance to disarm him. Another wave of sizzling green energy flicked the arrow aside, as though the blade itself refused to allow any direct shot to land. She narrowed her gaze, readied another arrow, but a new quake rattled the platform, making her footing uncertain.

A savage roar escaped Jackson's throat. His demon-fire spiraled around him in a hazy crimson swirl. He closed the distance again, sword raised high, ignoring the stabs of necromantic energy biting at his limbs. The tower groaned in protest, rubble cascading from the upper vault. Elinora threw her arms over her head, bracing herself as more dust and shards crashed nearer.

Corgrave bared his teeth, brandishing the Dreadblade in a final, defiant arc. The aura crackled dangerously at the tip, intensifying so much that the jagged runes on the blade glowed white-hot. "The realm is built on treachery!" he roared. "Burn with me, knight!" The next instant, he launched himself forward in a reckless lunge.

Jackson parried the blow with a jarring *clang* that sent tremors through his shoulders. For a breathless second, they stood locked face-to-face, each forcing the other's blade away inch by inch. Energy crackled in swirling eddies around them, scorching the stone beneath their feet.

Green arcs seared the edges of Jackson's vision. *I can't let him keep the blade.* He mustered every shred of infernal strength, driving his sword in a sharp upward angle that bashed aside Corgrave's guard.

An instant later, his palm flared with unholy power. The demon-fire coiled around the blade of his weapon and struck Corgrave's side in an explosive burst. Corgrave screamed, stumbling backward. The Dreadblade slipped from his grip, dripping runic sparks. The entire dais lurched, and more of the floor collapsed away in a thundering crunch.

From behind, Elarius cried out a warning, "If he drops it now..."

He never finished. Corgrave somehow wrenched the blade back under control, even as agony twisted his features. Sweat streaked his face, and his breathing grew ragged. But he refused to let go. Energy rippled in harsh waves from the Dreadblade's runes, scorching more lines into the walls.

Jackson clenched his teeth. Elinora and Elarius were still fighting to divert the final explosion, but time was running out. "Riven, keep him pinned!" he bellowed. Another quake rattled the stones underfoot. Luke hissed a curse as he nearly lost his footing trying to rush to Jackson's flank.

Corgrave's eyes gleamed with vengeful light. "You'll never drown my house in shame again," he spat. The circling runes flared, a maelstrom poised to tip over the edge.

Jackson glimpsed the mania in Corgrave's stare. *This ends now.* Heat pricked every inch of his body. His gauntlet glowed with a furious red hue, responding to his own rage. Holding his sword in a two-handed grip, he launched forward in a savage combination, forging a blur of steel and infernal flame.

Corgrave parried desperately, but the raw violence of Jackson's strikes hammered him against the altar. Sparks rained from the Dreadblade, each discharge bright enough to burn afterimages across the chamber.

Above them, the ring whined, arcs of lightning ripping across the ceiling. The exiled lord refused to yield. He pressed the blade into a final lock, tension shaking through both men's arms.

Jackson roared, channeling an unholy surge into his blade. Demon-fire surged through his veins, fueling one last blow. Steel met steel with a thunderous clash.

Corgrave's defense finally fractured under the assault. He staggered back, eyes wide, as the meltdown's energy churned to a blistering crescendo around them.

CHAPTER TWENTY-NINE

Cracked stone rained from the rafters as a roar filled the fortress like an onrushing tide. The entire structure trembled under the runaway arcane energy spewing from the Dreadblade, which lay near Corgrave's motionless form. Jackson stood over the body, gasping for breath, eyes locked on the sword's sinister glow. What should have been a victory felt far from safe.

A sudden burst of violet sparks lanced upward from the blade, scouring a crooked path to the ceiling. With a heavy groan, gargoyles perched high on the stone supports lost their footing and crashed in a deafening avalanche of rubble.

All around, energy spilled out in twisting arcs that slammed into pillars, walls, and unfortunate souls still huddled behind fallen debris. The fortress courtyard had become a war zone of crackling mana and swirling dust.

Corgrave's limp figure slumped on the ground, cloaked in a swirling haze of spent necromancy. Jackson still half-expected the man's eyes to flick open in one last, brutal hex, but the exiled lord's chest did not rise again.

The faint stench of brimstone clung to the remains of the Dreadblade. Arcs of molten green traced across the weapon, an unstable beacon calling doom upon the tower. Each snap of energy made the hair on Jackson's arms prickle. He gave Corgrave's body one final glare, as though daring it to move, then turned to scan the chaos beyond.

"Jackson, look at the altar!" Elinora's voice cut through the thunderous din. She dashed forward, ignoring the shards of broken tile scraping her palms. Runes lay scorched into the floor, and greenish cracks crawling with arcane heat webbed outward.

Elinora's arms shook under the strain, partly from pain, partly from pure adrenaline. *We don't have time*, her eyes said as she scooped up a runic chisel from the ground. Its handle was scorched black, but she clutched it like a lifeline.

Elarius crouched beside her, shoulders trembling. "The loop is feeding off the blade's core, twisting every scrap of magic left!" Grit stained the older runeforger's cheeks, and fresh sweat gleamed across his brow. His voice trembled, but his hands found surprising steadiness while he gripped a second small chisel. Distress flickered across his face as the tower's stones groaned and split around them.

Riven thrust past a collapsed beam. "We have to seal it before the entire fortress collapses." Her voice was all focus.

A ragged shout came from further down the courtyard as Luke wrestled a trembling guard away from the meltdown zone. The guard's face was pale with terror, runic rifle half-forgotten in his hands. "Out!" Luke barked. "Move! Unless you want to get incinerated along with your boss!"

He practically hurled the guard aside. Then, he spun, trying to corral more panicked mercenaries who sprinted in all directions, uncertain whether fleeing or fighting might keep them alive. Some still clung to their rifles, firing haphazardly at phantoms in the swirling haze. The muzzle flashes revealed twisted expressions of fear.

Luke's face contorted as he dodged an errant blast that

scorched the stone behind him. "Fine, keep blasting at thin air if you want to die. I'm done babysitting!"

Across from him, several Thornvein militia crouched behind scalded chunks of masonry, scanning for pockets of danger. Their crossbow strings were taut, but the meltdown's arcs careened unpredictably, forcing them to abandon any neat formation. The constant thunder of collapsing architecture turned everything into a swirl of dust and terror.

Jackson's gaze flicked to the Dreadblade, still spitting crackling mana. *We can't let the explosion rip this place apart.* He gritted his teeth. Corgrave's final contingency threatened to render their victory meaningless. The fortress was falling, and with it, any chance to keep the devastation contained.

He allowed himself a shaky breath, then commanded his Hell-Forged armor to release. A low rumble started at the base of his throat, and the black plates covering his body flickered. Cracks of red light shimmered along the edges, the runes etched into the metal pulsing in dissonant unison.

Then, as though drawn by invisible strings, the pieces peeled away from his frame. Each plate lurched into the air in a swirl of brimstone fog, then spiraled into a twisting funnel over Jackson's shoulder.

He closed his eyes and exhaled, letting the demon-fire embedded in his blood coax the armor back to its infernal source. Plate by plate, it vanished in flickers of embers until no black metal remained. A faint tang of sulfur wafted off him. His breathing grew raw, but relief coursed through every nerve as the punishing weight lifted.

Next to Corgrave's corpse, the Dreadblade snapped and hissed, nearly overshadowing the swirling cinder-lights of Jackson's armor returning to the ether.

He tasted grit on his tongue, but that was nothing new. Every muscle ached as he stepped toward the runic altar. At its center,

Elinora and Elarius hammered at the floor, chisels scraping arcs into the stone that glowed with dim runic lines.

Riven drove another chisel in place, her fingers precise and quick, sweat glistening on her cheeks. Each blow was a desperate attempt to carve out a counter-seal that might channel the meltdown's runaway energy. With the tower trembling around them, it seemed a fool's errand. Yet none of them paused.

Elinora's gaze locked with Jackson as he approached. "We need your fire," she shouted over the clamor. She pressed a chunk of Riftwyn crystal into his free hand. "If we merge it with your infernal spark, maybe we can contain this."

He nodded, swallowing. "Guide me."

She placed an unsteady hand on his wrist, and he felt the chill of the crystal. A jolt of mana flared through him, stirring the embers of the demon-fire coiled around his heart. He inhaled. The lingering warmth of the armor's departure still resided in his veins, a stubborn reservoir of power resisting total dispersal.

Elarius had once explained that infernal flame could devour twisted magic like a wolf snapping at a wounded creature. It was dangerous, but they had run out of safe options.

The runeforger glanced up. "Keep it steady, Jackson. You have to filter the arcs before channeling them to our seals." He struck his chisel against the stone again, weaving runes in a frantic dance with Riven. "Elinora, bolster him with the crystals. We'll angle the flow into the ground. Hurry!"

Another quake rattled the floor. Luke dove behind a fallen statue in time to avoid a falling catwalk. Sparks spewed from a half-collapsed corridor, sending shrill whistles into the choking air. Bits of corrupted stone flickered with green light, scorching the floor wherever they landed. Across the way, a handful of mercenaries finally dropped their rifles, stumbling away from the crumbling battlements with hands raised in surrender.

Jackson exhaled and summoned a faint flicker of demon-fire around his left palm. It glowed ruddy orange, like the last coal in a dying forge. Elinora pressed the carved crystal wedge against his flame, letting her own faint magic flow into the union. She whined in pain, maybe from stress or from the lacerations scoring her arms, but she held firm.

Together, they coaxed the swirling arcs to shift direction, drag toward the funnel of infernal heat that flared against the darkened air.

A terrible buzzing noise came from the Dreadblade's tip. Blackish tendrils of necromantic discharge lashed out, snapping at the edges of Jackson's flame. The two forces wrestled, spitting and crackling until Jackson forced more of his infernal power forward, forging a bridge to the runic circle Elinora and Elarius crafted at their feet.

The arcs writhed like serpents in a net, then collapsed toward the single point of demonic incandescence. The ground shook again, pitching them into a precarious lean.

"Just a bit more!" Elinora hissed, lines of concentration etched across her face. A swirl of crystal-laced mana spiraled around her chisel as she hammered the final glyph. The shapes glowed with a flickering green that warred against the red of Jackson's demonfire.

An ear-splitting crack rang out from the fortress walls, an entire section of rampart peeled away in a thunderous crash, falling into the black abyss beyond. Wind and dust clawed inside, swirling fragments of mortar and broken beams. The power pulsed in a moment of near-panic, as if it would tear everything to pieces.

Jackson grunted, bracing one foot against a shattered chunk of tile. *Hold, damn it.*

Elarius drove his chisel one last time. "Now!" He pressed his palm against the etched lines, pushing a final surge of will.

Jackson roared, channeling everything left in him. Fear, rage, the dogged loyalty that refused to let them all die here. His hand flared in a luminous spiral of red-orange flame, the Riftwyn crystal intensifying the heat until it burned too bright to look at. Each arc collided with that swirling glow and fed into the runic seal.

The next wave slammed forward, but this time, it didn't erupt outward. Instead, the arcs curled in, streaming into the circle Elinora, Riven, and Elarius had completed. The unholy energies spiraled tighter, spinning with a wild hiss. Floor tiles cracked further, spreading spiderweb lines across the dais.

Then, with a deafening whoosh, the fiery swirl collapsed into itself, dragging the Dreadblade's glow into a final, furious knot. Fire flared, and for an instant, the night turned as bright as noon.

Jackson clenched his teeth, sweat trickling down his brow. He felt the energy buckle, felt it yield to the synergy of crystal magic and demon-fire. A heartbeat later, the unholy power rippled, shuddered, then imploded in a gush of harmless sparks. The ground sagged, then jolted upright, as though the tower's very foundations exhaled a breath of relief.

The swirling haze dissipated in a slow swirl of dust. Only a handful of sputtering embers remained. No roaring arcs of corrupted power, no twisted necromantic glow. The cursed Dreadblade slumped by Corgrave's side, its steel cracked down the length, runes extinguished.

In the courtyard beyond, pockets of arcane flames still smoldered, but the meltdown was conquered. As a patch of dust cleared, Luke and a few Thornvein militia rushed forward, stamping out lingering embers from stray runic rifles. One soldier groaned in relief when the final arcs fizzled from his steel breastplate. Another, face streaked with soot, collapsed to his knees, letting out a disbelieving laugh.

Jackson's vision wavered. He sank, knees colliding with the floor. A wave of exhaustion deeper than any he'd felt in previous fights crashed over him. He forced his head up enough to see Elinora's soot-streaked face. She caught his shoulder with trembling hands and gave him the barest nod of encouragement.

From behind them, Luke emerged. The rogue surveyed the ruin, eyes wide at the cratered sides of the courtyard. Above, mangled rafters and walls were barely upright. He reached down to help press a strip of cloth against a shallow gash on Jackson's forearm. "You, uh, about gave me a heart attack."

Jackson slumped forward, letting Elinora straighten him. She brushed loose curls of hair from her damp forehead, her own arms trembling with the aftershock of raw magic. "We ended it," she whispered, glancing at the crippled Dreadblade. "It's powerless."

They turned at a scraping sound. Riven limped over from the collapsed archway, short of breath, bandaging a scrape on her temple. She surveyed the shattered rifles and the ragged mercenaries stepping out with hands raised. Soot tinted her silver hair. She didn't speak, but her eyes shone with fierce satisfaction.

Luke dropped to a knee, joining them in an exhausted circle. He released a half-laugh, half-sigh. "If that had gotten any worse, I'd have been flatter than a halfling's pancake." His grin twisted into a feigned glare at Jackson. "And you. *Now* you decided to fling that armor around? Seriously?"

Jackson sagged, exhaling a heavy breath. "It pulls from Hell," he managed. "The more I use it..." He swallowed, voice raw. "The more I risk my soul."

Luke's eyes widened as he rubbed the back of his neck. "Oh." He glanced at the patch of ground where the last sulfuric sparks had vanished. "Yeah, my bad."

CHAPTER THIRTY

Jackson stood among the rubble, breathing air that tasted of ash and lingering sparks. The dawn light came slowly. Its weak glow settled over toppled walls and charred debris. Blistered stone sloped away from him in every direction, the remains of a once-imposing tower that groaned through the night.

It wasn't long before reinforcements from House Morrivale and Baroness Thornvein's militia arrived, their boots crunching on scorched gravel as they secured the smoldering ruins.

Some of Corgrave's devotees shuffled across the rubble in small, broken groups, their heads lowered. They paused in fearful awe at the sight of the remains lying crumpled near the collapsed altar. Only a few hours ago, the man threatened to bring down the entire tower with his meltdown weapon. Now, all his ambitions had burned away.

Jackson watched in grim silence as the mercenaries dropped their spears or runic rifles. They muttered frantic promises of surrender to anyone willing to listen. He felt an odd relief at their submission, but no satisfaction. The blitz of destruction he unleashed could have wiped them all out.

Luke limped across the courtyard with a tired grin on his face.

He clutched his side, probably bruised to the bone, and mustered his signature brand of cheer. How he found it within himself, Jackson couldn't tell.

"I never found a danger pay contract that covered potential explosions," Luke remarked, waving at the militia. "We almost got incinerated, so does that mean I get a bonus?" He shook his head, then winked. "Too bad there was low opportunity for horizontal activities on this job. I could have at least used that as part of my hazard pay."

Jackson snorted. "Your ambition is truly inspirational, Luke." His voice sounded hoarse. His throat had not recovered from yelling warnings as the arcs swarmed them through the night.

Luke laughed under his breath, then nudged Jackson with one elbow. "I can't raise morale by standing around frowning, you moody Hellspawn. Someone's gotta lighten the mood." He glanced at several Thornvein soldiers carefully sweeping piles of rubble. "They're making sure the residue is stable. They said it can still flare up unpredictably?"

Jackson nodded. "It might." His gauntlet, scorched from summoning his cursed armor, ached at the memory. "Master Elarius can help with that. If the remnants are bled off with the right ritual, we won't see any more cracks of wild magic." His gaze drifted to a makeshift canopy stitched together from tarps. Elarius stood beneath it, hair disheveled and robes torn. He was greeting new arrivals, offering teary thanks.

Elarius noticed Jackson and waved him closer. The knight trudged over the uneven ground, stepping around a collapsed column. The old runeforger's eyes shone with hope behind his spectacles. His hands still trembled, probably from working so long under Corgrave's brutal captivity. How long had it been since he'd last slept or had a proper meal? Probably too long. It was a wonder the man was still alive. Jackson had seen stranger things, though.

"Thank you," he rasped as Jackson drew near. "You and your

allies saved more than me. This could have buried half the region." He rubbed the raw scalds on his wrists. "I promise my forging experience will go toward rebuilding what was nearly ruined. We can restore at least some of these wards properly and see that no one abuses them again."

His relief was contagious. Jackson rested a hand on his shoulder, ignoring the throbbing in his arm, and forced a small smile. "We trust you, Master Elarius. The kingdom does, too." His voice caught.

Past Elarius, Jackson glimpsed a figure in leathers, silvery hair cascading over her bandaged temple. Riven stood watch at the tower's crumbled edge, bow at her side. A thin line of dried blood edged her forehead, but she looked composed, confident, and lethal. No one dared approach her but Jackson.

She leveled him with an even stare as he neared.

"Glad to see you upright," Jackson managed, attempting a quiet greeting.

She nodded. "Better to see you not buried under falling debris." Then, to his surprise, one corner of her mouth lifted.

Jackson inclined his head in thanks, then stepped aside when she returned her focus to scanning the perimeter. He noticed none of the militia men or Morrivale soldiers had tried to talk to her. She had a daunting aura. Still, she exuded the trustworthiness that came from an archer who never missed.

A flash of light drew his attention away from the elf. Elinora knelt near what remained of the dais, beside a broken mass of twisted metal. She carefully lifted a jagged piece of the once-dreaded blade and inspected it as green sparks flickered along the fractured length. Closing her eyes, she channeled a runic glow from her pendant and touched it to the blackened shard. The noxious green aura sputtered, then died.

Jackson moved beside her. He noticed the set of her jaw, how the corners of her eyes tightened with tension. She had never looked more determined, or more exhausted.

She glanced up. "I think we have all the major fragments. No telling what stray bits might be buried under half a tower of stone, but we have the core of the Dreadblade." She lowered the largest shard into a warded chest protected by runic etchings. A hum resonated when the metal touched the container.

"House Riftwyn has a sealed vault for dark artifacts," she continued. Her voice was subdued, edged with relief. "We will lock these pieces away. No one should ever attempt to put it back together."

Jackson studied the remnants. One twisted sliver about the size of his palm rested in her hand. "Would it be wise if I kept a piece?" he asked. He turned the shard carefully, almost feeling the residue of necromantic forging. "If it is split up, there is less chance of reassembly."

Elinora pressed her lips together in thought, then nodded. "That is actually prudent. We can give the king the final say. He might store it under close guard. Our vault at Riftwyn Manor can handle the rest." She nestled the smaller shard in a cloth embroidered with faint protective runes, then handed it to him with careful fingers. "Keep it sealed until King Rodric decides what to do."

Jackson took the shard. "Thank you." He wrapped it quickly so he didn't have to look at the jagged edges a moment longer. *This is better in pieces.*

A cluster of Morrivale reinforcements passed by, their messenger leading them with short bursts of direction. One of the riders leaned over to speak to Elarius in hushed tones. Then, he stepped over to Jackson and Elinora, carefully threading his way through dusty wreckage.

He bowed to Elinora, then to the knight. "My lady, sir. Word from the capital. Our baroness has signaled the king. He knows of Corgrave's defeat and is sending envoys to commend you and investigate any conspirators."

Elinora exhaled a long breath. "That's the best news I've heard in a while. Thank you." She rubbed a soot smudge from her cheek. "At least we can deliver the proof of Corgrave's forging scheme without delay. Master Elarius will be able to explain everything when they question him."

The messenger bowed again, then hurried off to see Lord Morrivale's second-in-command. Nearby, Jackson spotted Luke sprawled on a chunk of broken stone, entertaining a few militiamen with an elaborate story that involved him nearly being eaten by the magical implosion. He waved his arms around for emphasis.

They seemed to enjoy his theatrics, though a few kept darting uncertain glances in Jackson's direction. He realize they probably noticed Elinora standing close. They must have wondered why she dared to be so near him.

Jackson cleared his throat. "You look tired." He adjusted his hold on the cloth-wrapped shard. "You should rest before the next wave of demands hits you."

She managed a small, rueful smile. "And you are the picture of restful serenity?" Her gaze drifted over his scorched gauntlet, the blackish soot staining his armor. "You nearly poured Hellfire through this entire place. Are you sure you do not need rest yourself?"

"I suppose," Jackson muttered. "That took a lot out of me. But for now, I can stand if you want to sit."

Elinora chuckled. "Those unstoppable big shoulders of yours, always ready for duty." She knelt to secure the warded container, checking each runic latch. When the final clasp clicked, she stood and motioned a silent invitation to walk. Jackson followed her across a ruined courtyard toward a partially collapsed archway.

They moved around patches of rubble where Thornvein's militia organized captured weapons. A few survivors from Corgrave's ranks shuffled aside, wrists bound in rope, guarded by stoic crossbowmen. At times, Jackson caught the faint green flicker of residue along the cracked stones. The swirling arcs had mostly died out, but once or twice, he glimpsed a wisp of mana spark across the ground.

They halted at the archway. Broken stones arched overhead in a precarious half-circle. Through it, the morning sky was thick with drifting haze. Sunbeams sliced through the gloom, illuminating motes of ash swirling in the air. The chaos from last night felt like a dream burned across every corner of the fortress.

Elinora turned to him. Her eyes were bright, and she looked on the verge of tears. Then she steadied herself and slipped her hand into his, touching his scorched gauntlet with a gentle, determined pressure.

His heart thudded. He was no longer braced for an enemy's strike, yet raw emotion surged. His instincts ordinarily warned him to keep a distance, but he couldn't deny the sense of closeness they had earned by fighting side by side. Or how much he wanted it.

"I was terrified when the magic flared," she admitted, her voice quivering. "Terrified I would lose more than my home and these crystals. Terrified I would lose allies, and…you." She tightened her grip on his fingers. "All that power swirling around us, I thought we would never make it out."

She exhaled, blinking away the haze in her eyes. Jackson brush the back of her hand with his thumb. *We lived*, he thought. *We stopped it.* Bit by bit, the tension unraveled.

Elinora's gaze moved from his hand to his eyes. Warmth stirred deep in his chest. The burdens of the night burned away, replaced by a quiet, hopeful awareness that for all the darkness swirling in his blood, he had not crossed the final line. He'd found a path to protect others instead of damning them. For now, that was enough.

She stepped closer. Jackson sensed the question in her posture, something unspoken about how they would move forward. It ignited a flutter of old fear inside him, yet he kept his hold on her hand. They stood together in silence, sharing the weight of their survival.

Luke's voice bounced across the courtyard with a casual call of his name, snapping Jackson out of the moment. Elinora's cheeks colored, yet she remained at his side, hand still entwined with his. Soldiers glanced in their direction, some with curiosity, others with cautious acceptance. He raised his chin. *Let them stare.*

She finally released him with a small sigh. "We have more to face outside these walls. But at least we have ended this chaos." Jackson nodded, ignoring the persistent ache in his limbs. She picked up the warded chest with both hands and gestured for them to head out.

As the company prepared to depart, Jackson felt an unexpected surge of contentment. Corgrave was gone. The threat was defused. The air carried the scent of dust and dawn instead of sulfur and fear. The tension in his infernal markings had ebbed, at least for now. His soul did not feel completely at peace, but it no longer bristled with the memory of arcane arcs searing the sky.

He acknowledged Riven's small bow of greeting, then nodded to Luke, who gave him a sly grin. "Ready to leave this heap behind?" he asked, shifting the weight of his pack. "I vote we find a decent inn, with pillows not made of rubble. I could use warm bread and a drink, too. Maybe more than one drink. We all deserve it."

Jackson almost laughed. "I appreciate your sense of priorities, Luke."

He tipped an imaginary hat, then jogged ahead to help two soldiers load crates onto a wagon rumbling in behind the reinforcements. By the cracked dais, Elinora held the chest close. She met his gaze, her expression bright despite the bruises across her cheek.

Jackson's gauntlet throbbed, reminding him of the cost. For once, he welcomed the ache. Elarius limped ahead, leaning on a staff. Luke and Riven walked in wary silence, scanning for any last trouble.

Elinora came to stand beside Jackson, gaze set on the path ahead. Together, they and the surviving allies began the slow trek back safer lands. As they departed, the sun spilled through the ragged tower spires, bathing the courtyard in a soft glow.

The realm breathed, free of Corgrave's shadow.

THE STORY CONTINUES

The Story Continues with book 2, *The Iron Key*, coming soon to Amazon

BOOKS BY MICHAEL ANDERLE

Sign up for the LMBPN email list to be notified of new releases and special deals!

https://lmbpn.com/email/

For a complete list of books by Michael Anderle, please visit:

www.lmbpn.com/ma-books/

CONNECT WITH THE AUTHOR

Connect with Michael Anderle

Website: http://lmbpn.com

Email List: https://michael.beehiiv.com/

https://www.facebook.com/LMBPNPublishing

https://twitter.com/MichaelAnderle

https://www.instagram.com/lmbpn_publishing/

https://www.bookbub.com/authors/michael-anderle

www.ingramcontent.com/pod-product-compliance
Lightning Source LLC
LaVergne TN
LVHW041908070526
838199LV00051BA/2544